A Sudden Thunder

by

D. A. Joy

Published by Domnall Publishing

Cover layout by Kyle R. Joy based on the original chromolithograph "The Monitor and Merrimac: The First Fight Between Ironclads", produced by Louis Prang & Co., Boston via Wikimedia Commons

ISBN-10:061584359X
ISBN-13:978-0615843599

To my wife, Terri

ACKNOWLEDGEMENTS

Chapter 1: The First Photograph Of President Lincoln From Www.En.Wikipedia.Org:

Chapter 2: The Fifth Avenue Hotel From Www.En.Wikipedia.Org:

Chapter 3: The Brooklyn Navy Yard In 1861 From Www.Navyandmarine.Org

Chapter 4: Fort Pickens In 1861 From Www.En.Wikimedia.Org

Chapter 5: *USS COHOCTON* Modified From A Drawing Of The *USS PAWNEE* From Www.En.Wikimedia.Org

Chapter 6: *USS MACEDONIAN* From Www.Navsource.Org

Chapter 7: The Relief Of Ft. Pickens By The United States Fleet From Www.Navsource.Org

Chapter 8: Destruction Of The Norfolk Navy Yard From Www.En.Wikimedia.Org

Chapter 9: Chasing A Blockade Runner In Harper's Weekly From Www.Sonofthesouth.Net

Chapter 10: A Typical Blockade Runner From Www.History.Navy.Mil

Chapter 11: The Hatteras Expedition From Www.Sonofthesouth.Net

Chapter 12: The Great Naval Expedition To Port Royal From Www.History.Navy.Mil

Chapter 13: *USS SAN JACINTO* Stops The *SS TRENT* From Www.Navsource.Org

Chapter 14: *CSS VIRGINIA* In Drydock From Www.Navsource.Org

Chapter 15: On The Deck Of The *CONGRESS* From Www.Americancivilwar.Com

Chapter 16: The Heart Of Battle, From An 1871 Wood Engraving Published By A.S. Barnes From Www.En.Wikimedia.Org

16th President of the United States, Abraham Lincoln

CHAPTER ONE

A cold and bitter December wind swept through the Brooklyn Navy Yard. To Lt. John Richards, it was as piercing and disquieting as the talk of dissolution sweeping the country. Another gust swirled about him and he tugged his great coat closer as he stared into the dry dock.

His sloop, the *USS COHOCTON*, lay there, the water drained and workmen pulling the old copper from her wooden hull. Three years growth of barnacles and seaweed marked the ship's recent return from the Mediterranean, but neither he nor the ship was prepared for what awaited them in the United States.

His deeply tanned skin contrasted with the fits of snow that came with the wind. He shivered in the cold, hunched against the breeze, his almost six foot frame seeming to shrink in the icy air. He stared at the ship, hardly noticing the workmen, barely aware of his breath fogging in front of him.

Lincoln was elected in November, a surprise to most everyone in the country. *COHOCTON* had already departed her station to return home and the crew did not discover the election results until just three days before when they arrived at Brooklyn. The Illinois Republican had created an unbelievable stir.

Already, southern states were declaring their intention to secede rather than submit to a government controlled by an abolitionist. As Richards tried to stiffen himself against another icy blast, so too he tried to reconcile his position with the fractured sentiments of his friends and shipmates, as well as the country at large.

He had spent the last eleven years at sea in one part of the world or another. He lived a profession that treated all states as part of a greater whole and he did not feel like he owed any state more of his allegiance than another.

To him, the matter of secession and dissolution of the Union was confusing, even vaguely ridiculous. His country was composed of the wooden hull of his ship and declared by the stars and stripes flying at the mast head. But now, he could not walk through the Navy Yard or even sit in his boarding house without being presented with the subject in a myriad of different fashions.

There was talk of war if secession came, and he was by profession a warrior. But with the splintered views of most everyone about him, how would his Navy react to the start of an internal war - a civil war? While the strengths and weaknesses of the various fleets they encountered as they cruised the seas of the world were often a subject of wardroom discussion, it never occurred to him (or anyone else he could remember) to consider using the fleet in home waters against another state in the Union.

"Lt. Richards?"

The voice that startled Richards from his reverie was quiet and high-pitched. He found a young boy of no more than twelve standing next to him. The boy was poorly dressed and stood shivering in the frigid wind.

"Yes?"

"Telegram, sir," continued the boy, extending a pink hand. He took the envelope as the boy looked down into the dry dock. "She's a beauty, lieutenant."

Richards paid little attention to the comment. He was reaching into his pocket for some coins. He tossed the boy a few pennies, and then watched him scamper away. Turning his attention to the telegram, he carefully tore it open. He held the paper tightly as it fluttered in the breeze.

John -

I would like to see you tonight on a matter of some urgency. If you could be at the Fifth Avenue Hotel this evening at 7:00 P.M. for the formal reception, I would be most appreciative.

Respectfully,

G. Welles

G. Welles - Gideon Welles, the man who was to be Secretary of Navy after Lincoln's inauguration and an old friend from Connecticut. Richards nodded, a slight smile crossing his lips. Welles was responsible for his appointment aboard the *COHOCTON*. It was to his best interests to see what Welles wanted.

His mind turned back to the small note in the morning *Times*. The Fifth Avenue Hotel was the site of a Republican victory celebration. He would need his dress uniform cleaned and readied within five hours. The uniform now lay in the bottom of his sea chest. He stuffed the message into his coat pocket and walked from the dry dock.

Richards entered his boarding house, stamping his feet to remove the snow and get the circulation going. Hanging his coat in the hall, he walked up the two flights of stairs to his room. A sea chest and duffle bag sat outside. He realized they belonged to his roommate, Lt. Judson Caldwell, *COHOCTON*'s second lieutenant. Richards entered the room.

"Going somewhere?" he asked.

The other man stood at the window, looking over the snow covered city. The men regarded one another, for they were cast from the same mold. Both had dark hair and eyes; they were close to same height; both had well-defined features with sharp jaw lines. In the Mediterranean, they were often mistaken for brothers, a fact which brought them closer. Now, Richards sensed something separating them.

"Yes, John," replied Caldwell easily. His voice was smooth and low, but carried the intonations of the deep south. "I must leave for Alabama tonight. I offered my resignation an hour ago."

Richards accepted the comment, belying the turmoil he felt. "What caused this sudden change? We planned to await developments."

Caldwell smiled. "I received a telegram from my father. Alabama is considering a resolution of secession and he wishes me home if it is approved."

"A family matter then?" Richards understood little of family matters. He had few living relatives, and his life in the Navy kept him apart.

"Family and honor. My loyalties are with my state and my family. My duty lies with them," explained Caldwell. "You are southern born, John. You should understand."

It was Richards' turn to smile. Though born in Virginia, he was raised in Connecticut. Both his mother and father had died while he was young, leaving his father's sister to rear him. His only other relative was his uncle Andrew, also a lieutenant in the Navy. He still owned the family farm in Virginia, the property signed over to him by his childless uncle. This ownership made Virginia his legal state of residence, but his only real life was the Navy.

"I am hardly a true southerner, Virginia born or not."

"I know, John, but I must to do what I believe is right."

There was a lump in Richards' throat at the thought of his good friend leaving. He remembered the telegram in his coat pocket and why he returned.

"I am invited to the Fifth Avenue Hotel this evening at seven. If you must not leave immediately, you are welcome to come along."

"The train departs at 10:30. I shall have to leave early to be on it."

Richards smiled. It was a small concession. "I will be happy to make apologies for you."

"Then I must get my dress uniform ready."

Shortly before six, the two officers left the boarding house and made their way to the ferry landing near the Navy Yard. They rode across the short stretch of water separating Brooklyn from the city of New York. As anticipated, cabs crowded around the landing on the far side. Caldwell arranged for his baggage to be sent to the train depot. Hiring a hackney, they settled in for the trip uptown.

The streets in Manhattan were rough. Though covered with snow, deep ruts were carved by the wheels of the coaches and the runners of the occasional sleigh. When the coach turned onto Broadway, Richards expected the ride to improve. Instead it grew worse, the cab lurching in and out of the ruts, tossing them about. In spite of the gas lights lining the street, the driver seemed to strike every dip and mound. Other than exchanging comments on the quality of the ride, the two men rode in silence, both lost in their own thoughts.

The progress north was slow in the heavy traffic clogging the street. The driver's curses ravaged the other vehicles as he wove in and out of the flow. After what seemed hours, the coach reached Fifth Avenue and stopped in front of the brightly lit hotel.

Richards paid the driver and they quickly entered the welcome warmth of the hotel. Music and crowd noise provided directions to the main hall. A quick survey of the room revealed Welles' tall figure on the opposite side. Carefully, he picked his way through the assembled dignitaries. He caught pieces of conversations and became aware of their common subject. Secession, revolution and disunion were the most common words, but they were spoken by a variety of people with an even greater variety of opinions. He was only halfway across the hall when a hand grabbed his arm.

"John!"

"Becky!" he said, surprised at her sudden appearance. He absorbed her bright smile for a moment, and then took a slight step backwards. "Your father did not mention you were here!"

She laughed and gave him a slight curtsy. "I wanted to surprise you."

He had not seen her for over two years. She was several inches shorter than his five-eleven. The black hair was shoulder length and made the smooth skin of her bare shoulders seem whiter. Her eyes were a bright, piercing blue and twinkled in the gas light. Her lips and cheeks were properly pink, betraying just the merest hint of make-up.

"I would like to introduce Judson Caldwell. I mentioned him in my letters."

She curtsied again, slightly deeper this time. "Lieutenant Caldwell," she said her voice a touch lower. "I feel as though I already know you."

"And I you," he returned, bowing deeply and taking her hand. She turned as Caldwell released her hand and gestured across the room. "Father wants to see you immediately, John." She did not wait for a reply and began to move in that direction. "Some urgent business he feels must be addressed tonight."

With her arms linked to the two Navy officers, Rebecca Welles led them to her father. The tall figure of Welles dominated the scene as he spoke with a small group of men. Richards again noted the sharp eyes and the fervor in his voice. The flowing beard seemed much whiter than the last time Richards had seen him. Rebecca coughed tactfully to interrupt.

"Father," she offered.

"John! I thought you would never arrive!" greeted Welles, the deep voice cutting the surrounding noise.

Welles took his hand in a firm grip and guided him towards the gathered dignitaries. In a few confusing minutes, Richards was introduced to half the notables in the State of New York.

"May I present Lieutenant Judson Caldwell, also of the *COHOCTON*," returned Richards.

Caldwell acknowledged the greeting, but his southern born accent was suddenly out of place in the room. It was strange, for it was the first time Richards really noticed the inflection. Nor was it lost on Caldwell as the southerner became stiffly formal with the New Yorkers.

"Lt. Richards has just returned from the Mediterranean." Welles explained to the people about them, his voice piercing the party's murmur as well as the uncomfortable silence of his group. "I must ask your pardon to discuss the situation there with him in private."

Richards had little time to speak. Rebecca took Caldwell by the arm and drew him onto the dance floor. Welles did not wait for an acknowledgment before leading him out the back of the ballroom.

"It is good to see you again, John," he said.

"And I am glad to see you, Sir," replied Richards.

Welles grinned. "And Rebecca?"

"Always," returned Richards, also smiling.

They went up a flight of stairs to a suite of rooms. Welles closed the door and cut off the sounds drifting up from the ballroom. A young officer stood as they entered. He was shorter than Richards with sandy hair and a round, open face.

"Lieutenant, this is Lt. RenError! LaForge. He is being assigned to COHOCTON."

"Pleased to meet you," said LaForge as they shook hands.

Richards detected the slight southern accent which overlaid the other voice. "Lieutenant," he responded cautiously.

"He is the son of a Louisiana business associate," explained Welles. "He is just returning from an assignment with ordnance."

"Yes!" LaForge brightened at the interest shown. "I have been working with Commander Dahlgren and Lt. Brooke at Gosport. It was all very routine with no room for advancement. Besides, I joined the Navy to see a bit of the world, not the Norfolk Navy Yard. Mr. Welles helped me gain this appointment."

Richards nodded. "As he has helped me on occasion."

Welles interrupted. "I did not bring you here to compare careers. What of COHOCTON? What condition is she in?"

Richards stood silently, arranging his thoughts. "The boilers are in good shape, as is the engine. Rigging, masts, hull are all fine. She needs to be coppered and the workmen are already working on it. No problems with her that a few days in dry dock will not correct."

Welles absorbed the report while pacing slowly across the carpet. He halted behind his desk when Richards stopped speaking. His words carried a quiet intensity Richards had never before experienced.

"Are you aware of the number of ships available to the Navy?" As before, Welles did not wait for an answer. "Forty-two! A third of those are sailing ships and laid up. Only nine are in home waters. The remainder are scattered across the globe by my predecessor."

"Nine?" asked LaForge in disbelief.

"Nine." The word carried finality. "Two are here; two more at Norfolk. The others are strewn along the coast."

The implications were immediate. If war did come, the North would control the Navy. Naval control of the southern coastline could bring a quick ending to any hostilities.

"I do not have to explain to you about the Navy, gentlemen." Welles pointed to a small map of the country lying on his desk. "In eight days, you must take COHOCTON south. Here," he emphasized, his finger stabbing the southern edge of the Florida panhandle, "is Ft. Pickens. It is a garrison fort outside the Pensacola Navy Yard. We must hold strong points along the southern coastline if we are to bring a quick conclusion to any fighting. You will transport reinforcements and supplies."

"I am not officially commanding COHOCTON..." began Richards.

Welles dismissed the objection. "Lieutenant Reynolds left yesterday," he said, pulling out his watch. "Lt. Caldwell will leave for Alabama yet this evening. You are left in command of the ship, lieutenant, with Mr. LaForge as your first."

It was what Richards had always worked towards, command of his own ship. But with Caldwell leaving, LaForge would become the senior lieutenant aboard the vessel. "You realize our mission is against the southern states?" he asked.

A serious expressed came to the young features. "I am not a Secessionist. In fact, Mr. Welles thought my southern heritage might insure my berth. My orders are to report in two days."

Richards accepted LaForge at his word, and the confirming nod from Welles. "And under whose orders will we be acting?"

Welles understood Richards' meaning. "Until the inauguration, I am powerless. But we have influence enough in the Navy and War Departments, enough so the orders for *COHOCTON* are on the way." Welles smiled. "It took a bit of planning to arrange for the right commander, however."

"Thank you for that, Mr. Secretary."

"A bit early for the title, John." His voice turned serious again. "Buchanan and his administration refuse to take steps to prevent a rebellion. I must do what I can to see it ended quickly." Welles' features were somber, matching the tone of his words. "You must keep this secret. Tell no one." He let a smile wash away the fear and determination on his face. "It is time we rejoin the party. I am assured you and Rebecca have much catching up to do. I will not monopolize you both with politics."

Richards reluctantly immersed himself in the noise and clamor of the ballroom, all the while searching for Becky. He finally spied her on the dance floor, gliding smoothly about in the arms of another Navy officer. Richards pressed through the crowd, reaching her as the dance ended.

"I thought you and father would be at it all night," she said, taking his hand.

"Not tonight," explained Richards. "Shall we dance?" he asked, extending his arm. He whirled her onto the dance floor.

"How are things in the Mediterranean?" She asked lightly.

"The temperature warmer; the conversation cooler."

She smiled at his comment, then let it fade from her face. "Father believes it will be war."

"I hope not. I did not join the Navy to kill Americans."

Her face remained serious. "And for whom will you fight, John? You are Virginian."

"An orphaned Virginian," corrected Richards, "and one raised in New England besides. No, my loyalty belongs with the Navy."

"Then you would fight for the Union," she concluded firmly.

Richards felt a momentary wave of doubt at the strength of the comment, but he kept his eyes on the pretty young girl in his arms. "I would prefer not to fight at all."

"No one wants war. What of your friend Judson? What will he do?"

Richards paused and it was a moment before he could phrase the words. "He is returning to Alabama. He resigned his commission this morning."

They finished the dance in silence. He was waiting for the next number to begin when a Marine officer cut in. He wanted to refuse, but it was to be expected. Not only was Becky beautiful, which was reason enough, but she was also the daughter of the new Secretary of Navy. Many military officers would be vying for her attention.

He spotted Caldwell with a mixed group of military

men standing to one side. Collecting a glass of wine, he walked over to join his friend.

"...and I say it will be war." The speaker was a rotund little man in a militia uniform. Richards did not know his state, but the voice was clearly New England. "States will not be allowed to secede from the Union."

"I strongly disagree, suh," stated an Army captain with a Virginian drawl. "Our forefathers thought it best to make their way separate from England. How can you justify preventing us if southern states decide to separate from the Union?"

"I any case, it will mean a war," intoned another officer, his cheeks flushed slightly from drink. The voice implied the Midwest. "The North must surely triumph over the South."

"I take great exception to your comment, sir," replied the captain.

Richards took that moment to break into the conversation. "Gentlemen! Lt. Caldwell!" he said, greeting his friend. "I trust our fellow officers are keeping you entertained?"

"My friend, Lieutenant Richards," introduced Caldwell. "Mr. Welles has finished with you then?"

"For the moment."

"And Miss Rebecca?"

"Abducted by a Marine."

"Ah." Caldwell took a glass of wine from a passing porter. "My friends and I were just discussing politics..."

"We were discussing war!" interrupted the fat militiaman.

This began another general discussion, but Caldwell turned to his friend and lowered his voice.

"What of Secretary Welles?" asked Caldwell.

Richards opened his mouth to make a reply. But he remembered Welles' caution and brought his glass to his lips instead. He suddenly considered Judson an Alabamian instead of a fellow officer. He took a sip and tried to speak smoothly.

"A brief question on the British and the status of the Anti-Slavery Patrol." He could not be sure if Caldwell believed him or not.

"And your thoughts?" asked the Virginian.

Richards realized the question from the other conversation was directed at him. The eyes of the other officers were focused on him expectantly. He used the same answer he had given Rebecca earlier.

"Our Navy was not meant to kill Americans."

"It would be a wonderful little fight," observed the Midwesterner, beginning another glass of wine.

The Virginian lifted his glass in a slight toast. "That it would be, though I have no *confusion* on who would be victorious."

The gathered officers laughed, the sound somewhat forced to Richards' ear. A pair of women came up and the men ceased their talk of war, returning to a more formal discussion of state's rights.

"I must say you and Miss Welles make a fine couple."

"Thank you."

Caldwell finished the glass of wine and deposited it on the tray. He faced Richards squarely.

"It is time I leave, John."

Richards took his friends hand, feeling the pressure of the grip. When would he see him again? And under what circumstances? It was obvious the same thoughts troubled Caldwell.

"Take care, Jud," he offered.

"And you. Until better times."

"Aye," returned Richards.

It was an effort to turn from thoughts of his friend to look for Rebecca on the dance floor. She was kept constantly busy, one gentleman or another taking her hand as each dance began. As he watched, he grew irritated over the actions of the other officers. They fawned over her while paying little real heed, paying more interest in her father. Finally, he managed to cut back in.

"We are not getting to see much of each other," he observed.

"I know." Richards nodded and steered away from an approaching Army captain. "Thank you for writing. It made the voyage less lonely."

"I looked forward to your letters."

"When are you to return to Hartford?" he asked.

"I am going to Washington with father."

The comment aroused his curiosity. "And what will you do there?"

"I will keep father's house since mother does not want to leave Hartford and all the children. But there is more to it," Becky continued. "People say things to me - in front of me - they would not say to father. You men overlook women; you think we do not have the intelligence to know what is happening. Father wants to use that."

He smiled uncertainly. "At times you seem so young, then there are times when you seem to have more understanding than a woman twice your age." He stopped, the words sticking in his throat. He was not saying what he felt, but he did not know what words to use. His discomfort grew as she laughed.

"Is that a compliment?" she asked, the merest hint of a blush on her cheeks.

Embarrassed, his voice was low when he answered. "I

suppose it is."

Her voice grew soft again. "If it was, I thank you for it."

Deep blue eyes stared up at him and it was like he had never seen her face before. They were both breathing harder than normal and it took him a moment to realize the music had stopped. He spoke quickly before someone cut in.

"I missed you over this past year." He kept his voice low. "Did your father tell you I leave within a week?"

"The war?"

"Hopefully, it will be stopped short of that."

"And tomorrow night?" she asked.

"Nothing shall keep me away."

He yielded Becky to a never ending string of officers and dignitaries with a new confidence. He even managed to keep a light heart when Welles had him dance with the matronly wives of two of the officials present. By the time the ball ended, he felt well pleased with the events of the evening. But trip down Broadway had a sobering effect on this euphoric mood. As the coach lurched along, he thought of the war looming on the horizon.

If there was war, it would mean fighting his own countrymen, his own friends - Caldwell for one. And what of his uncle? Andrew Richards had spent a good deal of his life in Virginia. What demands would be placed on him? The elder Richards was still in New York, but the subject had not been broached at their single meeting. Richards resolved to see him again before leaving.

His own feelings were in conflict. Though he had avoided the subject earlier, Richards relished the action of a war. His career thus far had been devoted to a peacetime Navy with few incidents beyond the routine. It was impossible to work and live aboard a ship of war without wondering at its performance in battle. The opportunity now lay before him. Yet there was another, deeper force driving him. It was the idea of Americans set against one another. He remembered the *Times* and the column devoted to the Senate committee working towards resolving the differences. Those differences could be, *must be,* settled. Perhaps the Secessionist movement would be a thing of the past by the time he reached Pensacola.

There was also Becky to consider. Marriage, for the first time in his life, presented itself as a possibility. Becky, as his wife, could ensure his career would proceed without problems. But he could not marry her for such a reason, no more than he could accept a position for which he was unfit. To use her in such a fashion would place him in the same category as the other officers earlier in the evening. He dismissed the thought as the cab drew up to the ferry. He could not use Becky that way; nor would Gideon Welles allow such a thing. And it went without saying, the headstrong Rebecca Welles would not permit it either.

Fifth Avenue Hotel in New York City

CHAPTER TWO

As promised, orders were waiting the next morning. *COHOCTON* would transport a company of New York artillery to Ft. Pickens. The ship would to put to sea at the earliest moment and no later than January Fourth. It left barely more than a week to prepare.

The workmen continued their labor across the bottom of the ship, fighting to remove overgrown and corroded copper sheets. They moved quickly and had already stripped more than half. The bare wooden hull was prepared for the new copper, caulking hammers echoing in the cold, empty spaces of the yard. New sheets took their place at the stern, the metal shining in the bright December sunlight.

The *COHOCTON* was one of the smaller ships on the Navy list, classed as a second-rate screw sloop. Displacing only 1200 tons, she was at the low end of the fleet's sloops. Officially rated at eight guns, she actually carried ten. The two deck rifles were not counted a part of her main armament of thirty-two pounders. Unlike some of her sisters, the main gun deck was fully enclosed. She drew only ten feet of water at the bow and slightly less than twelve aft. This slight draft would be useful if called upon to work in the shallow southern inlets.

She was capable of turning eleven knots at full pressure. With a stiff trailing breeze, she once produced almost fourteen under sail. Nonetheless, Richards was never happy with her sailing qualities. The combination of heavy guns and light draft made her wallow in heavy seas. COHOCTON would have the chance to prove this again, for they would pass Cape Hatteras, the one spot on the eastern seaboard seemingly in continual storms. He remembered his grandfather's ship had wrecked there some twenty-four years before.

Richards turned his attention from the dry dock to the small building he was to use until COHOCTON was floated out. He wrote orders and checked the bills of lading, along with the usual problem of completing a crew. The ship's compliment was normally over two hundred, seventy. There were less than one hundred sixty currently in the barracks to man her. And though disliking the paper work, Richards waded into the multitude of pages necessary to get COHOCTON back into the water and headed for Pensacola.

Men were assigned and positions filled. Coal, ammunition, food, water - all the necessities of life at sea were assembled. Though he dreaded the work, it proceeded quickly and it was well past noon when he realized he had not yet eaten. Richards decided to return to the boarding house for his meal. As he finished donning his coat, the door opened and Lt. Paul Reynolds entered. The sudden appearance of the ship's captain shocked Richards into silence. It took two attempts before he could stammer out a greeting.

"Good afternoon, sir."

Reynolds grunted. Stepping to the desk, he examined the papers silently for several minutes before speaking.

"I understand COHOCTON is being prepared for sea. Why was I not notified?"

Richards replied cautiously. "I did not find out until last night, captain. You had already departed."

Reynolds snorted. "Fortunately the Navy Department succeeded in contacting me. There was a message waiting when I reached Baltimore. I collected the crewmen from the train and we were able to return. You will find," he said, peering at the crew roster over his glasses, "we can finish filling many of these slots. Still, we will be short over sixty men." Reynolds rested his gaze on Richards, at last to noticing the heavy coat and the sweat on his forehead. "Where are you going?"

"Dinner, captain. I have not yet eaten today."

"Return as quickly as you can manage." Disdain was heavy in the captain's voice.

Richards disliked the curt dismissal. At the moment, however, he only wanted to escape this man who treated him like a recalcitrant pupil.

"Yes, sir," he responded, then left the building.

The cold outside was a welcome change after the heat of the building. The feeling lasted for only a moment; he was quickly chilled from the sweat that had formed during the brief discussion. Yet he hardly noticed the cold while his mind digested that Reynolds' return had cost him command of the COHOCTON.

While he ate his quick lunch at the boarding house, Richards considered his captain. He did not dislike Reynolds. In fact, he held a deep professional respect for the man, who had been in the Navy for thirty years. Reynolds position of Lieutenant Commanding belied his competence as an officer, but it was not an unusual situation. One could easily grow old and retire as a lieutenant in a peacetime Navy. But now, Richards was more concerned how Reynolds reappearance affected the mission. He jotted a short note to Welles informing him of the change.

The new copper extended for almost a third the ship's length. If the work continued all night as planned, it might be possible to warp the ship out of the dry dock by the next afternoon.

Reynolds was pacing near the dry dock observing the work. Richards studied the medium height and build of the man, noting the neatly tailored uniform. Reynolds' face was covered by a short beard, as neatly tailored as the uniform. He returned the junior officer's salute casually as Richards fell into step next to him.

"I have checked your paper work," said Reynolds. "Everything appears to be in proper order. A good job, Mr. Richards."

"Thank you." Richards paused for Reynolds to continue.

"You are from Virginia, are you not? Orphaned, though a member of a distinguished naval family."

Richards remained defensive. "So I am told."

Reynolds produced a pipe and filled it. He paused in the action and examined the younger man more closely. "Lieutenant Andrew Richards - is he a relative?"

"My uncle."

Reynolds digested the information. "I never made the connection before. We were together at Vera Cruz, then again in California. Your father, James, was killed at Vera Cruz."

"Yes, captain." Richards kept his answers short, waiting to see what Reynolds was working towards.

The senior lieutenant started walking again, completing the action of filling his pipe. "Would you mind telling me what you think of the secessionist matter, Mr. Richards?" He stopped again, peering at Richards over the top of his glasses while he lit the pipe.

Richards thought quickly. While his loyalties were mixed, he saw what Reynolds was attempting. He felt himself to be an honorable man and did not wish to lie about the matter. Neither could he commit himself openly to Reynolds.

"It is difficult to say," he replied, haltingly. "There are points to be made by both sides; points I can agree with." Reynolds nodded and began to retrace his steps. Richards continued. "I would not like this to become open rebellion."

Reynolds agreed quickly, perhaps too quickly. "Of course not! There are many things to consider, and I do not care to fight my own countrymen."

"Nor do I, but I also have my duty to perform."

"Yes. Our duty."

Richards realized they were speaking of different duties, different loyalties. In the same instant, he saw where his must lie. His previous doubt was gone, for his duty lay with his home, and his home was the Navy.

"Have I answered your question?" asked Richards.

"Yes, I think you have." There was only a slight note of sadness in Reynolds' voice.

Richards arrived for his dinner with Rebecca just before seven. Welles was waiting and Becky was nowhere to be seen. It gave him a few moments to discuss the day's developments with the future secretary.

"Reynolds returned," announced Richards bluntly, warming himself near the radiator. "He received word when he reached Baltimore."

"There can be no doubt where that word came from." Welles did not ask for confirmation. "What do you propose?"

"I am still the first officer and can make sure he does not jeopardize the mission. There is the possibility he is loyal to the Union - and the Navy - but I doubt it."

"If someone within the Navy Department informed Reynolds, then the mission is no longer a secret from the Secessionists."

Richards shrugged. "True, but we must continue as though it were. There is always the chance..."

Rebecca's entry interrupted the conversation. Welles kissed his daughter on the cheek before replying to Richards.

"Try not to let all this talk bother you. Enjoy the play."

Richards and Rebecca left the room. He guided her away from the elevator and towards the stairs. Though people used the machine everyday, Richards felt a vague distrust for the contraption. It was easier to take the three flights down to the lobby. They left the hotel and took a waiting cab. Richards helped her into the coach.

"Wallack's theater," he instructed the driver.

The play was called "Fast Men of the Olden Times", a musical adaption of the life of Charles the Second. Richards found the production to be terribly boring. However, he feigned interest for Becky's sake, which required laughing and clapping at the appropriate times. He even managed to remember enough to carry on an intelligent conversation afterwards. They returned to the hotel for a light dinner, easily locating seats in the vast dining hall.

"You did not care for it, did you?" she asked.

Richards fought his first impulse to lie and tried to keep his face serious. It was a short and unsuccessful struggle.

"I was bored silly," he answered truthfully. "But it was worth the trouble to spend the time with you," he finished quickly.

She cast her eyes down as a hint of pink touched her cheeks. "Your compliments are improving."

The young couple ate slowly and talked lightly. They skirted the issue of the war and Richards was thankful for it. After completing the meal, they enjoyed a last glass of wine before he escorted her to her room. They kissed for a long while before speaking.

"Tomorrow night?" asked Richards.

"Yes," she answered quickly, then disappeared inside.

Richards felt he did not have a care in the world. He thought briefly of visiting his uncle before returning to the boarding house, but it was too late in the evening. Instead, he returned to his room and stripped off his clothes, sliding between the warm sheets.

The morning *Times* announced the news that Alabama joined the growing list of southern states in secession. Once again, Richards thought of Judson Caldwell, the person who was easily his best friend in the world. Yet even these thoughts were swept aside in the crush of the day's events. The coppering was finished shortly after noon and the ship was ready to be refloated.

At the dry dock, a few remaining workmen scrambled from beneath the mass of the ship. Several stood at the lock, preparing to open the gates and let the waters of the East River reclaim the ship. Many of the ship's company gathered to watch the events.

"We do not need a crowd of gawkers, Mr. Richards," pointed out Reynolds. "Take some of these men aboard and be ready to take the line from the tug."

"Yes, captain." Richards examined the assembled men, spotting the more experienced hands among them.

"Sims, Archer, Healey! You heard the captain. Lay

onto some of these slackers and get aboard!"

The workmen laid planks to the ship. When finished, Richards stepped gingerly across the first one, ignoring the thirty foot drop on either side. The designated crewmen followed and watched as the planks were withdrawn. Richards walked, noting the strange, solid feel of the motionless deck.

"Not quite alive, is she, lieutenant?" said the seaman named Sims.

"We shall fix that in a moment," returned Richards. As he spoke, a light line was tossed from a dock worker. The seamen grabbed it, hauling in the successively thicker cables trailing after it.

The far end was fed from a steam winch. A tug approached along the river and a second line was made fast from it. Once satisfied, Richards gave the word. Another steam engine puffed to life and the sluice gates crept apart, the river rushing to fill the void beneath the ship.

The crewmen ashore waited for the waters to wash around the hull. At Reynolds' order, they picked up poles to fend the side while COHOCTON was pulled clear. Another tug approached as the gates opened completely.

The ship awakened as the water supported her weight. The first tug backed, smoke pouring from its stack and water churning around the stern. The second line grew taunt and COHOCTON slid backwards.

Richards watched the sides of the ship, but the men on the tug and winch worked their equipment expertly. The waiting crewmen did not have to use the poles once as the ship slipped from the dry dock. One tug moved in next to the sloop as the first pulled in its line.

"Man the helm, Sims," ordered Richards as the ship gathered way. It took only a few minutes to be pushed to the coaling station and made fast to the wharf.

The ordeal of stocking the ship's coal bunkers followed. Reynolds excused himself, leaving the messy task to his subordinate. Richards supervised the rigging of the coal chute from shore. Hands were detailed to shovel the coal into the chute while the regular coal heavers went below to move the fuel into the bunkers. The entire afternoon was spent in the arduous operation.

By this time, it was too late to see Becky that evening, so he jotted a quick note and detailed a man to run it to the telegraph office. A further two hours were spent returning the decks to their normally bleached white condition. Richards, along with the rest of the crew, was covered with grime from head to foot. Only the coal heavers, firemen and engineers seemed comfortable in that condition. The tired crew was released for the night and he headed for the boarding house.

An hour passed before he felt truly clean. Drying himself, he regarded the mess in the bottom of the bathtub, glad to have it off his skin. It was not yet eight-thirty. Too late to see Becky, but he had not seen his uncle in the past week. With the rush to get COHOCTON ready, there might not be another opportunity. Donning a clean uniform, he boarded a cab to Brooklyn.

The trip was not far. The boarding house was of higher stature than his own, but otherwise much the same. Richards climbed the steps to the room and knocked on the door. His uncle's voice answered.

"Enter." Even ashore, it carried a note of authority.

He sat near the window, the evening paper on his lap and a pipe clamped between his teeth. He looked up to see who it was.

"Well, John! Pull up a chair!" While Richards moved the chair, Andrew Richards continued. "I have seen little of you this past week. I hear they are preparing COHOCTON for sea."

"Yes, uncle," answered Richards. "We ship out within the week."

The elder Richards, a life long sailor, nodded knowingly. "More of this I suppose!" he said, shaking the paper. "The damned fools will have us killing each other before long."

"That is why I want to talk with you. I need to know what you are planning to do."

"Do?" The simple reply was a long time coming. He took the pipe from his mouth and banged it on the arm of the chair. "What do you expect?"

"I do not know. I suppose I came looking for advice."

Lieutenant Richards snorted. "I wish I had some for you." He pointed at the pile of tobacco ash on the floor. "I have sat here all evening thinking on it.

"I am from Virginia, John. There, you take your oaths and duty seriously. That duty is more than to the flag of the United States. It is to friend and family, to the state of birth as well." He waved back an interruption. "I know, son, I know. You were not raised that way in Connecticut. I need no explanation or excuses. It is not your fault. My sister raised you as she and her husband saw fit, and I think they did a good job."

Richards smiled, conscious of the praise. "You still have not answered my question, Uncle. Am I wrong if I bear arms against my state; against my countrymen?"

The older man's head shook sadly. "I have no answer. You took an oath to uphold and defend the Constitution, but don't the people of the nation make up that Constitution? I am no sea lawyer. I can only tell you what I feel."

He paused to refill and light his pipe. "I am getting on in years, John. I have been thinking of resigning the Navy for some time." He talked through another protest. "It has been in the back of my mind since watching your father die at Vera Cruz. This," he said, tapping the paper again, "is only the final straw.

"The men doing this are my friends. The men who will be fighting them are my friends, too. I cannot kill them. No, I shall resign my commission tomorrow. I will go back to the farm and stay out of this war."

"I can not do that," said Richards after a moment's silence. "My life is with the Navy, not some plot of land."

"You have to do what you feel is right, John," said Andrew. "I do not expect you to follow in my footsteps. Who knows?" he finished, a sad chuckle marking the phrase. "Maybe I can ensure you have the farm to return to when you want it."

Richards did not know what he expected from his uncle. It was certainly not what he received, but he tried to understand the decision.

"I wish you luck, sir."

The older Richards smiled sadly, accepting the sentiment from his nephew. His face brightened with a thought.

"I do have something for you," said Andrew, standing and walking to a sea chest in one corner. "This is our family birthright, more so even than the farm."

Slowly, he opened the chest. The interior was filled with flags, ensigns from different ships manned by Richards' family members through the years. John remembered seeing them as a child and often wondered what had become of the trunk.

"This flag," said Andrew, taking a tattered stars and stripes from the top, "was your father's. He died under it." His voice cracked under the strain. He returned it to the chest in silence.

"Thank you, uncle."

"Whatever you do, John, do it from your sense of

honor. Fight if you must, but fight for what you believe, Unionist or Secessionist. It is the best advice I can give you."

Richards nodded. "I shall miss you, uncle Andrew."

The two men clasped hands. "Take care, John," his uncle said, voice filled with emotion. "James would never forgive me if something happened to you."

"As you say, I must do what I feel is right."

"That you must." The older man gripped his hand firmly, then slowly released it. "I will have the chest sent over before I leave."

The following day was dull and gray, low clouds scudding across the sky, but the work continued. Richards arrived early to get his orders from Reynolds. Again, the captain excused himself, citing other pressing needs. It was left to the junior officer to supervise the rearming of the ship.

The COHOCTON moved from the coaling dock to make room for other ships. She sat alone, a bright streak of copper showing how light she was riding. The day's activities would solve that quickly enough.

Like so many other things, there was only so much steam could accomplish. It took man and horse power to move the heavy gun carriages to the dock. The thirty-two pounders comprising the main armament weighed over two tons each. But there were only six of the venerable weapons waiting for installation. Two nine-inch Dahlgrens were being placed on the ship, the new guns a shiny black even in the dull light. The Dahlgrens dwarfed the old cannon beside them. As Richards contemplated how to arrange the armament, Elijah Hardy, the ship's gunner, approached.

"Well, lieutenant," he said casually. His years in the Navy made Hardy quite familiar around junior officers.

Richards was not sure of the man's age, but knew it was approaching sixty. "What ye' think of me new babies?"

Hardy was a good sailor; he was good at his job and could be counted on when the going was rough. It was simple to overlook his easy going manner. "We will be able to do something with those in a fight, I venture," replied Richards. "I should think both midship aft to help maintain the balance."

Hardy scratched his beard and eyed the guns, then looked at the ship. "Aye, sir, that should do her fine, I'm athinkin'. It keeps the ammunition in the aft magazine."

"Well then, Mr. Hardy, proceed!"

It was hours of back breaking labor to remount the guns. The steam winch lifted the guns, but man power maneuvered the several tons of weight over the hatch. The winch lowered the weapons with the crewmen guiding the way. But after reaching the gun deck, only manpower was available to place the weapons at the proper site.

COHOCTON was pierced with a dozen gun ports to a side, but the larger guns meant few of them were actually occupied. The additional ports allowed the guns to be placed to the best advantage for the ship's balance.

Richards released the men for lunch. After their return, they completed installing the main guns. Only the two four-inch deck rifles remained to be placed. Hardy, after spending the day between decks supervising the installation of the main guns, reappeared.

"About them deck guns, lieutenant..." he started. Richards knew what Hardy was about to say, but he also knew the answer.

"We have had this discussion before, Mr. Hardy. The captain wants them both forward on standard carriages. He prefers them as bow chasers." He was not harsh with his comments. Both men understood their captain.

"We be the laughin' stock of the fleet, beggin' your

pardon," continued Hardy, but with no intention of apologizing. "It's jus' pivot mounts would be better."

"You have my permission to discuss the matter with Captain Reynolds."

Hardy was appalled at the prospect. "Jus' voicin' my opinion, lieutenant."

"Very good, Mr. Hardy. Get the guns mounted."

"Aye, sir."

Reynolds had yet to put in an appearance as the second deck rifle was lashed down. The men were set to bringing the ammunition aboard the ship. With three different sizes of guns, the magazine arrangement required a prolonged discussion to determine a layout which allowed a constant flow to each of the guns without interference to the others. To complicate the task, a light snow began to fall, swirling around in the breeze.

The snow did not help Richards' disposition. The men were moving quickly, trying to keep warm in the cold air. The deck became slippery, and he had to keep a cautious eye on the sailors moving the shot, shell and powder into the ship in an ever increasing stream. It was at this juncture LaForge chose to report aboard. Leaving Hardy in charge of the deck operation, Richards took the junior lieutenant to the wardroom.

"Tricky business," commented LaForge.

"Yes", replied Richards drily. He was thinking he could have used the other officer's help earlier when they were moving the guns. He suppressed the thought and reviewed the orders carefully to assure they were correct. "Glad to have you with us," he said simply, extending his hand.

LaForge shook it with enthusiasm. "Perhaps," he ventured, "you could answer a question for me. Why not mount the deck guns on pivots? They are five years behind the times this way."

Richards let out a sigh. "I just discussed this with our gunner, lieutenant. The captain prefers the present arrangement."

As if in answer to a summons, Reynolds opened the wardroom door and entered. He gave both Richards and LaForge a stern glance before speaking.

"And what arrangement is that, Mr. Richards?" The school-master's edge was hard in his voice.

"The arrangement of the deck guns," replied Richards quickly. He continued without a break to forestall any further questions. "May I present Lt. RenError! LaForge? He is assigned as our second lieutenant and has come off a tour with ordnance."

Reynolds eyed both LaForge and the orders critically. "Well, Mr. LaForge, we need another lieutenant, right enough. I would have preferred one with a bit of experience, however." He surveyed the orders again and let a long sigh escape. "I guess I must take what is available, though I wish the Navy Department had seen fit to send another engineer and a couple good petty officers with you."

LaForge seemed unaware of the rebuke. "I am glad to be aboard, captain."

Reynolds coughed nervously, unsure how to accept the open reply. "Mr. Richards will show you the ship and see to your training. I will take over the loading, lieutenant."

"Yes, sir," replied Richards smoothly. Reynolds left the room. "Let's start on the main deck," he said, walking past LaForge.

"Georgia?" asked LaForge as he followed, his voice barely a whisper.

"Aye," replied Richards in an equally low voice.

Richards started at the bow, explaining the rigging and spar arrangement. LaForge was a constant stream of questions, revealing an almost total ignorance of ship handling. Richards explained as best he could, uncomfortable and unsure of himself in the role of teacher.

Three bells rang in the noon watch and he noticed one of the ship's boys at the gangway blocking the entry of another boy. Welcoming a relief from the repetition of LaForge's education, Richards investigated and recognized the stranger as the telegram boy.

"Is there a problem, Jigs?" asked the lieutenant.

"This boy says he's alookin' for you, sir." While Jigs' language was rough, his tone and manner were properly respectful. "I fig'rd I should stop 'im."

"I can handle him. Return to work."

"Aye, aye, sir." Jigs ran to the bow where two other boys were working.

Richards looked down at the delivery boy, noting in more detail the poor quality of his clothing. But the lad's eyes were not looking at him. Instead they were trained on the three boys forward.

"Is he really a sailor?" asked the boy.

"Jigs? He is as much a sailor as any man on this ship."

"I thought of bein' a sailor - when I grow up, I mean," explained the boy quickly. "It's why I'm deliverin' the telegrams to the yard. I love watchin' the ships and all."

"What's your name?" asked Richards.

"Willie Potter, Sir."

"Where do you live, Potter?" Richards was sure of the answer but wished to confirm his thoughts.

"Me?" The young voice was incredulous. Potter could not believe anyone, particularly a naval lieutenant, would express an interest in his life. "In New York, with a group of me mates. On the streets, ya' know. I've been on the streets me whole life - as long as I can remember, anyway."

Packs of homeless boys roamed the streets of the city. Most survived as scavengers. Potter was luckier, with a job to help himself stay fed, if little more. The boy's clothes attested to that. Richards felt a bond of sympathy for the boy, perhaps because of his own orphan childhood.

"How old you are?"

Potter shrugged. "About twelve, I reckon. I can't rightly say for sure."

"Would you like to sign aboard the *COHOCTON*? You would be a powder boy, like Jigs."

His eyes went wide with wonder. "This ship? Now?"

"This ship, now," returned Richards. "You will get food and clothes, a bit of schooling and eight dollars a month besides."

"Eight dollars?" The amount seemed a fortune to the destitute youth.

"Go back to where you live and return with anything you want to bring along. I will see you are signed aboard."

"Yes, sir!" The boy was off at a run, causing Richards to laugh as he shouted after him.

"Wait, Potter! The telegram?"

The boy skidded to a halt. He came back with a sheepish grin on his face and handed Richards the envelope.

"Now, get back as soon as you can," said Richards. He left at a run, the only pace young boys seem to know. The exuberance was refreshing after the dull days of loading the ship and re-educating LaForge. He opened the envelope and withdrew the message.

John-

I must return to Connecticut on urgent business on the morrow. I shall not be back until after the fourth. Please attend the victory ball this evening at the Fifth Avenue Hotel that we may finalize your preparations. Have Mr. LaForge accompany you and extend an invitation to your good Captain.

Respectfully,

G. Welles

He folded the telegram and placed it in his pocket. There were no problems with which Welles could help him. He would have to deal with the captain himself, for the future Secretary of Navy could not change Reynolds' position.

"RenError!, there is a formal reception tonight at the Fifth Avenue Hotel. We are invited."

"Dress uniforms, I presume?"

"Of course." Richards wondered if his was still be presentable. When they reached the deck, Richards excused himself. "I must relay an invitation to the captain."

On the crowded gun deck, he tried to stay clear of the bustling crewmen who continued to move supplies into the hold. It took a few minutes to find the captain in the cramped space, and Richards was forced to wait until Reynolds chose to acknowledge his presence. He relayed the invitation quickly and without flourish.

"A gracious invitation," commented Reynolds while considering it. "Please express my thanks and my regrets on not being able to attend."

Richards did not wait for an explanation. In truth, he was just as happy his captain did not accept the invitation to the party. Besides, LaForge was waiting and, with a sigh of resignation, he returned to the tedious duty.

Richards entered the lobby of the hotel, following several well dressed notables. He felt a touch on his shoulder as he turned towards the stairwell.

"Lieutenant?" LaForge stood behind him, a pretty blond woman on his arm. "May I present my wife, Lorraine?"

"Mrs. LaForge," returned Richards. He took her hand and bowed. She curtsied slightly in return but did not say anything.

"Please forgive her silence, lieutenant. She is French and is working o learning English."

LaForge looked to his wife and spoke briefly in her native tongue. She answered back rapidly and Richards caught little of the response.

"She is happy to meet you," translated LaForge.

Richards engaged the junior lieutenant in conversation while guiding the couple to the stairs. The music and sound of conversation directed them to the ballroom.

The gathering was smaller than the previous one, but not by much. Welles greeted the guests at the door, assisted by Becky. Richards was not given a chance to say more than 'hello', for Welles took him by the arm and led him to a side room.

Welles kept his voice low to prevent anyone from overhearing. "What of *COHOCTON*?"

"She is ready for sea," replied the officer, "but the Army supplies and equipment will not arrive until tomorrow. We have not made the arrangements for the soldiers."

Welles nodded, his face set in deep thought. "And the crew? What are their loyalties?"

"Split, like the rest of the country." He stated the case simply, making sure Welles was fully aware of conditions on the vessel. "Reynolds brought many of the southern crewmen back with him - enough to run the ship if he must."

"And northerners?"

"Over half. The engineer and gunner are both New Yorkers. Most of the seamen are from New England. We can hold the ship, if we have to fight for it."

"You may have to, John." Welles shook his head sadly. "The situation grows worse with each passing day. There is actually talk Lincoln will never be inaugurated!" The older man's voice rose, but he forced it to remain level. "They are passing bills of secession in state legislatures without even the formality of a discussion." He finished in a colder tone. "There is one other thing I must make clear, John. If hostilities are to begin, we cannot fire the first shot, no matter the provocation."

"I cannot fire unless fired upon?"

Welles shook his head. "You will not fire unless the very survival of the ship and crew is in question!"

Richards absorbed the implications of the statement. He had observed the results of modern naval combat in the Mediterranean. His reply was even.

"Sir, I know you are not completely familiar with naval affairs. Shell fire from only two or three guns can reduce a ship the size of COHOCTON to a sinking hulk within minutes." The prospect was not pleasant.

"I am too well aware of it, John." There was a note of sadness, but his position did not change. "However, those will be your orders. And they will not come from the Navy Department; they shall come directly from Buchanan!"

Richards accepted the remarks. It was not the first time he had received orders hindering the completion of an assignment, nor would it be the last.

"Come," said Welles, letting a rare smile cross his stern features. "This may not come to pass. Becky will singe my tail feathers if I let it spoil her evening!" Placing a strong arm around the younger man's shoulders, Welles returned to the ballroom.

Richards searched the room for some sign of Becky. He caught sight of LaForge and Lorraine dancing slowly together. The couple looked happy, smiling widely at each other. Then there was Becky, also on the dance floor. She caught sight of him and excused herself from her partner with a polite curtsy. He bowed at her approach and, without a word, the two moved onto the floor.

They stayed together dance after dance. Becky did not allow any of the other men to interrupt. The press of her was thrilling and he smiled inwardly at her refusals to officer and dignitary alike. They talked lightly, on subjects of no consequence. Neither mentioned the threat of war or their coming separation. But midnight approached and the reception drew to a close, Becky could no longer ignore the topic.

"When do you leave?" she asked, her eyes cast low.

"Reynolds will wait until the last minute. Probably the night of the fourth."

She held herself close when the music ended, and his arms stayed about her. Finally, the dictates of proper society forced her away.

"Five days," she whispered. "I could not say everything I feel in a month."

"God, I shall miss you," he said, kissing her dark hair. "Have I ever told you how beautiful you are?"

She ignored his compliment. "They will be trying to kill you."

"Everything will be fine." He hoped his words sounded more positive than he felt.

"I do not want you hurt or..." Becky's voice choked off, but Richards' mind filled in the words. *"...or killed."*

"Be careful," she managed to conclude.

"I will, but the prospect of action..." He stopped, unable to put his feelings into words. He turned his thoughts from the Navy to the young woman beside him. His mind was a swirl of emotions as they threaded through the crowd. The last few days with Becky were the happiest in his memory; the threat of a long separation horrid. The decision came on what course he must follow.

"Becky." His throat was suddenly dry in his attempt to form the words. "Will you marry me?"

If she was surprised, it did not show, for her step did not falter. But her voice was filled with emotion, barely audible above the noise of the room.

"Whenever you want, John."

He took her hand, forcing her to stop when he brought it to his lips. Then, ignoring the crowd, he took her in his arms and kissed her. She returned it with equal passion. And with people's stares following them, they finished the walk to her father.

"Sir." Richards used the voice he normally saved for the main deck to cut through the surrounding conversations. Welles looked at him, either unaware or ignoring the moment of passion on the dance floor. "I would like to ask for Rebecca's hand in marriage."

Welles stared at them, feigning disapproval. "Does Rebecca wish to marry you?"

"More than anything, father!" The words exploded from her lips before Richards could reply.

Welles could not hold the stern visage any longer and a wide grin broke upon his normally restrained features. "Then nothing could make me happier." He slapped Richards firmly on the back. "When shall we set the ceremony?"

Richards hesitated, looking to Becky and noting her subdued expression but bright eyes.

"When I return," he stated firmly. A hurt expression crossed her face, but vanished just as quickly. She nodded, agreeing with his decision.

Richards was able to use the late hour to forestall an endless round of congratulations from the group assembled in the ballroom. Bidding Welles goodnight, he took Becky's hand and pressed it to his lips.

"You understand why I need to wait?"

She nodded. "Yes, I understand." The hurt appeared again, then her arms were around him and she was pressing close. Warm, wet tears were on his cheek when she spoke. "Come back to me. Please."

He held her tight and kissed her. "I will. I promise." Another surge of passion caught him and he crushed her tighter. "I love you, Becky."

Her lips stayed close to his. "I love you, John."

The Brooklyn Navy Yard

CHAPTER THREE

The artillery supplies arrived in the morning, the numerous wagons adding to an ever growing pile on the dockside. It was questionable whether all of the material could be held in the ship, but Reynolds continued to supervise the loading. Richards noted the bright streak of copper showing evenly along the waterline when he came aboard. LaForge waited for his lessons and the crewmen were already at the job of stowing the supplies.

The morning was spent on the standing rigging, the various stays supporting the masts. As before, LaForge found the descriptions returning to memory as he reviewed their names and functions. The crew moved around the two officers in ordered confusion to lift and haul the army stores and place them below.

The noon meal came and went, with little visible reduction in the pile of supplies waiting on the dock. The crewmen were not pressed at a particularly fast rate, especially those working under the southern mates. While Richards corrected this when it became too obvious to ignore, the ship's first lieutenant could not interfere too openly with the captain.

On the main deck, Reynolds released the crew for the night, the dock still half covered with supplies. It would take most of the next day to finish. Richards noted an odd feel to the deck as he crossed to the gangway. He called to LaForge and left the ship, the other lieutenant coming along, trying to catch up.

Richards examined COHOCTON while waiting. The bright streak of copper so evident that morning had disappeared at the stern. The line of new sheets was just visible below the water level, but the line angled upwards towards the stem, reappearing above the water halfway down the length of the ship.

The trim of the ship was bad. With her down by the stern, COHOCTON's already poor handling characteristics would be multiplied. But the captain had supervised the loading and to point out the mistake was unthinkable. Richards wanted to believe it was an error, but he could never recall Reynolds making such a mistake before.

"Do you have plans for tonight?" asked LaForge. He blew on his cupped hands to warm them against the increasing chill as the light died.

"Not this evening, RenError!," he answered. "It looks like a good night to stay by the radiator. Perhaps a trip to the bath house might not be such a bad idea. It would take the chill out of my bones. And you?"

"Lorraine and I are going to see some of New York. I know a good restaurant not far from the hotel, if you would care to join us."

Richards shook his head to decline the invitation. "Enjoy yourselves, but remember to be on the ship by eight."

LaForge grinned, the wide, friendly smile he had used when they met. "Aye, aye, sir." Then he, too, left at a run.

Monday dawned bright and clear, January First, 1861. The new year made little difference to the mood of the country, however. The newspapers were still dominated by the secession of the southern states and the threat of war.

COHOCTON was picturesque, the balance of the Army supplies finally stored aboard. To all intents and purposes, the ship lay ready for sea. The tugs moved her into the harbor and steam was raised to check the boilers. Richards awaited word from Reynolds on when they would depart. To him, it was a waste of coal to keep the boilers going if they remained in port for the next three days.

Late in the day, an Army officer came out from the shore. The thought came easily now they were no longer in direct contact with the land. Richards watched him disappear into the captain's cabin. Later yet, he and LaForge were called aft.

"Lieutenant," said Reynolds, standing as they entered his cabin. The Army officer stood also. "This is my first officer, Lieutenant John Richards, and my second, RenError! LaForge. Gentlemen, Lt. Philip Jameson of the New York state militia."

Richards shook hands, noting how the tall officer crouched beneath the beams in the cabin. Reynolds waved them into chairs.

"Lt. Jameson and myself were discussing the Army troops. He feels to bring them aboard before weighing anchor would compromise our mission."

"Yes," said Jameson. The voice was very deep, contrasting with the youthful face. "My orders are to be as unobtrusive as possible."

"Where are your troops now, lieutenant?" asked Richards.

"We are assigned at Staten Island. Perhaps the ship could load the troops there, at night?" ventured the Army officer.

Reynolds nodded, accepting the proposal. Richards disapproved.

"That would be a long operation with just the ship's boats, captain," he pointed out. "Perhaps they could be brought out to us by the ferry? It would be faster and create less stir."

"Of course!" agreed Jameson enthusiastically before Reynolds could comment. "We are always using the ferry to move our troops, captain." He leaned forward for emphasis. "No one could know what was happening until our rendezvous. There would be no opportunity to pass word to any spies."

Reynolds clearly did not approve but could think of no reasons not to implement it. "Yes." The word came slowly, reluctantly. "I suppose such a plan might work, if you want to take the risks of transferring at sea."

"We can arrange for a rendezvous within the harbor." Richards carefully aimed his words at Jameson rather than Reynolds. "The waters will be calm and there should be few problems with such a transfer."

"Definitely," said Jameson. "A few risks are worth while to maintain secrecy. Do you not agree, captain?"

Reynolds was boxed in. Richards kept his face straight as the lieutenant commanding answered.

"Yes, lieutenant. My orders are clear on the matter of secrecy." Richards had seen teeth pulled easier than those words.

"Then it is settled." Jameson slapped the top of the desk with an open palm. "When shall we leave?"

Here, Reynolds was in charge. The ship was his command and his responsibility. His word was law.

"We will be ready to go on the fourth. I would say that night will suffice."

Richards felt the ship was ready for sea, that very night if necessary. But he had no say in the matter; Reynolds was the captain.

"The night of the fourth it is then," agreed Jameson. "The last ferry leaves the island at midnight. My troops shall be aboard and we will rendezvous south of the island."

Jameson shook hands with Reynolds. The captain, with Richards and LaForge close behind, escorted the officer to the deck. Once the lieutenant was gone, Reynolds turned to Richards. He seemed ready to comment on the younger man's interference, but did not. Instead, he took the companionway below.

COHOCTON drifted in the Lower Bay just south of Staten Island, the black shape of the ferry boat turned transport hardly discernable against the darker night. They had weighed anchor just before sunset, a course set for Ft. Monroe as a part of the continuing secrecy surrounding the mission. But before leaving the harbor, they doubled back to make the midnight meeting.

The dim shapes of the soldiers moved slowly and cautiously across the connecting gangway. No one spoke in the eerie silence and only occasional sparks from the stacks of the two ships added a weak, shifting light to the proceedings. A scrape on the deck startled Richards. LaForge stood there, features all but hidden in the darkness.

"How many more do you think?" His voice was a hushed whisper.

"We are about half done."

Reynolds stood further forward, engaged in a conversation. It took a moment to identify the other man as

Merrill. Richards saw the absurdity of the potential conflict, the fact of people set against each other simply by their state of birth. He also saw there was nothing he could do to change it.

The tread of feet ended when the last of the soldiers stepped off the gangway and marched below. The silence was destroyed by the sound of wood scraping wood when the gangway was pulled back onto the ferry. Without a word passing between the ships, the paddles on the ferry started turning and it was swiftly swallowed by the darkness. Reynolds' calm words broke the quiet.

"Lt. LaForge."

"Sir?"

"You have the watch. Set course for Pensacola. No sail until sun up."

"Aye, aye, sir."

Reynolds stepped to the companionway and disappeared below. LaForge went to the helm and rang half speed on the engine room repeater. Richards waited, wanting to observe LaForge before trusting him with complete control of the ship. Healey was at the wheel and grunted while he turned it to bring the ship on course.

"How does she handle?" asked Richards.

"God awful stiff, sir," replied the helmsman.

The ship headed due east to clear the harbor. In less than an hour, COHOCTON was in the Atlantic and had her first alarming encounter with the ocean. The bow met the first wave and refused to follow the correct course. Healey fought the wheel, helpless as the ship slid into the trough, throwing her sideways to the approaching swells.

"Christ almighty!" cursed Healey, leaning his weight against the wheel as it spun in the opposite direction.

Richards jumped to help as LaForge stood by, seemingly unaware of the struggling sailor. The vessel rose on the next wave and crested the swell in a sickening, side-sliding lurch.

"Helmsman aft!" shouted Richards, helping to bring the ship back on course. The two men pulled the spokes through, but to Richards each spoke felt as heavy as a shot. Another man reached the helm and COHOCTON met the next wave head on.

The bow wavered uncertainly on the swell, unsure what course to follow. The sloop was down aft and the stem lifted quickly while the stern lingered, sinking into the oncoming waves. Reynolds' voice boomed from below.

"Mr. LaForge! What the devil is going on up there?"

"The trim, captain," shouted Richards, cutting off LaForge's reply. "I have had to place two men on the wheel."

There was a slight pause while Reynolds digested the news. "See to it in the morning, Mr. Richards. In the mean time, it is Lt. LaForge's watch."

Richards struggled, wanting to point out the error in stowage. But military discipline won out, and he managed a convincing "Aye, sir."

After observing LaForge and the ship's motion, Richards decided the younger officer could manage the rest of the watch. He went below and fell into his bunk, not relishing the thought of what lay ahead.

Breakfast was quiet, the three officers exchanging only a few professional comments on the transfer of materials needed to adjust the trim. Richards, assigned the duty, decided to inspect the holds and confirm the current distribution of supplies. He finished his meal of fresh eggs and bread knowing it would not be long before they would be living on canned food and salt meat. The atmosphere in the ward room was cold and oppressive. LaForge was embarrassed by his inability to handle the ship and

Reynolds took a haughty, indifferent attitude to both his subordinates.

Richards made his way to the after hold. The space forward was dominated by the steam engine and boiler, as well as the coal bunkers necessary to keep the boiler fed. The space around the magazine was crowded with equipment and supplies. It was impossible to even sort out the mess.

"Aye, and the forward hold is no better." Hardy stood slightly behind, shaking his head at the disarray.

"What is this, this..." His words failed in the attempt to describe the arrangement.

"The captain saw to the loading, Mr. Richards," replied the older man sadly. "The poor girl is probably dyin' of shame, her innards in such a shape."

"We could shift the Dahlgrens forward to correct it."

"Aye, that would help, lieutenant," agreed Hardy. "But the magazines were stocked for the current arrangement. If we move the guns for'd, they'll be a ways to their shot and powder."

Richards eyed the gunner. There was something in his manner which said he was holding back. "What else, Mr. Hardy?"

Hardy struggled. "It don't much matter." He was disgusted, his tone hardly respectful towards a superior officer. "The way them holds is stocked, we can't get to the damned magazines any ways!"

Richards observed more closely. An Army howitzer lay fully against the door of the after magazine. To reach the shot and powder, he would have rearrange the entire shipload of supplies.

"We shall do what we can, Mr. Hardy." The gunner stepped clear and followed the officer to the main deck.

Richards emerged into the sunlight and was

immediately struck by the absence of sails. A favorable wind blew from the northwest, the flag snapping and crackling and pointing towards the port bow. Reynolds strolled the quarterdeck and Richards fell into step alongside.

"Good morning, captain," he said, trying to sound amiable while the greeting expressed less than his true feelings.

"Mr. Richards, have you decided on the steps to improve the trim?"

"First thing after the crew has eaten, sir."

Reynolds nodded his approval. "They will work better on full bellies."

"This is a fresh northerly," observed Richards, attempting to sound casual. "We might be able to take advantage of it and spread some canvas."

Reynolds examined the rigging to consider the proposition. Then he looked at the two men standing by the helm and shook his head.

"I think not. With the ship so difficult under steam, she would be all but impossible under sail. I fear we shall just have to accept steaming all the way to Pensacola. Unless your efforts at redistribution have some dramatic effects, of course." Richards remained quiet, biting back a remark on the responsibility for the current situation. "Besides, lieutenant," finished Reynolds, "our orders are to proceed with all haste. Steaming will make for a faster passage."

"Yes, sir," Richards replied dryly. He was not worried about the length of their trip to Pensacola. His concern was the coal. With Secessionists trying to seize every bit of Federal property, it could prove difficult to replace the fuel.

"What actions are you taking with the cargo?" asked Reynolds, forcing a change in the subject. "*COHOCTON* was not intended to be a merchantman." It was a thin enough excuse for the state of the hold.

Richards outlined his plan for shifting the two Dahlgrens and some of the cargo forward. Reynolds listened quietly, offering no criticism of the plan. Neither did he offer any improvements.

The crewmen finished eating and the master's mates assigned work parties. Knots of soldiers appeared on deck as they, too, finished eating and were chased from the gun deck. Finally, the lower deck was sufficiently empty for the work to begin.

The men shifted the cargo carefully. Each party was controlled by one of the master's mates who assured each heavy cask, crate or gun was properly moved across the rolling deck. Richards controlled the overall direction of the transfer. It was fortunate the deck was pitching only slightly. Even a moderate sea would make it too dangerous to move the heavy supplies around.

LaForge was assigned to move the nine inch guns forward. He approached the problem systematically, methodically and safely. The task also took him twice as long to accomplish as a more experienced officer.

By the end of the day, the jib was spread to help balance the trim. With the pressure forward, the extra man was removed from the helm. But Reynolds' prediction was correct. The poor sailing qualities of the COHOCTON, combined with the trim, created a dangerous situation with any sail aloft. Richards eyed the stack, watching the smoke pour from it to be quickly blown down wind. Coal was now the COHOCTON's life blood and the smoke showed they were using it as fast as the coal heavers could feed the flames.

With the effort of moving the cargo behind them, the crew settled into the normal routine of sailing. Despite the inter-service rivalry, the sailors and soldiers coexisted well in the cramped spaces of the ship. The voyage took on the aspect of an ocean cruise instead of the desperate mission it was in reality. The thought kept Richards from lapsing into the prevailing holiday mood. That, and the thought of sailing past Hatteras.

Richards awoke with a start, slammed against the bulkhead. He lay in his dark cabin while the ship tossed wildly. The storm had been expected since the wind picked up in the afternoon, but the action of the ship showed it had surpassed expectations. But Richards was used to storms at sea and lay back in the bunk, closing his eyes to return to sleep.

He wondered how long it would be before he replaced LaForge on watch. He toyed with the idea, half asleep, while contemplating the time. Then the realization struck him. LaForge, on his first sea duty and easily the worst sailor in Richards' memory, was commanding the ship! He bolted upright at the thought and was nearly thrown from the bunk.

Quickly, Richards struggled to his feet and felt for his clothes in the dark cabin. *COHOCTON* was off Hatteras! He forced himself to remain calm while knowing LaForge was unequal to the task before him. The sloop tossed even more wildly as he finished pulling on his oilskins and staggered from the cabin. The trip to the companionway was shortened when a massive heave threw him forward. He struck the steps hard enough to knock the wind from him, but he grabbed the guide rope in a moment of wild groping.

Pain pounding in his chest, Richards pulled himself up the steps. He was struck by a blast of wind and water as a wave crashed across the bow. Holding the safety rope tightly, he struggled aft. The crewmen in the watch huddled in the lee of any available obstruction to escape the fury of the storm. Their faces could not be seen in the dark.

Waves crashed over the bow with appalling rapidity, water cascading the entire length of the ship. Each threatened to sweep his feet from beneath him, but skill and determination kept him upright. He was assailed by the roar of sea and wind, each blast sounding a new note in the rigging.

LaForge and two helmsmen stood aft. Hands gripped the wheel tightly, tendons and veins rigid and hard set. Healey's face was cast in fear and panic while Sims, less visibly concerned, stilled showed the stress of the situation on his features. LaForge stood holding the guideline with both hands, his expression a rigid mask of determination.

Richards assessed the situation. The compass showed north-east; the engine room repeater indicating full steam. They were running the jib at dusk and it was doubtful it had been reefed. Even as the thought crossed his mind, a thunderous bang came from the bow as the sail split.

"That solves that problem," he said aloud, though it could not be heard by anyone else. It would have been nearly impossible to work the sail at any rate. He pulled himself closer to the junior lieutenant.

"Go below!" The force of the storm sapped his strength and he kept his words to a minimum. "Tell the captain it is urgent!"

LaForge nodded and groped his way forward along the guideline. Richards bent over the speaking tube.

"Engine room!" He turned his head quickly to catch the faint reply.

"Aye, aye, sir!" The voice was all but lost in the raging storm. It was hardly recognizable as Wilson, the chief engineer.

"Report your situation!"

"Holding so far! Dangerous to keep the fires going...I have already had some injuries!"

"Are the pumps going?"

"No." Even the engineer kept his words short.

"Start them!" Richards looked up, staring into the eye

of the wind and feeling the sting of rain and sea. "We shall change course soon. I will give you as much warning as possible!"

Richards leaned into the wind. LaForge was not visible, apparently reaching the comparative safety of the gun deck. He faced Healey, who seemed on the verge of hysteria.

"Take it easy," he shouted as calmly as he could manage. "We will be fine!'

The helmsman answered with a nervous nod and a weak grin.

Richards waited for Reynolds to appear, wishing for the man's experience and knowledge. His knees buckled slightly with the shock of crashing into each succeeding wave. *COHOCTON* was weathering, being blown backwards by the force of the wind. The rugged coast of North Carolina lay somewhere behind them. If they did not change course soon, they would be wrecked.

Amidst the fury, Richards found himself thinking of his grandfather, a man whom he had never met. He had commanded a sailing sloop. Its wreckage lay somewhere nearby. He was experiencing the same fear and apprehension his ancestor must have felt. This was the feeling just before a ship was wrecked; the feeling of helplessness and fearful expectation. And there were thoughts of Becky and his promise to return to her.

Richards waited, delaying far longer than he wished. And as the time lengthened, anger grew. Reynolds must be awake and know what was happening. *Where was he?* Inwardly, Richards stormed and fumed, all the while trying to maintain a calm exterior for the helmsmen. He could not afford to have his anger mistaken for fear. Then two figures appeared at the hatchway, struggling rearward along the line. Neither was Reynolds.

The first was LaForge, marked by the hesitant yet determined way he pulled himself along. The second form was almost swept away by the first wave to catch him. Holding by pure strength alone, the form regained his footing and followed LaForge aft. By the cut of the uniform, it was Jameson, the Army officer.

"Well?" he shouted to LaForge.

The officer gulped to catch his breath before answering. "The captain leaves it to your judgment! He does not wish to be disturbed."

"He what?" The anger burst out before he could contain it. "Goddamn..." With an effort, Richards choked himself off in mid-word. It was the captain's place, the right of command. He was distracted by the approach of the dripping Army officer.

"Lieutenant, my men..." started the officer, but the words were lost in the storm. He took a deep breath and continued. "Most of them are sick; all of them scared! Is there not something you can do about the way the ship is behaving?"

Richards regarded the soaked soldier, who had come on deck without benefit of oilskins. It would be days before he would be dry again. He forced himself to more important considerations.

Whether their position was north or south of Hatteras, they were being driven ashore. He had only two options. Heading southeast would take them away from the coast. At the same time, the storm would strike from directly abeam. The ship was not handling well and could be laid over by the action. They had to turn and run with the wind. Yet if they were still to the north of Hatteras, they would run ashore even more quickly than if they stayed on their present course.

"Did you ever see the Hatteras light house?" he asked LaForge.

"No! The lookout thinks it has been extinguished."

Richards returned to Jameson. "I shall see what we

can do about making your men more comfortable!" he shouted. "Mr. LaForge, see the lieutenant back below and pass the word we will be changing course directly."

"Aye, sir!" LaForge started forward.

"Thank you!" shouted Jameson before following LaForge.

Healey was smiling broadly over the exchange. The tendons in his hands were no longer as rigid. Even the stolid Sims allowed a slight clucking sound to escape.

"After all," shouted Richards, expending the effort to lighten the mood, "we sometimes forget the comfort of our passengers!"

"Aye, sir!" Healey's death grip loosened visibly.

"On my order, come about on the starboard to southwest. Smartly done now; there will be no room for error!" Healey and Sims nodded. "Good. We will let her lay there for a bit, then see how close we can lay her to south."

"Aye. Starboard to southwest!"

LaForge followed Jameson below and Richards bent to the speaking tube.

"Engine room, get ready! We are coming about!"

Richards waited. He wanted everyone prepared before they changed course. He forced himself to remain calm, to give LaForge enough time to spread the word. He shouted orders to the crewmen on deck and made sure they were passed forward. The waiting crewmen strengthened their holds on whatever fixed object was available. And while he stood, he felt the coast creeping up. Then enough time had elapsed. He shouted to the helmsmen as they struck the next wave.

"Now!"

At the single word, the two men pulled on the wheel and the sloop turned. Slowly, too slowly, the bow shifted to starboard. *COHOCTON* slid down the backside of the wave at an uncomfortable angle. In the trough, the wind caught the remains of the sail forward and the ship spun faster, but it was not fast enough.

The next wave caught them broadside. Richards grabbed the speaking tube convulsively as the ship rolled. He forced his exterior to remain calm, but internally he was gripped by panic as *COHOCTON* heeled over, further than he had ever experienced. The deck tilted sharply towards the surrounding sea, as if the lower yards would actually touch the surface. Then the wave crest passed and she righted herself, pivoting more quickly with the force of the wind. The wheel now spun to port as the helmsmen straightened out on the new course.

"Southwest, lieutenant!" reported Healey. The relief on his face was not shared by the young officer.

Were they north or south of Hatteras? He bent to the speaking tube. "Full stop!" he shouted, pulling back on the repeater.

It was necessary to lean slightly backwards against the wind. The ship rode better in the following sea, going over the waves instead of crashing through them. *COHOCTON* had a swooping, almost graceful feel Richards would have appreciated on the open sea. But the location of the coast preyed heavily on his thoughts.

"A point port," he shouted.

The wheel turned and the ship came easily to the new course. After a moment of feeling the effects of the change, the order was repeated. Though stiffer, she still acted well. Again, he repeated the command. Fighting the wheel, the helmsmen managed the new course. He decided the ship could not be brought any closer to south. Standing quietly, he settled down to await the outcome of his actions.

His body took on a will of his own, not content to await the results. Richards fought down an almost overwhelming urge to pace. Then his hand, seemingly on its own, moved towards the speaking trumpet. He pulled it back self consciously, realizing the men on the foretop would never hear him over the storm. He wanted to fidget, to do something to expend the nervous energy suddenly developed within him. Instead he stood, quietly staring straight ahead with hands clasped firmly behind him. His eyes fixed on parts of the ship for brief instants, feigning professional interest.

At one point in the interminable wait, he allowed himself the luxury of slowly withdrawing his watch and deliberately checking the time. The action was careful and slow, all the while maintaining an air of disinterest. After a lingering examination, he replaced the watch in his pocket with equal deliberateness.

It was ten after six and the watch was half over. Six ten - and they had not yet run ashore. Six ten - and there would be light enough to see in another hour.

He made another inspection of the ship. The wind was less severe and the waves less frequent. Over the next hour, the force of the storm continued to ease. Richards let a long, involuntary sigh of relief escape. Then he rewarded himself with another luxury and took a brief stroll about the quarterdeck.

"Almost dawn," he said to Healey, breaking the self-imposed silence.

"Aye, and the storm looks to be breakin'."

"Yes, it does," he agreed. His spirits lifted at the thought. "Another point port, please. She should handle it easily now."

The wheel turned and *COHOCTON* casually accepted the new course. Richards gave a brief nod of approval and returned to his spot near the speaking tube.

It was definitely getting lighter as the wind slackened. Richards felt almost happy when the bow could be seen in the first, dim light of dawn. A shout came from the foretop, easily heard above the dying wind.

"Ahoy the deck! Land to starboard!"

Richards strained into the gloom, but he could not make it out from the deck. He picked up the speaking trumpet.

"Can you identify it?"

"Cape Lookout, sir!"

There was a rush of relief at the words. "Are you positive?"

"Aye! I'm familiar with the area."

Cape Lookout placed them south of Hatteras and, on their present course, moving away from land.

"Thank you!" he shouted. "Thank you very much."

He hoped his voice carried the relief he felt. It was a close thing. If he had waited to be awakened for his watch, it might have been too late.

Richards relaxed, enjoying the spray, the wind and the motion of the ship. Punctually at eight, a weary looking replacement arrived at the helm. The storm slackened to a stiff breeze, and only one man was needed to replace the two helmsmen who had seen them through the night. A few minutes later, Reynolds, looking fresh and well rested in a dry uniform, appeared to relieve Richards.

"Good morning, sir." Even while speaking, Richards felt the anger build, resentment over Reynolds' ignoring the crisis.

"Hmm, yes," replied Reynolds with disinterest. He examined the deck, his eyes coming to rest on the tattered sail hanging from the jib stay. "Why was that not reefed?"

Ribbons of canvas drooped from the halyard. Richards thought of the long night, of the past six hours, and his eyes met Reynolds'.

"It was too dangerous for the men, captain." He almost spat the last word out.

Reynolds let out a grunt of disapproval and called crewmen to replace the sail.

Reynolds, whether there was a war approaching or not, commanded the ship. Richards could not say anything without the risk of mutiny, but he controlled the urge with difficulty. Instead, he walked from the quarterdeck, intent on finding himself a hot cup of coffee and a dry bunk.

Fort Pickens, Pensacola, Florida

CHAPTER FOUR

The morning of the ninth dawned clear and bright as *COHOCTON* glided peacefully into Pensacola Bay. Richards examined the quiet waters of the harbor as Reynolds brought the ship past the fort guarding the entrance. Two other ships, *WYANDOTTE* and *SUPPLY*, were anchored outside the harbor. The few crewmen moving about their decks stopped only briefly to inspect the newcomer before returning to their tasks.

The ship slowed as the throb of the pistons died. She drifted slowly forward with her momentum until Reynolds' shouted order had the wheel put over. The bow turned and another order released the anchor. The sound of the hawse cable broke the stillness, followed by the splash of the anchor breaking the smooth waters of the bay. The *COHOCTON* tugged at her cable and came to a halt, resting between the naval yard to the north and the fort to the south.

"Mr. Richards," said Reynolds when the younger lieutenant returned to the quarterdeck. "I will have the launch lowered. You and I will report to the yard commander."

"Yes, sir."

Within the hour, Richards and Reynolds entered the office of the yard's commander, Commodore James Armstrong. The man was familiar by reputation only; his exploits during the Mexican war were well known. It was a shock to be introduced to a graying old man behind a desk, the image so at contrast with the tales of bold courage. Besides Armstrong, two other men stood in the room, one a Navy officer, the other with the Army. They waited silently while Reynolds handed Armstrong their orders.

The commodore took the envelope from Reynolds and stared at it absently. Remembering the presence of the others with a start, he glanced up at the assembled men.

"My apologies, gentlemen. Captain Reynolds, this is my executive, Commander Ebenezer Farrand. The other is Lt. Adam Slemmer, commanding Company "G" of the First Artillery. Lieutenants Reynolds and Richards of the sloop COHOCTON," he finished, directing his words to Farrand and Slemmer.

Richards accepted the handshakes of the two men. Farrand was a dark haired man in his forties with the shifty, disquieting look of the jackal about him. His deep drawl announced his origins. Richards made a mental note to be careful around him. Slemmer was a younger man of lighter coloring and obviously distraught. His voice indicated a northern home.

Armstrong opened their orders while they accepted the greetings from the two officers. The old commodore slowly read the contents, nodding as he completed each page and proceeded to the next. At length, he carefully folded the sheets and replaced them in the envelope before speaking.

"More troops for the fort," he said, for Farrand's and Slemmer's benefit. He continued to Reynolds. "Lt.

Slemmer is preparing to move his men and supplies to Pickens. Boat crews from *WYANDOTTE* and *SUPPLY* are to help him. Perhaps you could also spare some men?" Armstrong's words were weak; without conviction. The words did not form an order. They barely suggested a request.

"Lt. Richards can make any necessary arrangements with Lt. Slemmer," returned Reynolds evenly. It was as if he had no thought either way on the subject of the order. "I shall coordinate with the captains on *WYANDOTTE* and *SUPPLY*."

Richards agreed with his captain's request and the brief discussion ended. Reynolds departed, leaving the lieutenant time to examine the Navy Yard.

Civilians entered and left the yard in casual groups with no guards to challenge them. Small knots of men clustered outside the short wall, talking in low voices and casting nervous glances. Those sailors and marines present were strolling aimlessly about, either completely unoccupied or leisurely engaged in insignificant tasks. Slemmer appeared, walking quickly. Richards was hard pressed to catch up.

"Lt. Slemmer?"

Slemmer did not slow his pace. "Adam, please. John, isn't it?" Richards nodded. "How many men did you bring?"

"Forty, plus equipment and supplies." Richards found himself out of breath. Ships were too small to prepare for long walks at such a quick pace.

"I have only fifty-one myself. Let me show you the situation." Slemmer halted at the dock, pointing to the large fort dominating the harbor's entrance.

"There is Ft. Pickens. Last night as a precaution, I ordered some of my men to stand guard. It was none too soon, for a band of Secessionists came out to take possession of it. Fortunately, the guard was awake and frightened them off with a warning shot." He paused, taking a deep breath of relief at the narrow escape. "The next time, a single shot in the air will not be so effective."

"What of the navy yard itself? What actions are prepared to defend it?" asked Richards.

Slemmer let a long sigh escape. "Ft. Pickens is designed to hold a thousand troops." He pointed further down the bay, where a smaller fort stood on the opposite lip of the bay, barely visible from their position. "Ft. McRee requires another three hundred, but is now watched over by a caretaker and his wife." He turned and swept his hand across the expanse of the yard. "This is surrounded by a three foot wall and could not be held by the men from all three of your ships, much less my pitiful fifty-one."

Slemmer laughed, the first sign of humor shown. It was not a happy sound. "I came to my command because my captain and senior lieutenant are on leave. Of course, I consider it purely coincidental both are southerners and have voiced favorable attitudes towards the dissolution of the union."

He did not dwell on his sarcasm. "The only defensible point is Pickens. The only way there is across the water and I need boats to move my men and equipment. It will have to be up to the Navy to hold the yard." His final words were bitter.

"You do not think the Navy can hold it?" questioned Richards.

"The Navy must *want* to hold it. Armstrong..." Slemmer stopped, considering what he was about to say. When he continued, a note of sadness overlaid his words. "Well, I am not even sure Armstrong is in possession of all his faculties. He places his trust in Farrand and Farrand is a known Secessionist." Richards saw new life in Slemmer's eyes as he finished. "Maybe you, or Lt. Reynolds, can make Armstrong realize the danger!" His new found hope died when he saw Richards' expression.

"It is not possible. Reynolds has not declared for secession, but his sympathies lie there. I cannot go over his head, even if I thought Commodore Armstrong would listen to me." Slemmer nodded. The proprieties of the military hierarchy were the same for both services. "If what you say is true, it is unlikely he would take anything I present to heed."

"You are right, of course. It only confirms what I already feared. I have moved my wife and family out to *SUPPLY*. The situation here seems all but hopeless, yet I must try." He straightened his shoulders, his face set in resolve. "Let us return to my men and prepare for your boats."

In this single section of the yard, feverish and ordered activity was evident as the soldiers moved purposefully about and stacked their equipment in preparation for movement to Ft. Pickens. Richards found it an effort to stay clear of the frenzied movements. It was an hour later when Evans, the captain's coxswain sought him out. Richards returned the man's salute as he spoke.

"Lieutenant, Captain Reynolds' compliments and he would like you to return to the ship."

"What about the boats?" he demanded.

"The captain says the other ships aren't sendin' boats and he sees no reason to do so either."

Richards bit off his retort. The seaman was in no position to control the situation. Instead, he sought out Slemmer to apprise him of the changed plans.

"The ships are not sending any boats. I am ordered to return to *COHOCTON*."

Slemmer controlled his anger with difficulty. "I must get troops into that fort tonight! Tomorrow may be too late!"

"If we do not get your men moved," offered Richards, "we could land the troops on *COHOCTON*. They will be capable of holding out any unorganized group."

63

The Army lieutenant reluctantly agreed to the plan then left to speak with Armstrong. Richards followed the coxswain to the dock and returned to the sloop.

Tired and hungry, he stepped aboard COHOCTON and saluted the stern. It was six bells in the afternoon watch and the day all but wasted. Reynolds stood at the stern unconcerned, leaning on the gunwale and staring across the bay. The ship's captain appraised Richards critically, the schoolmaster's gaze more irritating than ever.

"When will we be sending boats to Lieutenant Slemmer?" Richards asked evenly.

"The other captains do not feel it necessary to waste their time moving the Army to Ft. Pickens. I concur. Lt. Slemmer is reacting to a non-existent threat." The captain did not turn to face him. His casual tone and actions reinforced the lack of concern Reynolds showed to their situation. The younger lieutenant was not easily dissuaded, however.

"Slemmer wants the troops and supplies from COHOCTON unloaded tonight. I gave my word we would do so." He stretched the point to force some action to be taken.

"Without my approval?" The tone was even but the irritation was evident.

"My word was given, captain, based on your orders to me when you returned to the ship. I intend to keep it!"

Reynolds straightened at the tone. "You insubordinate..." he started, his voice rising. He cut the comment short when several nearby seamen looked aft, the etiquette of the Navy asserting itself. After a deep breath to gain control, he continued in a lowered voice. "I have had my fill of your insubordinate attitude, lieutenant. You may move these troops because the word of a naval officer must be his bond, but I intend to replace you at the first possible moment!"

Reynolds' request could destroy his career, but Richards no longer cared. If war came, Reynolds' actions would speak for themselves.

"As you wish, captain. I shall make the arrangements with Lt. Jameson."

He left the deck. Several seamen risked quick glances in his direction, but would not meet his angry eyes. The story was plainly read in their faces. Some supported his actions, others did not. The command of the ship was split like the service, and nothing could weld it together again.

Unloading the troops that evening was accomplished with few problems. Richards, with Slemmer and Jameson on hand, took charge of the operation and quickly had the boats plying back and forth in the deepening night. Slemmer and Jameson agreed moving the supplies could be done in daylight once the structure was secured.

"Lieutenant! The captain wants you right away."

After seeing Slemmer off, Richards had returned to his cabin. He stripped off his clothes and fell into the bunk in an exhausted state. Now, he sat up wearily and checked his watch, focusing his sleep clogged eyes with difficulty. It was barely four hours. Shaking his head in an effort to wake up, he recognized Sims through his blurred vision.

"Get me a cup of coffee, Sims."

"I ain't no steward, lieutenant." The seaman spoke with respect, but also emphasized his position with a note of pride.

"You are now, damn it! I want a cup of coffee," repeated Richards, a hard edge to his voice. "Hot!"

"Aye, aye, sir." The helmsman meekly complied with the order.

Richards managed a quick shave and was pulling on

his clothes when Sims returned. First he sipped the steaming liquid, and then took a long drink, the burning fluid flowing down his throat with a satisfying pain.

"What is your first name, Sims?" asked Richards, his mood improving with each quick gulp.

Sims hesitated. "Gibney, Sir."

Richards smiled. "Gibney?" He drained the mug and handed it back. His mood improved as the coffee worked through his system. "I realize you are not a steward, Sims, but four hours sleep leaves me in very poor humor. I apologize for the inconvenience."

"Aye, sir."

"Inform the captain I will be there directly."

A boat was being lowered when he arrived on deck and Reynolds was engaged in discussion with LaForge. Only the last few words were caught.

"...continue unloading the supplies, but no boats are to be sent to the Army at the yard. Do you understand?"

LaForge, sufficiently cowed, managed a weak "Yes, sir." Reynolds, satisfied with the new lieutenant's reactions, turned on Richards.

"Captain Walke asked us over to *SUPPLY*. He and Capt. Berryman from *WYANDOTTE* want to discuss our position." He did not wait for a reply, gesturing to the entry port. Richards climbed into the boat ahead of his captain.

Both *SUPPLY* and *WYANDOTTE* were anchored outside the harbor and well away from Ft. Pickens. There was no indication as to the standing of the ships commanders, but their reluctance to aid the Army showed vacillation if not southern leanings.

SUPPLY was an old side-wheel store ship carrying only four guns. Not even a proper warship, she would present little threat in a fight. *WYANDOTTE* was one of several steamers bought for the Paraguay expedition two years before. Though a screw steamer and relatively new, the small vessel mounted just five guns. This left *COHOCTON* in the enviable position of being the major naval force on the station. That strength made little difference if there was no desire to exercise it.

They were directed to the captain's cabin aboard *SUPPLY*. Captain Henry Walke was a man in his early fifties while Berryman of *WYANDOTTE* was even older. The two commanders renewed their old acquaintance with Reynolds and it was some time before the three stopped reminiscing and addressed the questions at hand.

"What are your operating orders?" asked Walke. As the senior officer present, he was the de facto commodore of the unofficial squadron.

"We are to deliver troops and supplies for the fort." Reynolds voice was soothing, nothing in it indicating the urgency stressed in their orders. "Just forty men and supplies. Hardly worth the effort, really."

"Still, it will double the Army forces," observed Berryman.

"Might I ask your orders, captain?" continued Reynolds. "I was somewhat surprised at your presence here."

Walke, as senior, spoke for the both captains. "We are to assure the safety of the fort. How we are to accomplish that feat from afloat is not specified in our orders." He looked at the other two captains before continuing.

"We are faced with rebellion here," he said finally. "At least, that is what is claimed by some. What are we to do about it?"

Reynolds filled his pipe leisurely. "I think the danger is overestimated, Henry." His words were quiet and self assured. His use of Walke's first name showed their long acquaintance. "It is not our job to fight United States citizens."

Berryman was equally casual. "Agreed, but neither can we allow Federal property to be taken at the whim of distraught countrymen. We cannot allow them to seize and hold the nation's weapons of war."

Reynolds shrugged. "There has been talk of secession and disunion for the past eighty years, my friend. Why is this any different?"

"This is the first time states have voted for secession!" The words came from Henry Erben, *WYANDOTTE*'s first lieutenant. Reynolds ignored him, waiting instead for an answer from either of the captains.

Walke finally broke the long silence. "What Henry says is true. The situation is sensitive. Whatever action we decide upon, we must not inflame matters further."

The conversation continued its slow pace. Ideas were expressed, but no concrete plan of action developed. Richards sat silently and watched his captain. Reynolds voiced objections to any constructive thought put forward, while avoiding direct criticisms. Like his other actions, he subtly insinuated them into the discussion. Richards had seen too much of Reynolds' careful obfuscation over the past month. The disquiet he felt was still overridden by a lifetime of following naval discipline. He kept silent.

Both Walke and Berryman were either unable to see his actions or unwilling to believe their old friend was any thing but loyal to the Union they were sworn to uphold. Finally Erben expressed his ideas, pressing them with a refreshing energy. *COHOCTON*'s lieutenant let the other officer take the lead.

"At the moment, gentlemen," he stated, his voice maintaining a calm and even pace, "The Secessionists can not hurt us. They have no guns to reach out here. But neither can we prevent their taking the Navy Yard."

"And your point, sir?" asked Reynolds coolly.

"We must protect our ships, for the Navy needs them

all badly." Erben waited for a nod of agreement from Reynolds before continuing. Richards added his own for encouragement. "The yard contains guns and shot. If taken, the Secessionists will gain the means to damage or sink the lot of us!"

All of the ships' commanders were taken aback by the emotion of the appeal, but the younger man's words were swaying both Walke and Berryman. Even more to Richard's surprise, Erben expertly placed Reynolds into a position where he could not argue against the suggestions.

"What we must do," continued Erben, "is rob them of their ability to harm us. Then, we will not be forced into a position of defending ourselves and harming them."

The trap was complete and Reynolds took the bait. "And how do you plan to accomplish this?"

Richards marveled at how deftly the younger lieutenant maneuvered the senior officers into agreeing. He had to admit, even to himself, that he was envious of Erben's powers of persuasion.

"By destroying their source of powder!" said Erben rapidly. He paused, giving the import of his words time to register. Reynolds let out a grunt of disapproval, but Erben ignored it and leaned forward for emphasis.

"Across the mouth of the inlet is Ft. McRee. All the powder for the Navy Yard is stored there. With only a caretaker to guard it, we could move in tonight and dump the powder into the bay."

"Then we could not use it either!" said Reynolds, angrily tapping his pipe on the edge of the table. At last he had shaken the smooth words of the young officer, and rose to oppose them.

"Nor could it be used against us!" countered Erben. "We cannot hold the yard nor can we move enough materials away to do any good. We *can* destroy that powder! It is not only our best chance, sir," he concluded, directing his words straight to Walke, "It is our only chance."

Walke and Berryman were torn. It was time for Richards to lend open support.

"For the cost of a little powder, we can defuse the whole situation!" he said. *"COHOCTON* can supply a boat load of men for the occasion."

Reynolds visibly seethed but made no open admonition against Richards. Erben ignored the southern officer, thrilled at the offer of support of *COHOCTON'*s first lieutenant.

"One boat load from *COHOCTON* and another from *SUPPLY*. We could be ready to go by dark. All we need is your approval."

Walke nodded his head slowly in agreement, convinced by the ardor of his young lieutenant. On seeing this, Berryman voiced reluctant agreement. Only Reynolds resisted the notion.

"But to destroy government property! Surely there must be better alternatives, gentlemen. A guard supplied by the Army, perhaps..."

Richards, more than anyone else present, was familiar with the Army's problems. "Lt. Slemmer stated he has insufficient men to guard Pickens adequately, even with the reinforcements. He cannot possibly provide guards for McRee."

Reynolds huffed but would not argue with the facts. Neither was he ready to openly declare himself a Secessionist. Reluctantly, *COHOCTON'*s captain nodded agreement.

"Then it is settled," said Walke, relief heavy in his voice. As the senior captain present, he was de facto the commodore of the unofficial squadron at Pensacola. But rather than take an active leadership roll, he appeared most content with following the consensus of officers about him. "Tonight, men from *SUPPLY* and *COHOCTON* will proceed to Ft. McRee and destroy the powder store. Any further suggestions?"

There were no other comments. Walke, Berryman and Reynolds returned to their discussions of the old days. Richards had heard the stories of exploration and Mexico from his uncle and did not need to hear them again. With a gesture to Erben, the junior officers excused themselves.

"Thanks for your help," said Erben as they emerged into the sunlight. Erben glanced casually about the deck, noting the locations of the various seamen. The direction of his steps led away from any that might overhear.

"You are welcome," returned Richards.

Erben lowered his voice. "Is Lt. Reynolds always so obstinate?"

Richards nodded. "He will not set himself openly against the Union, but neither will he support it."

"Yes," commented Erben dryly. "It is extremely difficult getting Walke or Berryman to take action. They are more afraid of upsetting the locals than letting the Union collapse."

Richards had not seen his actions in that light. He had mostly considered his actions in terms of following orders. But he had to admit to himself, if not to those about him, that Erben's assessment was correct. Orders or not, he was supporting the Union and the Federal authority.

The two men determined the various details of the joint operation. Times were set and the number of men required agreed upon. As a final reminder of the seriousness of their expedition, the officers decided to arm their parties.

SUPPLY's boat was barely visible though less than ten yards to the port. Only the occasional splash from an oar betrayed its presence. The faces in *COHOCTON*'s boat were indistinct blurs, from Sims at the tiller to Hardy and MacDonald at the bow. Only twenty-five men all told occupied the cutter. They were few enough, but sufficient for the needs of the evening. Further, they were men Richards could trust; men of northern origins and with little or no connection to Reynolds or the south.

They grounded on the sandy beach a few yards from the fort. MacDonald jumped onto shore, ordering his five marines to guard positions. Richards gathered the seamen around him and followed Erben.

McRee was unimpressive, and even less so in the dark. The fort was little more than a glorified earthwork battery, but it was fully enclosed and the door was barred. *SUPPLY*'s first lieutenant pounded loudly on the solid oak, the sound echoing in the darkness. A crack of light appeared, widening only slightly in the night. There was a portion of a fat, old face.

"Watcha' want?" The woman's words were slurred, whether from sleep or drink was not apparent.

"We are from the Navy," replied Erben crisply. "Please step aside."

"The caretaker ain't here," replied the old woman, holding the door tightly. "He's gone to town and takes his orders from the Army. Come back in the morning!"

She started to pull the door closed, but Erben grabbed the edge and tugged it open further. "I am afraid our business must be concluded tonight," he replied coolly. With a finally lurch, he wretched the door free. "Get to work, men."

The elderly woman stepped out to face the officers as the seamen streamed inside. "What are you doing?" she shrieked. "Get out of here!"

Richards and Hardy pushed past the woman, the only defense the fort had. Behind them, a line of seamen from

SUPPLY and *COHOCTON* followed a few with lanterns to light the way. Richards looked about and pointed towards a door leading deeper into the sand of the spit on which the fort was built.

Hardy opened the door into the powder room. Richards nodded with unconscious approval as the old gunners mate barred the men with the battle lanterns from entering the magazine. There was no cause to worry inside. Soon, a steady flow of seamen walked from the fort, rolling the kegs of powder to the water's edge. Seeing this, the old woman started screaming, her shrill voice piercing the night.

"You can't do this! Help!"

"Be quiet!" hissed Erben.

The young lieutenant grabbed for her while Richards watched in amusement. There was the sharp sound of a hand striking flesh and Erben staggered backwards, shocked by the force of her slap. In the same instant, she ran from the fort.

Richards was surprised by the assault and was slow in starting after her. She was swifter than her years and weight implied and made for the fort's small dock. Several seamen in a position to grab her only stood and laughed at the sight of a naval lieutenant slipping on the sand while trying to catch an old woman in her night clothes.

By the time Richards reached the dock, she was in a small boat and paddling furiously towards the dim lights of the town in the far distance. The visible splashes from he strokes showed she was less than efficient in her rowing.

"She got away," he explained on Erben's approach. Noting her lack of progress, he was not too worried by her departure. He could not suppress a grin as Erben rubbed his face.

"It appears she rows more slowly than she runs," noted Erben ruefully. "We will be long gone before she can send any interference."

Richards smiled. "Unless we continue to dally here."

Erben chuckled. "No doubt, lieutenant!" He gestured back in the direction of the fort.

The two officers returned to the task at hand. All casks were opened and dumped into the still waters. The sailors, unused to tasks of destruction, found the change in routine a pleasurable lark. It was an effort to keep the exuberance under control to assure proper caution. The last kegs were rolled out an hour later when MacDonald appeared.

"Lieutenant! Boats from shore!"

"How many?" Richards snapped, his eyes turning towards the water.

"Three, maybe four. Could be eighty or ninety men."

"That old woman cannot have reached shore!" observed Erben, goading the men to hurry.

"Then someone told them." Richards looked about, noting the ramrod straight silhouette of the Marine against the darker night. "MacDonald, recall your guards and stand over the boats."

With only a snapped reply, the Marine disappeared into the darkness.

"Get your men to the boats," said Erben. "I shall finish here and follow directly."

Richards touched his cap to the other lieutenant, and then ran to the dimly lit doorway of the fort. "Hardy! Visitors from shore. Are you ready?"

"That was the last of it, lieutenant!" The old gunner appeared, his clothes stained gray from the powder.

"Back to the boat with you, then. Let's go, lads!" He made sure all his seamen left the fort before following the scampering sailors up the short stretch of beach. Beyond the dim light around the fort was the dark outline of a boat gliding to the dock.

The men tumbled noisily into the boat and Richards looked to Hardy and MacDonald. "Shove off!"

The long boat slid into the dark waters of Pensacola Bay, the oars digging in to carry them from the shoreline. Sims angled away from the landing spot. Richards sat in the stern sheets, nervously glancing to where Erben and his men were jumping into their cutter.

"They're off, sir," said Sims quietly, pointing at a line of oar slashes to the left.

"Pull, now! Roundly, lads!" ordered Richards.

USS COHOCTON at anchor off Pensacola

CHAPTER FIVE

COHOCTON's boat leapt under the urging of the oarsmen. The creaking of the oars in their locks and the grunts of the men sounded loud in the still night. The reassuring sound of the water sluicing by the side helped as they drew further from the beach. A flash ashore heralded the sharp crack of a musket.

"Oars!" Richards hissed.

The whisper seemed nearly a shout, but the rowing stopped instantly, the oars held parallel to the water. The only sounds were the heavy breathing of the men and the water dripping from the motionless blades. Even that felt too loud in the black night.

The shore was not discernable, but a man there might see the white splashes from their oars. It might even be possible to follow the sounds of the boat. In the sudden silence, *SUPPLY*'s boat was clearly heard before they, too, stopped. The quiet was shattered by a ragged volley along the shore line, each gun momentarily marked by the flash. Richards saw the splashes from the shots fall short of Erben's boat, then saw a Marine raise his rifle in response to the fire from the Secessionists.

"I'll get one of those buggers, sir!"

Richards pushed the gun into the air. "Don't fire, you fool! They will mark us by the flash!"

He fought his anger while trying to keep the sound of his words from carrying across the water. At the same time, he was relieved the weapon did not fire when he grabbed it.

Sheepishly, the Marine lowered the rifle, wise enough to make no reply.

The two boats sat motionless for what felt like eternity, but no further shots came from the party on the beach. Torches were lit ashore and the dark silhouettes of men gathered around the fort. Their agitation was apparent even at a distance by their rapid motions, though nothing more than indistinct ranting could be heard.

"Give way easy," ordered Richards at length, his voice still hushed. "Pull us farther into the bay.

The sailors bent to their work, the stroke slow and even. Only the occasional grate of an oar broke the stillness. As they moved, the lights of the torches formed indistinct points and relief washed across the boat's occupants. The form of the other boat appeared as a darker shape alongside. Welcome recognition showed it to be SUPPLY's cutter.

"Richards?" Erben's voice came quietly across the narrow gap. "What happened?"

COHOCTON's senior lieutenant did not need long to decide. He had thought of little else since the southern boats appeared at the small dock by the fort.

"Someone told." His mind was a tumult. "There was no other way for them to be there so quickly."

"Then we should best do something about the yard. If the Secessionists were willing to take McRee..." Erben's voice stopped, the thought requiring no completion. He continued a new determination in his tone. "I am going to speak to Armstrong again. Do you want to come along?"

Richard's nodded, little considering that the action would not be visible in the night. "I shall ride with you."

Placing Hardy in command of the *COHOCTON*'s portion of the small expedition, Richards stepped across the gunwale into the other boat.

At the navy yard's dock, Erben left his seamen with the boat. Quickly, the two officers walked towards the commodore's office, surprised at finding lights still burning at the late hour.

Erben rapped crisply on the door and it was answered by Commander Ebenzer Farrand. The men exchanged but a few words before Farrand ushered them into Armstrong's office. The commodore ignored them while he finished reading a telegram. Farrand spoke as the old sailor laid the sheet aside.

"What is it you want?" he demanded.

Erben addressed himself directly to Armstrong instead of the southern commander. "We have come on a matter of some urgency, commodore."

Richards broke into the conversation. "We destroyed the powder stored at McRee. We must now consider the material here at the yard, commodore."

There was a glazed look in Armstrong's eyes. "You what?"

"We destroyed the powder to keep it from falling into the Secessionists' hands." Erben pointedly ignored Farrand, interrupting the commander as he opened his mouth to speak. "Neither can we allow the yard to be taken, commodore."

Armstrong straightened in his chair. "Are you mad?"

"Mad?" questioned Erben. "We cannot allow the yard

to be used against the Union. I submit we must prepare it for demolition first thing in the morning."

"Demolition?" snorted Farrand. "Commodore, if not mad these two must be drunk! I have no wish to hear any more of this drivel!"

"Yes, my friend, you may leave." Armstrong dismissed his second in command with a casual wave of his hand. For the first time, Armstrong showed some emotions.

"You want to blow up the yard?" the commodore asked scathingly. "Surely you must be mad, lieutenant, to even consider such a thing." He rose, facing them across his desk. The fire in his eyes gave a hint of the man behind the reputation. He reached down and lifted the telegram, crushing the paper in his fist beneath their noses.

"Do you know what this is, gentlemen? This message is from Washington, direct from the Navy Department! They urge me to take every precaution to protect the Federal property under my control. And you two rush in asking my permission to destroy it?" The effort seemed too much and his voice faltered. "Farrand wants me to seek the protection of the state. The Washington government wants..." His words died out, confused. There was a long silence, then Armstrong sank slowly back into his chair.

The old man held his face in his hands and sobbed. "What am I to do? Please tell me! What is the right choice?"

Richards looked at the tired old man before him. Armstrong's eyes rested on each of them in turn. He reached across and touched Erben's shoulder.

"We can do nothing more here, Henry."

"You could answer my question!" shouted Armstrong, lurching back to his feet. "Hot blooded young lieutenants! Think you know everything, do you? Well, what is the right choice when the Union is disintegrating before my eyes?"

"We have made ours," said Erben, his voice quiet and

gentle. "I cannot tell you what is correct. You are in command here, sir." He stepped back from the desk and touching his cap. "By your leave, commodore."

Armstrong sank back into his chair, fear, confusion, even panic on his face. It was an effort for Richards to leave the office.

Erben shook his head sadly on the slow walk to the boat. "That poor, old man," he said finally, his voice heavy with emotion.

"I am afraid we did not help him much," returned Richards.

Unexpectedly, a form stepped from the shadows, blocking their path. Richards and Erben stopped short. It took a moment to recognize Farrand's voice when he spoke.

"What do you intend to do?" the commander asked, his southern tones both smooth and threatening at the same moment.

Erben answered automatically. "Preserve the Union! Now step aside."

Erben stepped forward to pass and Farrand placed a hand on the lieutenant's chest. "You will make no attempts to destroy this yard or to bother the commodore. Is that clear?"

"I believe I have made my position clear." Erben removed Farrand's hand.

Perhaps it was the humiliation of being struck earlier by the old woman increasing Erben's awareness, but he stepped back and easily warded off a sudden blow from Farrand. His return punch caught the commander on the jaw and knocked him to the ground. Farrand sat rubbing his face, showing no willingness to continue the fight.

"You *are* mad," Farrand said as he regained his feet. "Mad, drunk or both!" As Erben stepped forward to threaten him, Farrand back pedaled, his voice rising to a shout. "Guards! Guards! They are trying to blow up the yard!" At the same time, Farrand turned and rushed away from the two officers, his voice rising even louder in alarm.

Richards grabbed Erben by the shoulder when he started after Farrand. "We had best be gone! The guards will not believe our story!"

Erben, angry over Farrand's action, hesitated. Then he ran after Richards towards the dock and the waiting boat. Within minutes, they were safely into the bay.

"What now?" asked Erben, the tiller turned towards COHOCTON.

"We have accomplished quite enough for one evening, Henry," said Richards evenly.

Erben returned a smile and they finished the short passage in silence. The shape of the sloop separated itself from the surrounding blackness. At the entry port, Richards noted captain's gig was missing. LaForge, standing the watch, waited expectantly, as he came through the entry port and saluted the stern.

"What happened?" asked LaForge.

"Unexpected guests." He eyed the other lieutenant, aware of something else in the man's manner. "Is there a problem?"

"I do not know, John. Right after you left..." The younger officer hesitated, then sucked in a deep breath. "Reynolds and Merrill took the gig to the navy yard. I thought you should know." He gestured at the still empty davits meaningfully.

"How soon after we left?"

"Not more than five minutes."

Richards calculated swiftly. The timing was right for the appearance of the Secessionists at the fort. He touched the man's arm. "Thanks, RenError!."

He seethed at the treachery, made all the worse because there was no way to prove it. Ultimately, he felt confused by the evening's events. The whole nation was divided between those wanting secession, those trying to prevent it and those, like Armstrong, who were caught in the middle.

The next day, Richards detailed the ship's boats to help move Slemmer and his command to Ft. Pickens. Slemmer's rude collection of boats and rafts sat waiting, already partially loaded from the previous day's efforts. The officer waited impatiently when Richards' boat drew up.

"We just received the word this morning. Florida passed a bill of secession yesterday." Slemmer was agitated as he relayed the information. He did not give Richards a chance to respond before continuing. "It is only a matter of time before they try to take over the Federal property."

The importance of the act required no explanation. As other boats drew up, Richards placed the men under Slemmer's command. Soon the motley collection moved across the bay carrying the artillery company to the comparative safety of the fort.

Slemmer and Richards had little free time until the sailors were hauling supplies into the fort. They watched the men work, assuring that little effort was wasted. Slemmer sounded more relaxed as he spoke.

"Things have been rough the past few days."

"We had some rough times of our own last night."

The Army officer smiled, the first time he had shown the genuine humor. "I heard about your little escapade last evening. I wish you had invited me."

Richards laughed. "Come now, lieutenant. The Navy must take care of its own."

"True, Lieutenant Richards, but it was an *Army* fort."

Richards laughed, tipping his hat slightly at the well earned jest.

"Lt. Slemmer!" The voice came from above and they both strained towards the ramparts. Jameson stood there, holding a telescope and pointing out to the sea. "Ships," he announced. "At least three of them!"

A narrow path twisted through the stacked supplies to the steps leading upwards in Ft. Pickens. When they reached the top, Jameson handed Richards the telescope. At first, he found it difficult to keep the ships centered in his field of view. It took a moment to realize it was the rock hard steadiness beneath his feet upsetting his sighting. He forced his hands to hold still, to keep from compensating for a moving deck.

There were three ships hull down, closing on the bay, standing out clearly under their pyramids of canvas. He judged the silhouettes carefully, recognizing the first two easily.

"The leader is *SABINE*, Adam," he explained. "A sailing frigate of fifty guns."

"Fifty guns? That is more than are mounted in the fort presently."

"Aye, but she can only move with the wind. She may carry enough artillery to level this place, but it will do little good if she can not deliver it where it is needed."

Richards brought the glass back to his eye. "The next is the *MACEDONIAN*. A sloop of twenty-two guns, but also a rag wagon."

"*MACEDONIAN*?" questioned Jameson. "Surely, I have heard the name before!"

Richards found himself smiling again. "Old Ironsides captured her from the British during the 1812 unpleasantness."

Slemmer was shocked. "But that would make the ship over fifty years old!"

"The English build well, Adam, and she was reconstructed in thirty-six and again in fifty-two."

"I feel so much better." There was no lack of sarcasm in his reply.

Richards examined the third ship. He was reassured by the sight of a small stack even though she, too, proceeded under sail.

"I am unsure about the last one, but at least she is a steamer. She might be *ST. LOUIS* or *PREBLE*, perhaps. Either is about twenty guns."

"It is an improvement over your *COHOCTON* and her ten, wouldn't you say?" asked Jameson.

"She probably carries eighteen pounders; we carry thirty-two's." He returned the telescope to its owner. "Our broadside is heavier, though guns are fewer."

Slemmer nodded. "So where does this leave us?"

"It increases our guns afloat, Adam, but you outlined the problem the other day." He glanced to sea at the warships. "We must be willing to employ those guns."

Their attention was drawn from the approaching vessels by a commotion on the beach. A group of men was trying to catch a wildly braying and kicking animal.

"You brought the donkey?" asked Richards, watching a soldier unsuccessfully trying to grab its bridle.

Slemmer smiled again. "You never know what might prove useful, John."

The new arrivals anchored outside the harbor joining the veterans of the station. The water at the bows of the newcomers was barely still before a flag hoist from *SABINE* called for all captains. It took little time to determine Captain Adams of the *SABINE* was now the senior on station. In a service obsessed with the hierarchy of command, it was always of the utmost importance to know who the senior officer was. In this case, it was obviously as important to the officer exercising that command as those who would be receiving the orders.

Reynolds wasted no time calling away his boat to report to the new commodore. Richards preceded his captain into the boat and sat silently while they passed the new arrivals on their way to *SABINE*. He noted none of the newcomers had soldiers aboard. If they did contain soldiers, the vessels were keeping the additional troops below decks.

The *MACEDONIAN* had a much heavier look to her than was common for frigates. He seemed to remember she was originally a ship of the line with a deck removed to convert her into a frigate. A razee, if he remembered the term correctly. Her timbers probably came from the Baltic, he reasoned, and would have held up well with proper maintenance since her capture in 1813. Still, she was over fifty years old, and her armament was most likely outdated.

The young lieutenant followed his captain aboard the *SABINE*. This vessel was newer and was one of the last generation of pure sailing vessels built for the Navy. By comparison to *COHOCTON*, her deck was spacious, as was the space between decks. The captain's cabin was positively cavernous compared to the one aboard *COHOCTON*. He nodded a greeting to Erben and Walker, taking a glass of wine offered by a well dressed steward. Captain Adams entered, indicating the waiting chairs for the other captains. The first officers were allowed to remain standing.

"Gentlemen," Adams began crisply. "I have orders to protect the fort and the navy yard. I need a report on the situation before I can determine our plan of action."

Henry Walke stood, nodding to the Reynolds and Berryman. It took him only a few brief minutes to relay the status of the fort and the loss of the yard. Adams nodded, seemingly asleep during the short explanation. But he sat up straight and spoke clearly as Walke sat back down.

"I see. My orders are quite clear on the matter of avoid confrontation with the local populace. How many men does the army have in the fort?"

"About sixty-five, captain," responded Walke.

Adams snickered at the low count. "Hardly enough to cause all this concern," he said. "I shall go ashore in the morning to discuss the situation with whoever might be in charge. In the meantime, we will take no action unless we see the fort directly threatened." He looked to each man in turn. "Is that most clear?"

They murmured their assent though Richards did not say anything. First, it was not his place to speak for the COHOCTON, but he also had another reason. He did not want to abandon the Army officers and troops to their own resources. It was clear to the Secessionists ashore that Ft. Pickens did not contain a large quantity of supplies, even with the extra provision unloaded from COHOCTON. If the Navy remained inactive, it was only a matter of time before those provisions were exhausted and the inadequate force holding the fort would be obliged to abandon it.

More wine was passed among the gathered officers. The discussion devolved into meeting old acquaintances arrived on the new vessels. The older captains grouped together to exchange stories, while the younger officers split up into a couple of small groups determining how the new commodore would affect their lives and actions.

Richards remained fairly quiet. He had no way to directly influence Adams one way or the other. It was plain, however, that the new commodore did not support the plan to hold the fort on the Florida coast. It was apparent that if forced to decide between maintaining control of the fort and firing upon a civil, even if Secessionist, population, Adams would allow the fort to go the same way as the navy yard and make no move to defend it.

The sun set and lamps were lit aboard *COHOCTON*. The crew gathered near the bow, singing songs accompanied by a few fiddles. Other men idled about, slowly smoking their pipes and watching the meager festivities of shipboard life. Reynolds had excused himself early, retiring to the solitude of his cabin. Richards stood near the wheel, pacing slowly along the quarterdeck and listening to the sounds from the lighted area forward.

The men were in good spirits, treating their adventure as a lark. It was good to see them so, but disquieting all the same. Their adventure could turn serious very quickly. Yet, Richards was also happy to spend a quiet watch, particularly after the efforts of the past several days.

Richards checked ship's clock. It was almost eight bells and time to relieve LaForge. The bosun came aft to ring the bell. The sound was echoed by the other ships around them. The party forward broke up, the men drifting below decks to their hammocks.

"Did the captain say when he would return?" LaForge showed little concern for the answer.

Richards found himself still adjusting to LaForge's southern accent. He shuddered at the thought of judging a man simply by the inflections in his voice.

"No, RenError!." He was suddenly very tired and yawned. The need to work ashore during the day did not relieve him of his watch that night. Normally, the first lieutenant was not required to stand a watch, but with the sloop short two lieutenants, Richards had to take his turn as a watch officer. He stretched and bid LaForge goodnight, then began walking along the quarterdeck. The captain returned late, but said nothing and went directly to his cabin.

Richards was still pacing slowly when the sun broke

the horizon. The bosun's whistle sounded and the men stirred, rising to the normal routine of stowing the hammocks and holystoning the decks before breakfast. Reynolds appeared to relieve him, the routine of ship's life continuing. But Richards halted at a shout from the masthead.

"Ahoy the deck! There's something funny in the yard!"

Richards grabbed a telescope, wondering why Reynolds walked to the opposite side. Grabbing a stay, he pulled himself onto the bulwark and trained the telescope towards shore. He swept it across the yard, expecting some sign of trouble. Instead, all appeared quiet and peaceful.

"The flagpole, lieutenant!" shouted the lookout.

The pole came into view, Richards moving slowly up its length. The flag was not the stars and stripes. It might be the state flag of Florida, but he could not be sure at the distance. Regardless, the meaning was clear. During the night, the Secessionists had simply walked in and taken over. Not a single shot was fired in defense of the place.

The tour of duty became routine aboard *COHOCTON*. Once the Navy Yard fell, the citizens of Florida made only one attempt to get the Army to surrender Ft. Pickens. Farrand led a group of prominent citizens to ask Slemmer to leave. Slemmer refused, quietly and with no discussion. The large naval presence insured no attempts were made to force the issue.

The ship benefited from easy truce with the local citizenry, one allowing them to receive fresh food and regular mail. The men fell into the holiday mood of the trip from New York. Regular drill and maintenance, even according to the strict schedule maintained by Reynolds, left them with too much free time on their hands.

The senior lieutenant watched the deck. The boys

played freely and noisily at the bow. The duty watch lolled about, their chores completed. They worked on their various crafts of knots and whittling, enjoying the warmth of the Florida sunshine. Across the bay, McRee stood, now in controlled by the state but without any visible changes from the Secessionists.

"John?" LaForge stood to his side, hesitant at interrupting his thoughts. "The captain wants to see all the officers in the wardroom."

The interior of the ship was cool after the warmth of the sun. Richards crowded into the wardroom and found all the petty officers also present. Reynolds stood at the stern windows, waiting until the gathering was complete.

"Gentlemen." His voice was smooth and easy, lacking the normal business-like crispness. "I would like to take the opportunity examine the ship's condition. We have had things very easy so far, but there is no indication it will not remain so. Mr. Richards?"

"Ship's condition is fit, captain," he replied. He kept his voice even, answering only what he was asked. "All guns, cordage and spars are checked and maintained on a daily basis."

"Mr. Merrill?"

The paymaster coughed nervously. "We continue to experience some desertion, captain. Another man disappeared last night. So far, it is just the southern hands."

Richards brought a hand up to cover the smile he knew was on his lips. He could not imagine *northern* crewmen deserting a thousand miles away from their homes.

"Well, we can not keep them from following their loyalties," said Reynolds, eyeing Richards carefully.

"We might call the hands together and ask if any want to be released, captain," suggested Richards. "At least they would not risk drowning by swimming for shore."

Reynolds cleared his throat. "I shall wait before we try such a *drastic* measure, lieutenant. Mr. Ambrose?"

The surgeon was a rarely seen man aboard the sloop. He maintained a self-imposed isolation in his small sick bay forward.

"The crew is remarkably free of disease, captain. Undoubtedly this is due to the good weather and the fresh food from shore."

And so the reports continued, covering the magazines, the food, the water. At length, Reynolds reached Wilson, the engineer.

First Assistant Engineer Jeremy Wilson was a thin, pale man. He was permanently grimy from his work below deck, but he loved the engine like a woman. There was never any doubt the ship's machinery was in good hands with Wilson.

"The engine is in good shape, captain, but we do need to discuss the coal..."

"Yes?" The word was a dare, a single syllable seemed stretched to the length of a sentence.

"We have less than twenty tons aboard at the moment, captain," continued Wilson. "I think we should shut down the boilers to conserve the supply."

Richards nodded at the suggestion. The ship only carried a hundred, sixty-five tons when fully loaded. With the heavy usage on their trip and Reynolds insistence the boiler be constantly lit, it was no surprise they were critically short.

"I will take it under consideration. How much longer would you estimate it will last?"

"Another three or four days at best," said the engineer. "Only two days of actual steaming, and then we would have to keep the speed down."

Reynolds nodded. "That concludes this meeting, gentlemen. You are all doing well at keeping the ship in shape." He regarded LaForge. "Lieutenant, after you pick up the food today, stop by *MACEDONIAN*. Ask Captain Adams if I might speak to him in the morning."

LaForge, slightly confused at the lack of explanation, managed to stammer a reply. "Yes, sir."

"That is all."

Richards left the wardroom wondering what Reynolds was planning. The end of the meeting was too swift, too clean for the suspicions he nursed.

The sailing frigate *USS MACEDONIAN*

CHAPTER SIX

Richards came on deck the next morning, watching the crew holystone the deck before being released to breakfast. The smell of fresh pork and eggs rose from the galley funnel and he breathed it in deeply, grateful for at least one benefit from the truce. Hardy came from below, saluting as he approached the wheel.

"Crew report, lieutenant." The voice was strained.

"Where is Mr. Merrill?" demanded Richards. "He normally makes the report."

Hardy hesitated, shuffling slightly before replying. "Gone, sir. He went over the side last night."

"That is absurd! I saw him speaking with the captain just before turning in!"

Hardy shrugged. "Ain't my fault, lieutenant. He's run and that's all there is to it."

Richards nodded to the inevitable. Hardy had no more control than he over such matters. All the same, the incident struck a disquieting cord. "I will report it to the captain. Inform the assistant paymaster to take over Merrill's duties and to see me if there are any questions."

"Aye aye, sir." Hardy paused, taking a deep breath. He smiled at the smells wafting from the galley funnel. "At least the cook's not run!"

After the crew ate, Richards started them on gun drill. As usual, they grumbled as they walked to their stations. Reynolds appeared and examined the exercise for a moment before speaking.

"Call away my gig, lieutenant. Captain Adams will be waiting."

Richards called for the boat's crew. "Might I accompany you, captain?" he asked, still curious. "I would appreciate a change in scenery."

Reynolds eyed him critically and Richards thought he was going to refuse. Instead, he replied in a neutral tone.

"If you wish, lieutenant. It might be a good experience for Mr. LaForge if he spent some time in charge."

The trip to the old *MACEDONIAN* was short. Reynolds was piped aboard with proper courtesy and Richards followed at the proper distance. They were greeted by the first lieutenant and quickly led to the captains' quarters. Captain Adams held out a hand to Reynolds.

"Glad to see you, Paul," he said, shaking it warmly.

"You are too kind, sir," replied Reynolds. He gestured to his officer. "Lt. John Richards, my first."

Adams nodded, pointing towards two chairs. "Be seated, gentlemen. I would offer brandy, but it is a bit early in the day. We shall have to be satisfied with coffee." A steward dutifully appeared and poured each of the officers a cup, withdrawing silently when finished. "Now, Paul, what seems to be the problem?"

"Coal," returned Reynolds. The comment was simple and direct, without the small talk so evident in other recent discussions with senior officers. "Because of our load coming south, we had an unusually high use. My engineer states we have only twenty tons left aboard."

"And a steamer without coal is just another sailing ship," finished Adams. "We have few enough steamers as it is. What do you propose?"

"We have a day's worth for steaming. It is enough for us to reach Mobile."

"Mobile?" Richards was startled at the suggestion. "It is barely a week since Alabama passed their law of secession. Is that truly safe for the ship and crew?"

Even Adams looked uncomfortable with the idea. Reynolds, on the other hand, sat quietly waiting for an answer and making no attempt to force the issue.

"Mobile is definitely the closest open port available." Adams' voice was hesitant, even when he reached his decision. "Yes, it will have to be Mobile. You may proceed at once, Paul. But for God's sake, be cautious. You can not be sure what the Secessionists might try."

"Extremely cautious," returned Reynolds. "We will leave after dark tonight, so as not to create a stir."

Adams glanced upward, calculating swiftly. "Aye, and it will put you into Mobile after dawn tomorrow. With luck, you can be on your way back tomorrow evening. Allowing for the bureaucracy, you should return in no later than three days. I will expect you then."

Richards voiced no further doubts in front of Captain Adams, but the plan to proceed to Mobile unsettled him. They were sailing into the lion's den, their hands tied by Buchanan's orders. He shook his head. Was it only two months since meeting Welles and seeing Becky? He turned his thoughts to more important matters. Mobile was indeed the closest port, but events were too set, too convenient. There seemed just precisely enough coal in the bunkers to reach Mobile, the fact adding to his suspicions. The port lay open to Union vessels despite the vote of secession, but he intended to remain extremely cautious.

The ship weighed anchor after dark. Richards smiled at the thought of slipping away unnoticed. The noise would alert everyone within miles the ship was on the move. Smoke and sparks drifted from the funnel and the deck throbbed beneath his feet as they began the short beat west to Mobile Bay.

The men of the watch were quiet as they went about their duties. Richards noted the muted tones of their speech, the hesitance of their actions as they moved about. *They think they are going into action.* He had to admit the same concerns crossed his mind.

"Good evening, sir." It was MacDonald, his Marine uniform pressed and proper even at this late hour.

"Lieutenant." It was an odd occurrence to have the Marine speak to him, emphasized by the fact the officer should be asleep below.

"If I might have a word, lieutenant," he continued, his voice lowered so no one could overhear. Richards nodded, glancing about to assure they were alone. "I would speak with the captain, but I believe my concerns would fall on deaf ears."

"And what are those concerns, Lt. MacDonald?"

"Mobile, sir. We are taking the ship into the heart of Secessionist territory tomorrow."

"I am too well aware of that fact, lieutenant."

MacDonald cleared his throat, looking about them again before he continued. "I know, sir. But what are we to do, lieutenant? What steps may we take to protect the men and the ship?"

Richards placed his hands on the bulwark, feeling the beat of the engine in the wood. The dark shoreline to the north was hardly visible in the night. But it was no longer the friendly shore of home. It was no something different, something uncertain.

"I am not entirely sure, lieutenant," he replied. "I do not command this vessel."

MacDonald did not respond immediately. It went unsaid between the two men that they were in unknown territory. They had to doubt their countrymen, their shipmates – even their own captain.

"Is there anything we might do without challenging the command of the vessel?"

Richard took in a deep breath, letting it out slowly. "I do not know, Daniel. We have very specific instructions to do nothing that might endanger the lives of citizens; even those know to favor secession."

MacDonald glanced nervously about them, his voice more intense as he continued. "And we are to do nothing to protect ourselves?"

"I do share your *apprehension*," he answered, choosing the word carefully. "Let me consider the situation tonight, before we reach Mobile. In the meantime, I would suggest you remain alert."

"A Marine is always that, lieutenant." Some of MacDonald's customary huffiness returned in the comment.

Richards smiled. "As I well know. But perhaps you might raise your level of alertness to a new height for tomorrow's activities."

MacDonald returned the smiled, saluting. "As you wish, Sir. We shall see what tomorrow brings."

He returned the salute and the Marine officer turned and went below.

The night watch continued without further interruption as the ship cruised through the quiet water. The sky was cloudless and the stars shown brightly in the crisp air as if suspended in the complex of rigging and masts. With the need to conserve fuel, the engine turned over slowly and set a leisurely pace, the dull throb lulling the senses. The eastern horizon was a bright line when they reached the mouth of the bay.

"Shore lights off the starboard bow!" The shout from the masthead broke the stillness on the deck. Richards lifted a telescope to examine the lights.

"It seems they are still concerned for safe navigation in Alabama," he noted, thankful not to have to maneuver the tricky mouth of the bay without aids. "Bring her starboard; steer due north."

"Due north, aye." The wheel spun in the Sims' hands, stopping with sharp precision as the bow started to turn. Just as quickly, the wheel turned back. "Due north, full an' by, lieutenant."

It would be a long run up the bay to Mobile. A quick calculation showed they should make it before noon. He lifted the telescope again, examining the large fort guarding the eastern edge of the bay: *Fort Morgan*. All seemed still in the structure and Richards breathed a sigh of relief. Any activity might mean they would soon come under a rain of shot and shell. A flag moved slowly up the staff to break open in the light of a new day. But it was not the stars and stripes; it was the state flag of Alabama.

"The watch is aft, Mr. Richards." Reynolds stood quietly to one side, his usual neat, trim appearance. His voice was slightly miffed, like impatience, or perhaps anticipation. It was the first emotion shown in weeks.

"Captain, I stand relieved." The words were formal, coming with easy practice to his lips. "I was noting the state has taken possession of the forts, sir."

"Not too unusual these days, surely," huffed Reynolds, inspecting the deck as the sailors began the daily task of scrubbing.

"By your leave." Richards touched his hat and started below. He met LaForge coming from the wardroom.

"RenError!, wake me when we reach Mobile."

LaForge looked at him, surprised at the request. "But you are off watch until this afternoon..."

Richards nodded, his face set. "Thank you for your concern, but I will be on deck when we reach Mobile."

LaForge shrugged, resigned to Richards' request. "As you wish, John."

Sims awakened Richards later. The sun shown brightly through the wardroom windows as he sat at the table drinking a lukewarm cup of left over coffee. Richards felt tired: he had not had enough sleep. But this day might be critical. Setting down the coffee mug, he pulled on his uniform coat and returned to the quarterdeck.

COHOCTON was in the final stages of warping to the loading dock, the coaling tower level with the tops of the masts. There were several black bodies working at moving coal up into the tower. They might have been slaves or merely covered with coal dust.

Reynolds saw him as the ship bumped against the dock. There was a momentary surprise in his expression but it disappeared in a flash. The captain shifted his attention to the deck. Crewmen grabbed the lines tossed from the dock and made the ship fast. Others opened hatches, preparing for the coal to be loaded. Still more arranged shovels, mops, brooms and buckets in readiness for the messy job ahead.

"You should have slept longer." Reynolds' tone was angry rather than concern. "I am going ashore to arrange for payment. You may supervise the loading."

Richards touched his hat, but Reynolds ignored him and stepped to the hastily rigged gangway. After saluting the quarterdeck, Reynolds crossed the short space, heading briskly towards the dockyard office.

"Mr. Wilson!" The thin engineer turned to him, blinking in the bright sunlight like a mole too long underground. "Get the coal chutes rigged and start loading."

Wilson saluted and turned to his men, shouting orders and creating a stir of activity both on deck and below. LaForge stepped forward, already grimy from working around the hold.

"RenError!," started Richards, his voice even, but his tone low. "We must be cautious this day. I want men stationed at the main and jibs. Put good men with axes at the lines so we are prepared to cast off quickly." LaForge turned to shout the orders but Richards placed a hand on his shoulder.

"Quietly and without fanfare, RenError!. Everything must appear normal and routine. After the loading begins, be sure to rotate the men at regular intervals so no one is too exhausted by the work."

LaForge nodded, issuing the orders to the men and petty officers. Richards was satisfied as sailors took the designated stations in an easy manner. Little would be visible from shore to indicate the preparations.

Richards looked about for MacDonald and found him not far away on the quarterdeck. He walked over and led him away from the working sailors. "I want your Marines together below deck. Hold them in the wardroom, armed and ready."

"Yes, sir."

"Daniel, do not load your weapons. We cannot risk an accidental shooting."

"I understand." MacDonald looked about them, lowering his voice further. "We shall remain *alert*, lieutenant."

"Well you should, lieutenant." Richards glanced across MacDonald's shoulder at the yard. Civilians strolled about or clustered into small groups, but there were far too many onlookers. "Maybe there is nothing better for men to do in Mobile than hang about the docks, so let us just say I am being cautious." MacDonald smiled at the slight joke and left to carry out his instructions; Richards stopped him. "And Daniel, choose only those you know are trustworthy."

"They are all trustworthy, lieutenant," snapped MacDonald in a huff. "They are *Marines!*"

The coal slid down the chute at a satisfying rate and Richards watched thankfully as it disappeared into the hold. A dirty black cloud of coal dust enveloped the deck and crewmen were kept busy with shovels and brooms to contain it as the unsightly mess marred the spotlessly white deck.

Wilson came back to the quarterdeck, his teeth bright against the grimy blackness of his face. "My coal heavers have it well in hand, lieutenant." He hefted a lump of coal in one hand, breaking off a piece with the other. "But this is what they're givin' us." He held up the broken section. "Lignite. It's going to smoke like the devil when we light up the boilers."

"Best store it in bunkers separate from the remainder of the anthracite. We will save that for an emergency."

Wilson's smile widened just the tiniest bit. "Already done, lieutenant." Without so much as a by your leave, Wilson went back to his work.

The crowd on the dock grew noticeably, though they tried to stand in small, unobtrusive groups. The men cast nervous glances at the sloop and more arrived every minute. Richards was uneasy, and he nursed more than a feeling they were expected.

The coaling was not progressing fast enough to suit him in spite of the tiring pace maintained by the sailors. As the crowd grew, the watchers became bolder and hurled cat calls and obscenities at the laboring crewmen. They pressed closer, the sailors casting nervous glances at the threatening mob.

Richards was alert for the first sign of trouble. He scanned back and forth across the faces, his nerves stretched to the limit. Suddenly, he recognized a face, the features distinct from the press of people around him. *Merrill.* Their eyes met and locked across the fifty feet separating them. At the flash of recognition, the paymaster let out a shout and the civilians rushed the vessel.

"Get aboard!" shouted Richards, but the seamen ashore needed no urging from him. He grabbed the speaking trumpet. "Marines on deck!" he yelled, turning towards the bow as his men scrambled aboard the sloop. "Main and jib home! Cast off bow line!"

There was a thud from an axe and the bowline parted. Two sails cracked open in the wind and the bow pushed away from the dock. But the Secessionists were already there, jumping the narrow gap of water. The gangway fell away and the Marines rushed on deck, their rifles ready, and bayonets glinting in the sunlight.

"Hand to hand, damn it!" he shouted. "Repel boarders!" With a shrug and a wave, MacDonald led his men into the struggling melee of sailors and civilians rapidly spreading across the deck.

The bow pressed further towards the bay, and Richards shouted aft. "Cast off stern line!"

He had waited a moment too long. The crewman raised his axe but was swept aside by another group of civilians crossing from the dock. Richards pushed through them, grabbing the axe from the deck and swinging it. Too late, an arm grabbed him. The blade bit into the cable and it parted. *COHOCTON* drifted slowly away from the wharf.

Richards struck an assailant with his fist, wincing at the contact with the man's jaw. The deck was covered with fighting figures while the ship slowly drifted into the bay, out of control. True loyalties surfaced when a few sailors helped the boarders. A quick glance aft was a relief, for the ship had moved too far away for more people to come aboard. The greater bulk of the mob was left angry and shouting while the ship made its slow way down wind.

The fight came under control. Disciplined sailors and Marines won out over the disorganized crowd. Union sailors tossed a steady stream of luckless civilians over the side, their success marked by a line of swimmers pointing towards shore. Reluctantly, Richards called a halt to the simple procedure. They were far enough into the bay he feared someone might drown. The Marines gathered the remaining attackers.

"Lt. MacDonald! Group the civilians forward. Make sure they do nothing to damage the ship!"

"Sir!" Their rifles ready with bayonets fixed, the Marines formed a sturdy cordon around the spiritless Secessionists.

Richards inspected the littered deck. Smeared with coal dust and, in a few cases, patches of blood, it was an untidy mess. The ship was now well into the bay. Sims took the helm, smiling over the brief fisticuffs, one eye slightly swollen from a blow. A reassuring glance aft showed no pursuit developing from the remaining mob ashore.

"Take in the fore course and the jib! Helm alee and let go!"

The sailors swarmed aloft and the sails disappeared. It was not as quick as usual, the crewmen working around the untidy group of boarders. The sound of the anchor splashing alongside greeted Richards as he strode forward to inspect the prisoners.

Potter and the other boys stood in a group, more than a single bruise visible among even the boys. They stood just beyond the cordon of Marines hurling insults at the Secessionists. He smiled at their youthful exuberance.

Most of the civilians refused to meet his gaze as he walked past the captives. There was only one man in whom he was interested, and he finally spotted Merrill trying to hide behind two of his fellows.

"Lt. MacDonald, we have a deserter in this group. Escort Mr. Merrill to the wardroom!"

MacDonald, accompanied by two burly Marines, thrust through the group and grabbed the paymaster. Merrill's face was etched in panic as he was dragged aft.

"Wilson!" The engineer appeared, apparently no worse the wear for the brief fight. "Get the men busy cleaning this mess. Anyone with a serious injury can be sent down to the surgeon."

"No more than a few cuts and bruises, I'm thinkin'," replied Wilson. He started shouting orders to the seaman.

"Mr. LaForge, you will come aft with me." Richards did not wait for a reply, leading the way below to the wardroom.

He sat across the table from Merrill, leaving the paymaster flanked by his two guards. The paymaster's appearance in Mobile confirmed his suspicions. Everything since leaving New York, from the badly trimmed ship to this final attempt to seize control, was planned. But more than his suppositions were needed to prove it.

He stared at the man, waiting before speaking to him; making sure the man was visibly sweating with fear before uttering a word. The first sound from his mouth made the paymaster jump visibly.

"Dying at the end of a rope is not pleasant." He let the comment sit, preying on Merrill's nerves. "That is what shall happen to you, Merrill. Those men on deck will go free; even the sailors. But not you. You are a deserter. Worse! A filthy rotten traitor!" He was on his feet, his shouted words ringing in the enclosed space. "I will hang you myself!"

Merrill's face was the color of a sun bleached sheet. He tried to speak and could not. Swallowing hard, he managed to stammer a comment.

"No, lieutenant. I was..." His words failed him, but he finished in a flurry. "I was only supporting what I believed in..."

"Traitor!" interrupted Richards. "I am going to enjoy every second while you dance!" He spoke to the marines. "Put him in irons and toss him in the brig!" He turned to the stern windows and the sunlight glancing off the water.

"You can not do this," pleaded Merrill, struggling against the two guards. "Please, I will do anything. Anything!"

With deliberate slowness, Richards looked over his shoulder at him. "I want only one thing and will give you only one chance. Who planned this?" Stark fear lay in the other man's eyes. Merrill swallowed hard, undecided. When he did not speak, Richards waved his hand. "Take him away."

The two marines grabbed the prisoner roughly and pulled him towards the door.

"Reynolds!" shouted Merrill, jumping away from the Marines. "I swear it was Reynolds! He told me he would bring the ship here. He sent me ahead to make arrangements to take her." Merrill sank to his knees, sobbing. "God, sir! Please! I was only doin' what I believed was right."

"So am I," replied Richards, his voice so low it could

barely be heard above the paymaster's sobs. "RenError!, MacDonald, did you hear his confession?" The two officers nodded without comment. Richards gestured to Merrill. "Put him forward with the others."

Sims appeared in the door as Merrill was taken away. "Boat from shore, lieutenant. It be the captain."

"Thank you, Sims. Return to your duties." With the seaman gone, Richards glanced out at the approaching boat. "I am on dangerous ground here, RenError!."

"You mean *we* are, John." There was a grim smile on LaForge's face.

"Not this time, RenError!. If Reynolds wants, he can insist on returning with us."

LaForge interrupted. "How can you say that with what Merrill has confessed?"

"Merill will stay here, or he will hang. You know that as well as I." Richards shook his head. "No, a court martial might look on what I am about to do as mutiny. I do not want you on my conscience." He took a deep breath, to prepare himself for what must come next.

"Allow Reynolds to come below. I will meet him in his cabin. But I want everyone - and I mean everyone - out of earshot. Is that understood?"

"Aye." LaForge paused, ready to speak again. But he held his voice and instead headed for the main deck.

Richards watched him leave, and then went up a deck to the captain's cabin. Everything was reaching a climax, the end of a path he foresaw in December when Reynolds appeared to take command of the sloop. Now it would be the same as it was then: the two men would confront each other for control of the ship. He took a deep breath, facing the same choice thrown before him so many times since COHOCTON returned from the Mediterranean. Union or Secession. There were only two choices. He entered the captain's cabin and stood waiting behind the desk.

Reynolds appeared his face livid. LaForge was closed behind. He shut the door and both men waited for the footsteps to recede before speaking.

"I will have you arrested," started Reynolds. "Court martialled for sure..."

"And I will see you hung," returned Richards flatly. He leaned across the desk, not giving an inch under the rage of his captain. He could not contain the malice carried in his tone and words. "Everything you have done was treason, pure and simple."

The captain's face grew redder, if possible. "How dare you..." Reynolds' tirade got no further.

"How dare you!" shouted Richards. Once given vent, he could not stop the flood of his emotions. "You planned from the beginning to have this ship seized! We have Merrill and he has confessed his part. You deliberately trimmed the ship badly, used the coal in useless maneuvering, all to get the COHOCTON here. No, if anyone is arrested, it will be you!"

Reynolds stood quite still, as if struck by a physical blow instead of mere words. He sank slowly into a chair, his words weak and hollow. "I did what I felt was my duty..."

"Duty?" From Richards' lips, the words were a sneer. He bit back further comments, forcing himself to calm down. In a lower note, he continued. "You have but two choices. You may resign your commission here and now. You may return to Georgia, unable to support the Union against your home state. It will be an honorable retirement and I will make no mention of your part in this day's events."

"And the other?" There was only resignation in Reynolds' words.

"I will place you under arrest. When the ship returns to Pickens, you will face charges of treason."

"Damned little choice." The voice was low and without emotion.

"You betrayed a trust, captain. Not only of your nation, but of the men under your command."

A heavy silence hung between the two before Reynolds spoke. "I will collect my belongings."

"I will detail a man to help you."

Richards went on deck and sent Sims below to assist Reynolds. LaForge, MacDonald and Wilson approached expectancy in their faces.

"It is done. The captain will go ashore here."

"You are letting him go?" questioned LaForge.

"There is nothing to be served by placing him in chains." Richards took another deep breath. It was time to clear the air. "Call the men, RenError!. They must make their choice also."

The bosun's mate blew his whistle and the crewmen assembled. Loyalties could not be ascertained from their faces.

"It has come to this, men." He paused, gauging the moment to continue. "You are either for the Union or against it. The regulations state you are all signed on for the length of the cruise, but we are in an extraordinary situation. Any man wishing to leave this ship and return to a southern state, now is the time to speak. You will be mustered out and put ashore. But be warned, any further acts against this vessel will be considered treason and treated accordingly. Those leaving will have fifteen minutes to collect their possessions." He paused, then spoke to LaForge. "Dismiss the men. If necessary, swing out another boat to take them ashore."

Most men dispersed to their jobs. Others went below to collect their kits. Only a few remained on deck, confused and undecided by the train of events. They slowly returned to their work. Richards watched them, aware of their feelings. Common sailors, north or south, were not plagued by the oaths and promises of their officers. To them, a ship was their home. To them, there was no where else to go.

Reynolds appeared, his sea chest carried by Sims and another sailor. He went over the side in silence. Richards wanted to say something, to express an understanding of the man's actions, but any such attempt would be seen as the lie it was. So he remained silent, watching the boats with Reynolds, the civilians and the few departing crewmen row towards shore.

"Mr. Wilson, I need a report on our coal stores."

Wilson touched his cap less head. "About a two thirds load, sir. Over a hundred tons by my reckoning. The men are still settling it below."

"Take what extra hands you need to finish it, and get the steam up. I want to maneuver the outbound channel while we still have light."

"Aye, sir." Wilson disappeared into the accustomed world of his engine and boilers.

"Was that wise?" asked LaForge. "Letting the seamen go, I mean."

Richards shrugged. "Who knows? At least we can trust all those who remained. Muster the hands and reassign the watch bills. We make sail within the hour."

Richards paced the quarterdeck. Ft. Morgan still stood at the entrance to the bay and the telegraph would alert them to the failure of the attempt to capture the sloop. Nor would the Secessionists be so obliging with the shore lights for an exit. No, he knew the run must be made before dark. And once the decision was made, another was equally obvious.

"Sims!"

"Sir?"

"Move my things to the captain's cabin." He held up his hand as the sailor's mouth opened in protest. "You are a coxswain now, damn you. See to it!"

Sims grinned at the sudden change of status. "If you say so, cap'n!" Then he was gone.

Thick, black smoke rolled from the funnel. Wilson was ready to get under way. In his mind, Richards composed the report he would have to submit to Adams in the morning.

"The boats are back and hoisted in," reported LaForge. "Ready to sail, John."

Richards nodded. He was the lieutenant commanding now. The side of his mouth curled up in a slight smile. The change of command was not quite what he had expected.

"Weigh anchor and steer south. Ring up half speed. Once clear of the channel, we will douse the boilers and get the sails on her. We will not be able to return here for coal again."

LaForge grinned. "I would think not."

Richards supervised as LaForge gave the orders to get under way. Though slow, LaForge gave the right commands at the right time. He is learning, thought Richards. *As are we all.*

The trip down the bay was aided by a backing wind, carrying the smoke away from the deck. Dusk approach as Ft. Morgan came into view.

"Beat to quarters, Mr. LaForge." The lieutenant looked at him, unsure how to take the order. "We will return any fire received from the fort. Load with shell, but do not run out except on my command."

The bosun's whistle broke the silence on deck and the men scurried about, preparing the ship for battle. They were by their guns, ready, when they came within long cannon fire of the fort.

Richards stood at the wheel, the fort slipping by the port side. Men stood on the bastions, their faces hidden in the growing dusk as they watched the ship make its way through the main channel. Though the guns were manned, they were not required. No shots were fired from the fort. The dark bastion slipped past their port side, and they were in the open waters beyond Mobile Bay. *COHOCTON* turned her bow east, towards Pensacola.

As Alabama slipped astern, there was time to consider it was Caldwell's home. He wondered if his friend had arrived safely.

Powhatan   *Cohocton*

The Relief of Ft Pickens, April 17th, 1861

CHAPTER SEVEN

Richards filed his report on the events leading to the captain's resignation with no mention of Reynolds' role in the attempt to seize the sloop. Adams accepted the report without comment. The Navy had come to accept such actions and the loss of an additional officer was no surprise. Richards remained as lieutenant commanding the *COHOCTON*. It had little effect, for they were still under the overall command of Captain Adams. That officer continued to display his apathy, if not outright Southern sympathies.

On their return, *COHOCTON* was placed between the fleet and Ft. Pickens, abandoning the more sheltered anchorage inside the bay. The remainder of the ships were positioned in the Gulf, two miles away from the beleaguered fortress and too far to be of any immediate help in an emergency. The captain's one submission to sanity was placing *COHOCTON* at the halfway point, ready to relay messages if necessary.

March opened with the situation around Pensacola remaining the same. The rebels ashore made no attempt to seize the fort while the Union made no further attempt to reinforce it. It was a stalemate, and a steady flow of communications passing between the non-warring parties. Adams refused to allow the troops to disembark, confining them to the already overcrowded quarters of the ships. Inwardly, Richards was relieved they had unloaded their cargo of troops before Adams' arrival or *COHOCTON* would be faced with the same extra mouths and bodies to maintain on the fixed resources of the vessel.

Richards paced the quarterdeck, the action a not quite unconscious habit developed by the enforced inactivity. The growing preparations around the navy yard were quite different. More soldiers arrived daily. Earthworks, punctuated by the black snouts of cannon, sprouted along the shoreline, the barrels all directed across the bay at Pickens. A fleet of small boats multiplied on the docks and beach, but no overt actions were taken.

Every day, Richards climbed the mast to inspect the changes wrought ashore. Every day, he reported those changes to *MACEDONIAN*. Every day, Adams maintained his indifference to the preparations and took no action or notice of the secessionist activities.

This day was the exception to that routine, however. On this day, *COHOCTON* provided the mail boat that went to each ship in the squadron and the fort and exchanged the Unionists' out going mail for the mail received by the Secessionists in the navy yard. This was also Richards' day to break his routine by accompanying the mail boat. On this day, Richards would have a much closer view of the preparations than provided through his telescope.

He gave Sims the order to prepare the longboat, stopping to pass a few comments with LaForge while waiting for the evolution to be completed. As he was speaking with the lieutenant, he noticed Potter walking past.

"Potter," he called after the boy. It had been several days since he had been able to check on the boy's progress. When the boy turned to face him, he noticed the deep blue-black surrounding his left eye and other bruises on the boy's face. "What has happened to your face, Potter?"

The boy hesitated, his voice sounding more like the lad taken aboard in New York than the developing sailor of recent weeks. "I tripped, sir. Nothing important."

Richards knew the words were a lie, but also did not wish to press the boy on the matter. Instead, he sent Potter on his way, searching for Hardy before leaving. He found the gunner checking the lashings on the newly mounted forward pivot gun.

"Mr. Hardy," he said.

The old gunner touched his cap. "'mornin, captain. Kin I help ye'?"

Richards looked about; assuring most of the men were out of earshot. "I just spoke with young Potter and noticed the bruising on his face."

Hardy appeared surprised. "Did the boy tell you how it happened?"

"He said he tripped, Mr. Hardy. I have a concern that this *fall* was helped along by some of the other boys."

"Cap'n," said Hardy, lowering his voice, "I've been seein' men and boys into and out of this navy for fifty years. I know your concern for young Potter, but it is something the lads must sort out. He can handle himself, I'm thinkin'."

Richards nodded. The boys were Hardy's responsibility and, as the old man said, he had seen to that duty for half a century. "As you say, Mr. Hardy. A matter for the lads to sort out."

"Aye, sir." Hardy touched his cap again. "Will that be all, sir?"

"Yes. Carry on, Mr. Hardy."

The long boat moved over the easy swell towards SUPPLY, the first stop on their journey. Richards sat in the stern sheets, Sims beside him with his hand the tiller. Just as Richards and the other officers took their turns on the duty, Sims allowed all hands to take turns at the oars to give the entire crew an opportunity to break their routine. They approached the side of elderly ship and Sims cupped his hands as they approached.

"*COHOCTON!*"

A familiar voice returned the hail. "Are you coming aboard?"

"Just the daily mail run, sir!" replied Sims.

Erben stood at the entry port as they bumped the side of the vessel. A mate handed down the mail bag and one of oarsmen took it.

"How goes it, John?" asked Erben.

Richards looked up at his friend, who seemed a bit more tanned than when they first met. "As well as we might expect, Henry, for lying at anchor instead of returning to the sea."

Erben shrugged. "Our fate appears to be to await events that will never occur, John. If *SUPPLY* sits here much longer, I am afraid the bottom will rot off."

Sims pushed the boat away from the ship's side.

"I shall send a boat on Thursday," said Richards as they moved towards the next ship. "You may come over for dinner, if Captain Walke will release you. Better yet, ask him along, also."

"I shall signal a reply later today," concluded Erben as

the ship fell behind them.

And so it went from ship to ship as the boat stopped and collected a mail bag from each in turn. As they finished with the *SABINE*, Sims pointed the bow across the larger stretch of water to the fort. It took longer to cover the distance and it was Jameson at the dock to greet them.

"Captain Richards! How go matters with the Navy?"

"No change, lieutenant. And with the Army?"

"No change. We are still short handed and could use the men and equipment that Captain Adams holds captive."

Though intended as a jest, the statement was essentially true. Adams, by making his agreement with the Secessionists ashore, held more men, guns and supplies on his ships than were actually present in the fort.

"Perhaps you can negotiate their parole," said Richards. The jest left a bitter taste in his mouth. Barring orders from a superior authority, Adams would maintain the status quo of inactivity around Pensacola. "I have asked some fellow officers to dinner this Thursday," he finished as Sims prepared to move away from the dock. "The offer is open to Lieutenant Slemmer and yourself if your duties allow."

Jameson saluted as the boat moved away. "I shall discuss the matter with him and send a reply this afternoon."

The boat moved into the smoother waters of the sheltered bay and Richards smiled to himself. The Army still lacked a means of signaling on par with the naval system of flags. They still relied on written, hand carried messages to communicate across distances.

Sims steered the boat towards the yard's main dock and Richards turned his attention to shore. Several new batteries lined the perimeter of the naval yard, the black or bronze snouts of cannon visible through the embrasures.

He made notes, trying to count the number and determine the size of the weapons. He was surprised at the large variety of weapons, with an equally surprising range of ages. Keeping such a diverse collection of guns served with shot and powder would not be an easy proposition, even for an experienced commander.

At the dock, a militia officer in an overly flamboyant uniform awaited their arrival, a number of mail bags at his feet. Richards stepped onto the dock for a few moments while the boats crew traded bags with the garrison.

"Suh," said the secesh officer, saluting.

"Captain," returned Richards. He had spoken with the officer on two other occasions, but still did not know his name.

Along with the mail bags, the officer also handed him a rough bundle of newspapers. "Our latest newspapers, lieutenant, as you requested at your last visit."

"Thank you," he replied, taking the bundle and handing it down to Sims in the boat. "Your kindness is most appreciated."

"You are our *guests*," said the militiaman, saluting again. "We may have our differences, but you will not speak ill of our hospitality."

"Nor shall I," replied Richards, returning the salute.

The boat headed back into the bay to retrace its steps and drop off the mail received the shore. Richards looked at the top paper, at headlines proclaiming the creation of the Confederate States and the election of Jefferson Davis. While his ship lay at Pensacola, the secessionists met in Montgomery to proclaim a new nation and government. Before he could read more, Sims spoke to him.

"Are we to drill during the afternoon watch, sir?"

While Reynolds ran the ship, they had run gunnery drills weekly. Now Richards ran them every day. This day, he had announced plans to strike the topmasts and yards, a difficult task that would require the crew to spend a good deal of time the following day to reset them.

"I see no reason to abandon my scheduled drills, Mr. Sims." He tapped the newspaper headline. "This would seem to indicate those skills will be needed soon enough."

"Aye, sir." Sims seemed dejected at the prospect of the afternoon's heavy work. "Me and the lads were just hopin' for a day to stand down."

Richards fought back a smile. "No doubt, you are depressed that you drill while the other crews lounge about as if on holiday."

"No, sir, beggin' your pardon," countered Sims. "We just have been drillin' every day except Sunday for weeks now. I think we have the concept, if you take my meanin', captain."

Some of the oarsmen laughed at Sims' discussion with the captain. Richards was unsure whether to be upset or amused by the pleadings of his coxswain. "I shall make the crew an offer, Sims," he said. "If the men better their time on striking the topmasts, they may stand down the day after tomorrow."

"The day *after* tomorrow, Captain?"

The young commander shrugged. "We shall still have to reset the topmasts tomorrow, Sims."

The oarsmen laughed at their captain's bargain, chatting between themselves and making bets as to which division would complete their task in the best time. Richards let the men chat as the friendly rivalry between the men would accomplish more than his strict urgings. But the moment passed quickly as Sims touched his shoulder.

"Over there, captain. A commotion on the shore!"

Richards followed the pointed finger. A number of men were on the beach, jumping and yelling in agitation. Oarsmen strained over their shoulders, the stroke interrupted by their attempts to see what was happening.

"Eyes aft!" snapped Sims, bring the men's focus back on there rowing.

"There's the cause," said Richards, pointing to a struggling figure. "Swimmer to port."

The man in the water stood out clearly, the flailing arms and legs apparently directed to bring him across the two miles of water to Ft. Pickens. Ashore, the milling figures were trying to launch a boat with little success into the surf.

"That man will never make it, Sims. Change course and pick him up."

"Aye, sir." His wrist turned the tiller and a snapped order increase the stroke. It took the Union boat a few minutes to reach the swimmer. The people ashore were still trying to launch their own boat as the crewmen leaned across the gunwales to pull man into the boat.

The man was a black, dripping wet and breathing heavily from his swim. Sims and another sailor helped sit him across from Richards, who held out a hand to steady the exhausted man.

"Back to COHOCTON," directed Richards. The man seemed too tired to speak and was shivering in the open air boat. Richards pulled up a piece of canvas to wrap around him. "Let's get him to the surgeon as quickly as possible."

Sims grinned. "You heard the captain, men! Roundly now!"

The oars bit deeply into the waters, and the long boat skimmed across the surface on the way back to the sloop.

"Take him to the surgeon," directed Richards as they cam aboard the warship. "I will be there in a few moments." He looked to RenError!. "What do you make of that one?"

LaForge shrugged. "Probably an escaped slave."

"Probably." Richards smiled. "But maybe one that has kept his eyes open?"

The sick bay of the sloop was forward and below the water-line. It was the traditional place, damp and smelly, lying below the vessel's waterline and above the water sloshing in the bilge. The black man sat on the surgeon's table while Ambrose poked and prodded. The new arrival held a mug, drinking deeply from the contents. The reek of the whiskey hung heavy in the still air.

"Well, Mr. Ambrose?" asked Richards.

"Fit enough, lieutenant. No broken bones and none the worse for his swim. Just that." The surgeon gestured towards the man's back while taking a bottle and some swabs from his cabinet.

When the man turned so the doctor could minister to his back, Richards saw what Ambrose was referring to. The flesh was a mass of scars from his neck to his buttocks, a criss-cross of lines laid out by a whip or a cat-o'-nine-tails. Most were healed, looking like white blisters against the ebony skin. Others were brown scabs, pink around the edges. Still more were fresh, blood welling up slowly through the massed scar tissue.

"Hmpf!" The surgeon's grunt broke into the stillness while he dabbed at the bleeding wounds. "Probably painful enough when he received them, lieutenant. I prefer not to think what they feel like after emersion in salt water." He dabbed at the wounds. "I have never been much of an abolitionist, but I may have to reconsider that position!"

"They hurts bad!" exclaimed the black, handing a seaman the empty mug for a refill. "But I does it again if'n I has to!" Ambrose's assistant looked at the mug questioningly and Richards nodded his approval. Once full, Richards handed it back to the man.

"Were you working in the navy yard?"

"Yez, massuh." He gulped the whiskey, wiping his mouth with the back of his hand. "I works wood. I'm a good 'un, too!"

Richards had never been addressed as "master" before. He found he did not like it. "No masters here. Captain will do"

"Yes, massuh – I meanz cap'n."

"How much do you know of the preparations in the yard?" The man looked at him blankly. "Do you know how many men are there? How many cannon?"

"Big guns, cap'n. Big!" He opened and closed his hand three times. "'Bout that many. I was helpin' cut the wood for the..." His limited vocabulary failed him.

"Carriages?" offered Richards, only to receive another blank stare. "The wooden things the guns sit in," he explained.

"Thas' right, cap'n, the careeges! I build 'em good, I'm tellin' ya'll."

Richards smiled at the rough language. Despite his mistreatment, the black man maintained a good nature. Living in Connecticut and serving at sea, Richards had given little thought to the actual condition of Negroes in the south. Even while serving on Anti-Slavery Patrol off the coast of Africa, his thoughts were more directed towards the performance of his duties than the actual fates of people kidnapped from their homes. The man before him was not necessarily a typical case, it took little imagination to realize that there was nothing in the "peculiar institution" to prevent such treatment from being widespread.

"What is your name?"

A Sudden Thunder

"They's calls me Joshua, like in the good book." Joshua finished the second mug of whiskey, tilting slightly as he passed it back for another round. "Thas' good, cap'n."

"Can you tell me any more about the cannon, Joshua?" asked Richards.

"My massah was an officer. But he's always frettin' 'bout the big guns. He got no powder to put in 'em. Plenny balls, but no powder." He eyed the empty mug hungrily.

"Well, Mr. Ambrose? What about it?"

"He will be fine with some rest and given a chance for all this to heal proper."

Richards nodded. "Well, Joshua, what am I to do with you?"

"Suh?"

"What do you want to do?

The slave looked at his surroundings, his eyes starting to glaze over from the effects of the alcohol. "Ize don' know, cap'n. Ize just heard Mistah Lincum waz settin' us free." His words slurred. Between the whiskey and his exertions, he nodded his eyes half closed.

"You can sign aboard with us, if you like." He held up his hand to keep the man from interrupting. "Do not say anything now. Sleep tonight and wait until you are more settled." Richards looked back to the doctor. "Will another tot of whiskey hurt?"

Ambrose snorted loudly. "After all he's been through; I should think he deserves it!"

"Give him another," instructed Richards. "Mr. Sims, after he has slept it off, have a black crewman talk with him. If he understands and wants to sign aboard, see to it."

Richards returned to the deck, squinting into the bright sunshine.

"Well?" asked LaForge.

"It seems they are having some trouble with powder over there, Mr. LaForge."

LaForge chuckled. "That *is* too bad." Before he could continue, the lookout's cry again came to the deck.

"Ship off the port beam!"

"It looks like we are to have a busy day," commented Richards as he picked up his telescope to examine the newcomer.

At first, Richards could see only the slight smudge of smoke on the horizon to mark the approach of the vessel. Soon, however, details of the arrival became clear. She was a sloop steaming directly for Pensacola. Richards recognized the BROOKLYN from previous meetings. In a navy with so few vessels, there was never a ship new to everyone on board.

"The BROOKLYN, Captain William Walker," reported LaForge after consulting the signal book. "Unless it has changed sine these were printed.":

"I cannot say I ever made his acquaintance," returned Richards. BROOKLYN. They had left Brooklyn ten weeks before, now the city's namesake joined them at Pensacola. "She appears to have a large number of idlers on his deck in blue uniforms. She must be engaged as a transport, much as ourselves."

LaForge examined the ship. "So it would appear." He lowered the telescope. "I wonder Captain Walker will do any better at getting the troops landed?"

"I think I shall make the attempt to find out, Lieutenant. Our catch this morning provides an excuse to visit our flag officer." Richards replaced his telescope in the rack. "Find that slacker Sims and have him prepare my boat. I shall be up as soon as I change my coat." Richards hesitated before going below. "And you can tell him that we will not drill today. That should make him happy!"

Walker from the *BROOKLYN* was already aboard the *MACEDONIAN* when Richards arrived. The lieutenant commanding *COHOCTON* was shown into the captain's cabin while the interview was still in progress, an unusual state of affairs.

"...My orders are also from Washington," explained Adams, "and signed by both the Secretaries of Navy and War, so do not tell me about my *duty*, Captain!" Adams tapped his index finger across the papers lying on his desk. "I might also add they were dated later than these!" He picked the pages up and returned them to Walker.

"I want to protest this decision, captain! I have seventy-five extra men aboard my ship. I will not be held accountable for the continued health of so many men confined in that small space!"

"It is not your decision, *captain*!" Adams rose to his feet and stepped around the desk to face Walker directly. "We have an agreement here and I do not intend to break it!" Walker flushed at the direct confrontation, but refrained from further comment. "That will be all," concluded Adams, returning to his seat.

Walker stood for a long second, ready to vent his mind. Instead, Navy discipline won out. He saluted and left. As he did, Adams turned his attention to Richards, the ire built up from the previous discussion venting on the new arrival.

"What do you want?" he snapped. Before Richards could answer, his memory returned and he continued. "Yes - you picked up a swimmer or some such this morning. What news?"

"An escaping slave, sir," reported Richards evenly. "He informs me the secessionists have 15 heavy guns mounted ashore." Adams raised an eyebrow to question the comment, but Richards continued with his explanation. "He is a carpenter of sorts and was helping to construct the gun carriages. He also says the secessionists are short of powder."

Adams snorted. "It seems yours and Mr. Erben's work this past January was not totally wasted." He stopped, his gaze fixed on the deck above for a moment while he considered the situation. "You will see to it the slave is returned to his rightful owner." Richards opened his mouth to protest, but Adams raised his voice to cut him off. "I am tired of arguing with junior officers, lieutenant! I will not have trouble caused with the local citizens if it can be avoided by returning some damned black. The Fugitive Slave laws are quite clear. Do I make myself understood?"

Richards fought back an angry retort. Instead, he forced his voice to remain level. "The man was very badly used ashore, captain. I shall have him landed when my surgeon is ready to release him."

"Oh, very well, damn you! I suppose they would rather get their property back in good condition. But I shall not be happy if I discover this is just a delaying move, lieutenant."

"Of course not, captain. I was sure you would want the information he provided."

"Yes, of course. That will be all." The dismissal was abrupt and rude, matching any Richards had experienced from Reynolds.

Richards returned to *COHOCTON*, examining the *BROOKLYN* as they slid past her. Another ship had joined their growing fleet at Pensacola. Again his suspicions were raised. With the country badly needing its Navy on the move, what was the purpose in tying up have the active vessels at this location?

"Signal from Lieutenant Slemmer, John."

LaForge's words were not unexpected. Early that morning, a small boat had left the navy yard for the fort. Richards examined it at length, noting a naval officer in the stern. Fighting down his curiosity, he went to breakfast, forcing himself to eat while awaiting developments. The eight weeks since *BROOKLYN*'s arrival was marked by even greater inactivity on the part of the forces around Pensacola. The ships sat motionless, the daily routine hardly broken on the Union warships. Adams enforced the inactivity as the warships observed Pickens, their supplies diminished with each passing day.

During that time, Lincoln was inaugurated as president of the Union. Three weeks before that, Jefferson Davis assumed the presidency of the newborn Confederate States. Alabama (and his friend Caldwell) joined the southern states and the new government. Only one action occurred, though it was one that sent a shudder through the Richard's spine. On the 20th of March in Mobile, the *USS ISABELLA* was obtaining supplies for the fleet at Pensacola and was seized by secessionist forces. *COHOCTON*'s experience from early February was repeated with much different results.

COHOCTON made good use of the time, however. Under LaForge's and Hardy's expert guidance, tracks were built forward and aft for the rifles and they were remounted as pivot guns. The supplies, so haphazardly arranged by Reynolds, were properly redistributed to serve the guns and trim the sloop. And he drilled his crew, instilled in them the skills they would need for a war that now seemed inevitable. Now Richards hoped the arrival of this boat at Ft. Pickens would prove a turning point to their enforced inactivity.

"I know Sims has been ready for the past hour," he said, wiping his mouth and setting the napkin on the table. "Have him lower the boat. I will be up directly."

"I thought maybe I..." LaForge let the words trail off.

"Sorry, lieutenant, but the privileges of rank prevail. I need to know what is happening even more badly than you do."

Sitting in the stern sheets, he wondered what news had brought the officer to Pensacola. It was close to half a mile to reach the small dock near one of the fort's sally ports. Slemmer's figure was easily recognized as they approached. The Navy officer, a lieutenant, stood next to him.

"John Richards, John Worden," introduced Slemmer quickly. "Lt. Worden brings us word from up north, John."

"Good or bad?" asked Richards. Worden stepped into the boat without waiting for an invitation.

"That is for Captain Adams to decide," explained Worden, settling in.

Sims guided the boat away from the fort and headed across the two mile stretch of open water towards *SABINE*.

"Any news from Washington?" ventured Richards.

"None good." Worden was older than Richards. He guessed by as much as twenty years. The weathered face was covered by a heavy beard, but heavy lines of concern or fatigue marked the officer's features. "It seems we are to have war," continued Worden after a pause. "The new government will reinforce both Pickens and Sumter." He shook his head sadly. "I do not know details of your situation other than what Lt. Slemmer has kindly shared this morning, but the Charlestonians will have none of it. They will surely start something."

"We have heard rumors of war for the past three months..."

"They will not be rumors much longer, Richards," returned Worden. There was no doubt of his sincerity. "Captain Adams has bandied words with Washington for almost a month about the troops aboard *BROOKLYN*. I am here to resolve the situation." The boat bumped against the frigate.

Richards followed Worden to the deck. He passed a few minutes with her senior lieutenant but did not have to wait long. Adams appeared with Worden close behind. The commodore's face was red from either embarrassment or anger.

"Make a signal to BROOKLYN," ordered Adams loudly. "Close on Fort. Disembark troops." He swung back to Worden. "Is that sufficient, lieutenant?" Worden ignored the remark.

"I am to return directly to Washington, captain. If I can borrow Lt. Richards and his boat?" Without waiting, Worden saluted and walked to the side.

"That did not take long," commented Richards as they pushed off.

Worden smiled, his lips mostly hidden in the depths of his heavy beard. "It is harder to mince spoken words than written ones."

"It is war for sure then." His tone was neither resignation nor regret. It voiced a simple matter of fact.

Worden eyed Richards questioningly. "You do not seem upset at the prospect."

Richards shrugged. After three months of vacillation on the part of the Navy department, the Union was little beyond the situation that existed in December, before Richards received orders to aid in relief of the fort and COHOCTON left New York. During that time, thirteen states had seceded, ceased Federal property, set up their own government and taken up arms against the national government in Washington.

"Perhaps I am tired of the charade. It is time we have it out and determine whether this shall be one country or many."

"We shall have it out, lieutenant. Of that, I have no doubt!"

There was a long silence between the men, the only sound being the splash of the oars. At length, Richards changed the subject. "My fiancé is in Washington. Would you carry a letter for me?"

Worden agreed easily. "Certainly."

Sims brought the boat alongside the *COHOCTON*. Worden came up the side while Richards went below for his letter. It took only a moment to jot a hasty closing to his letter in progress and to seal the envelope. He returned to the deck and handed it to Worden, who was speaking with LaForge.

"It seems you are mistreating your first, Lt. Richards. He also has a letter for a lady in Washington."

"I am sorry, RenError!," he apologized. "It is just the pace of events. Take a moment to complete you letter and find out if anyone else has mail for delivery to Washington."

Worden glanced at the back of Richards' letter while LaForge went below. "Rebecca Welles? The Secretary's daughter?" Worden placed the envelope in his pocket. "A lovely young lady as I remember." LaForge reappeared shortly and handed the bearded lieutenant a small bundle of letters. "I shall have to remember your connections in the future, Richards."

"If you know Gideon Welles as I do," retorted Richards, "you know that is an empty threat. But you are in a hurry, John. Perhaps you will let my abused lieutenant accompany you to the fort?"

Worden winked at LaForge. "I shall be honored by his company."

"Good fortune, lieutenant," concluded Richards, shaking his hand.

The boat left the ship, making a leisurely trip across the water. *BROOKLYN* was already on the move, steaming the short stretch to Pickens. Her boats were afloat before LaForge returned.

"It will be war then," he said, his voice serious. "Before the year closes, this shall all be behind us."

"A year." The words were flat and toneless. Richards noted Joshua on the deck, newly clothed in his white ducks. The big black hands ran a plane skillfully across a sheet of lumber under the watchful eyes of the ship's carpenter. The examination was unnecessary, for the former slave easily lived up to his boasting.

"The rebels are as dedicated to their cause as we to ours," he said. He was surprised at the emotion in his words. "They have weapons, ammunition and the will to use them. No, RenError!," he concluded, voicing the disquiet he felt in his breast. "I fear it will be longer than a year!"

*   *   *   *   *   *   *

The atmosphere altered drastically after Worden's departure. There was no longer friendly coexistence between the Unionists and the Secessionists. Mail and deliveries of fresh food were suspended. Troops continued to arrive at the Navy Yard, but reports persisted about the shortages of powder. Then the rebels sent word Charleston had fired on Ft. Sumter. War had come.

Two more ships arrived on the sixteenth of April. *POWHATAN* had been laid up in New York when Richards had last seen her. Rumors were she was being sent to Ft. Sumter, but now she had appeared in Florida. The other ship was unknown, but a crew member identified her as the *ATLANTIC*, a transport from New York. Troops crowded the deck and ports of the vessel.

A boat left *POWHATAN* for *SABINE*. As with Worden's visit, the conversation was short. Flags quickly fluttered to the yards of the flagship.

"What have they to say, RenError!?" *POWHATAN*, steam still up, closed to the fort with the transport a short distance behind.

"Our signal. 'Close on Flag'." There was disbelief in the voice.

"He can not be serious!" protested Richards. "Slemmer is left all but alone as it is!"

LaForge re-examined the flags, unsure of his reading. He even double checked the signal book. "That is the signal, John."

Richards let out a deep sigh. "Acknowledge, lieutenant. Shake out the fore course. Maneuver down to them under sail."

Boats from the transport plied the waters between the fort and the anchored vessels. This was not a half-hearted attempt at reinforcement like theirs or *BROOKLYN*'s. Hundreds of troops were placed in the fortress. Slemmer was probably losing his command, but it was a show of force that would create little doubt of the outcome. The supplies that followed the troops sent another clear message to the rebellion: the troops were there to stay. They were planning to stay for a long time.

Richards expected *POWHATAN* also brought orders for the other vessels, but no call to the flagship came that day. The next morning, the leisurely course of events around Pensacola reached their conclusion. While Richards made his daily inspection of the yard, a large collection of small boats, each crammed with men, pushed off. They headed across the bay towards Pickens.

"This is it!" shouted LaForge, jumping onto the railing for a better view.

"Signal the flagship, Mr. LaForge," instructed Richards. "'Enemy in Sight to Starboard'. By God, if that fails to get a reaction from Adams, I will fire a damned signal gun into him!"

The small flotilla moved quickly through the water, but the commander of *POWHATAN* was more sure of his duty than Adams. A gun barrel poked through an open port.

There was a blast of smoke and flame. The gun was aimed high but true and the shell exploded above the clustered boats.

There was terror in the boats as realization of the situation struck. Confusion and pandemonium followed. They reversed course, returning to safety of the mainland.

Another shell was fired from *POWHATAN*. It landed in the center of the yard, sending up a shower of dust and debris.

"Whoever is in command of *POWHATAN* has no doubts about what to do," commented LaForge.

Richards was surprised to find his mouth suddenly dry. "Well, we have our war!"

LaForge pointed to *SABINE*. "Signal, John. 'Captains Repair on Board'!"

"Damn!" The expletive escaped before he could stop it. "It is well past time! Sims, see to the boat." The sailor stepped from the crowd along the side, calling for his boat's crew. "Mr. LaForge, put the rest of these idlers to work!" He scanned the deck, making sure of every man's attention. "Gunnery practice, I should think. It would appear we are going to need it!"

Adams was quiet and withdrawn, far different from the last meeting. The captains from the other five ships waited for him to speak, their faces drawn with concern.

"We are at war, gentlemen." The words were choked, heavy with emotion. "I do not know all the states involved, but active rebellion has occurred." He paused again, momentarily unable to continue.

"Yesterday, Lt. Porter of *POWHATAN* brought orders for the disposition of our fleet. We are to blockade the southern coastline." Heavy envelopes were lifted from his desk and handed to the assemble captains.

"*SABINE, POWHATAN* and *BROOKLYN* are to

remain here for the time being, placing Pensacola under close blockade. *SUPPLY* and *COHOCTON* are ordered north to Norfolk, to serve in the Atlantic. *ST. LOUIS* and *MACEDONIAN* will make for the Mississippi and New Orleans."

With a deep breath, Adams concluded the short meeting. "You have your orders, gentlemen. Godspeed with your endeavors. I trust we shall meet again in happier times."

Richards opened the envelope in the boat, reading the pages during the short haul to the sloop. The ship was to proceed forthwith to the Gosport Navy Yard for resupply. Once prepared, she would be reassigned to the newly declared blockade of the Atlantic coast. There were several pages on the legal requirements of the blockade, but Richards ignored them for the time being. The orders read 'forthwith'.

"Captain?" LaForge's voice was heavy with expectancy as Richards came through the entry port.

"We are ordered north, lieutenant. Send a boy for the engineer and prepare the ship to get under way."

LaForge started the preparations while the quarter boat was lifted from the water. It hung dripping from the davits while Sims and his men secured it. Richards wondered about their future in that moment but shook the thought from his head. He went below to the chart room. The course was plotted when Wilson appeared, his coal stained features hard to discern in the dimly lit room.

"Captain?" It was the same hesitant expectancy shown by LaForge. Richards had to admit even he felt it.

"Gosport, Mr. Wilson, and with all due dispatch."

"Aye, sir." The brief comment was enough and Wilson turned to leave. Richards stopped him with a final encouragement.

"Do not spare the coal, Mr. Wilson. Where we are

heading, we will be able to replace it with your precious anthracite!"

The offer of a free reign for his engine was sufficient incentive for Wilson.

"Yes, sir!"

It was barely the start of the forenoon watch when LaForge reported all was ready. The anchor was hove short and a signal made to SABINE, the new receiving ship on the station. With the acknowledgment received, the order was given. The anchor was hoisted and catted and the head of the ship pointed south. Smoke poured freely from the funnel and the screw churned the waters at their stern.

The trip from Pensacola was rapid and trouble free. After three months of lying at anchor, Richards relished the opportunity to give COHOCTON her head. Fair winds and weather aided there voyage north, and the young captain was more than pleased by the performance of his ship and crew.

The COHOCTON entered the Chesapeake shortly after midnight and their first warning came upon entering the mouth of the James River. The masts of a sunken ship jutted gloomily from the smooth black surface, the marker of the burial spot of some vessel.

"What does this mean?" asked LaForge.

"I do not know," responded Richards. He touched LaForge's shoulder. "Take in all remaining sails and place two good men forward."

LaForge repeated the orders and creating a flurry of activity as top men swarmed aloft to take in the top sails. Richards nodded his approval and looked back to Sims.

"Dead slow, Mr. Sims."

"Aye, captain," replied the New Englander. He rang

the repeater and the throb from the engine decreased.

COHOCTON skirted other sunken hulks, slowly feeling her way forward. Whether the hulks were to keep someone out, or block someone in, was unknown. Then the southern horizon took on an orange glow.

The Gosport Navy Yard in Flames

CHAPTER EIGHT

To a sailor, the sight before them was a scene from the darkest reaches of hell. A clear view of the Navy Yard opened and burning ships lay everywhere, the night sky bright from the flames. *COHOCTON* coasted through the still, dark waters on the approaches to the Gosport Navy Yard and every member of the crew stood at the side, silently watching the spectacle. The crackle of flames mingled with the shipboard sounds and shouts of fear and excitement combined to create a cacophony that assaulted their ears. Everywhere was flame.

The yard itself was burning, red fingers reaching high into the night air. Anchored ships in the harbor were aflame, the masts and rigging engulfed, bright orange tongues licked hungrily along them and eating away at their fabric. Richards shuddered as flaming cinders arched across the open water and drifted about them.

"Clear away the deck rifles!" he ordered. He saw

Hardy near one side. "Mr. Hardy, see that is done."

Hardy tapped the shoulder of a boy near him and Richards noted briefly it Potter, his face no longer bruised. Another boy, Jogs, stood with him. The captain caught sight of a black eye on the other boy as the two lads took off at a run to get their powder charges.

LaForge stood before him, saluting. "Clear for action?"

"No," snapped Richards, looking at the flaming wrecks around them. "Rig pumps and organize the bucket brigades. Be ready to dowse any flames."

"Yes, sir."

"Have the starboard watch break out the pikes and be prepared to fend off any of these vessels that come too close."

LaForge, too, departed at a run, the ordered chaos of the deck adding to the hellish ferocity of the scene as the crewmen move purposefully in the orange, shifting light of the fire.

Richards took his telescope and leveled it on the yard proper. If the ordered confusion of COHOCTON's deck appeared as something from Dante's Inferno, the vision ashore was so much worse.

Large groups of men were visible, but they seemed set at cross purposes. Some groups fought the growing fires, trying to save ships at the docks or the structures in the yard. Other groups moved faster, carrying torches to spread the flames. It was another chapter of madness added to the events of the young year. He felt warmth growing on his cheek and lowered the telescope. A flaming brig lay close on the starboard side.

"Watch the helm!" he ordered. "These waters are tight and we need to keep clear of the flames!" Sims moved the wheel, and the ship fell away as they moved into the center of the harbor.

"Over there, John!" pointed LaForge. In the dancing lights from the flames, two ships sat dark and motionless to starboard. One was a steam sloop, marked by her funnel. The other was a sailing sloop lying close astern. In the midst of the flames and chaos of the yard, they lay still and untouched in deeper water.

"Three points to starboard." He pulled down on the engine room repeater and rang for full stop.

"Damn!"

It was LaForge with an uncustomary curse. Following his glance inland revealed an unusually large ship in flames near the dock. It was one of the steam frigates, her identity unknown. And all the while, running figures, silhouettes marked against the roaring fires, continued the macabre activities.

"Helm alee and drop anchor, Mr. LaForge," ordered Richards as they drew close to the untouched vessels. Though further from the burning vessels, the breeze carried the smell and the warmth of the fires across *COHOCTON*'s deck. Richards coughed as a dense cloud of smoke engulfed the deck, followed by another shower of sparks. "Call away my barge. Keep the men alert for any signs of flames, RenError!."

The splash of the anchor went unnoticed in the surrounding confusion. It impossible to keep his eyes from the scene about them while rowing towards the steam sloop.

In one place, an old ship of the line, masts and sides fully involved, burned through its cable. It drifted slowly in the current, bumping up against another ship. The second was the *PENNSYLVANIA*, the only first rate built for the sailing navy. The drifting ship made little difference, for *PENNSYLVANIA* was wreathed in fire and settling lower in the water. The collision did little more than add to the cloud of sparks swirling in the air.

In another spot, three small vessels burned together,

their anchor cables burned through. As he watched, one disappeared below the water, accompanied by a cloud of steam and smoke as the sea extinguished the flames. A challenge from the sloop drew attention away from the spectacle.

"Boat ahoy!"

"*COHOCTON!*" returned Sims through cupped hands.

Richards jumped to the entry port. There was no ceremony when he came aboard. Instead, he was immediately met by an older man with captain's stripes. His hair was in disarray and it, as well as his prominent side whiskers, glowed orange in the flickering light. The bald expanse across the top of his head glistened with sweat.

"My God man, what are you doing here?" he demanded.

"*COHOCTON*, up from Pensacola," replied Richards. "We had orders to resupply."

"*COHOCTON*? That is Reynolds' ship."

"I am Lt. John Richards. Captain Reynolds resigned his commission."

The old captain nodded his head knowingly. "Commodore Hiram Paulding," he said, introducing himself. He glanced towards the ruins of the yard. "Too bad you did not arrive a few hours earlier. We could have towed out another of the sloops."

"What happened?" ventured Richards cautiously.

Paulding was wild eyed, though Richards cautioned himself that much of the impression must be due to the shifting light from the fires. All the same, the commodore was less than calm as he explained the situation, his voice rushing forward as if there could be delay in the telling.

"I was sent down from Washington to watch over the yard. The commandant would take no action and the

Secessionists threatened an attack at any moment." He was distracted as a small sloop, its flames low, suddenly flared brightly.

The fire exploded across its deck, rigging, and masts in a massive sheet, a shower of sparks shooting high into the air. Every eye was drawn to the sight. Perhaps the sailors were horrified at the success of their own efforts. Pulling himself away from the terrible image, Paulding continued.

"I had the authority and saw no other options. I burned the yard to keep it from being used against the Union."

"In Pensacola, it was given to them without a shot," returned Richards. He became silent, mute to the events surrounding him.

"We are getting under way, lieutenant." Paulding was, if nothing else, a man of some action. It was a refreshing change after the months of vacillation at Pensacola. "We have CUMBERLAND in tow and are planning to anchor below Ft. Monroe. I will review your orders there."

"Yes, sir."

But Paulding was not listening. He was giving orders to prepare his ships. Richards climbed down to his boat, Sims directing it away from the sloop.

"Looks like most of the Navy's in flames here," said the helmsman, his voice hushed in awe. It was barely a whisper and Richards was not sure an answer was expected. He gave one anyway.

"It is, Sims."

The small sloop that had erupted into flames so spectacularly slowly turned on its side. Burned to the water line, the masts collapsed. With a loud hissing and accompanied clouds of steam, the water rushed in to make the final claim on the fire's victim.

"Prepare to up anchor," said Richards as he came

aboard the *COHOCTON*. "We shall follow the commodore to Ft. Monroe."

"Aye, sir."

The words were quiet. LaForge, too, was subdued by the events surrounding them.

In the yard, the conflagration diminished, the fuel consumed. The large steam frigate was no longer visible, for it had sunk at the dock. Only one of its masts still stood to mark the location. The *UNITED STATES*, an old frigate from the turn of the century, lay aground across the harbor, her masts gone and flames still eating at her hull. There was a lump in his throat at the sight of the old rag wagon. She had fought the British in 1812 and he had served aboard her as a midshipman. Now, like her namesake, she was in ruins. He turned angrily inboard.

"Get us under way, LaForge," he shouted. "There is nothing more to be done here!"

"That was a quick passage."

Paulding's comment was simple and matter of fact. In the light of the next morning, the commodore was neat and trim, the wildness of the previous night gone as if it had never existed.

"Yes, my engineer worked very hard to achieve it. We had favorable winds aiding us, also."

"Your engineer appears very able, lieutenant. I would suggest you keep him happy. Capable men are hard to find."

"Yes, sir."

The interview continued in this fashion with no comments of any substance exchanged. Finally, after reviewing the papers before him for the better part of half an hour, Paulding pushed away from his desk and stood up. He went to the stern windows and gazed across the waters of the bay.

"You shan't replenish at Norfolk, that is clear. The next most obvious port would be Baltimore." He considered for a moment, but Paulding shook his head to dismiss that idea. "No, Maryland is a state with mixed purpose and feelings at the moment. We cannot be sure of your reception there." He turned back to Richards. "Have you ever maneuvered the Potomac, Mr. Richards?"

"No, sir."

"Then it is best time you learn it. Evans!" The final word was a shout and unexpected. But barely a second passed before a thin face appeared in the cabin doorway. "Have you finished that report?"

The clerk nodded in a quick, nervous fashion common to his breed. "The ink is barely dry, commodore."

"Good. Write order's for this young man's sloop, the *COHOCTON*. He is to carry my dispatches to Washington and resupply there."

"Yes, commodore," deferred the clerk. "His name, sir?"

"Lieutenant Commanding John Richards," returned the commodore.

"Yes, sir." The face disappeared.

"We shall finish two birds with the same stone, Lieutenant." The commodore took a deep breath, the let it out slowly. "I do not know what Secretary Welles will think of my actions, but I best explain as quickly as possible."

"Of course, commodore." In spite of his simple reply, Richards felt a growing excitement within. *Washington.* Becky would be there.

"Things are not going well at the present, Mr. Richards," explained Paulding further. "Do not be surprised at what you see and hear, even in the capitol. Loyalties are split everywhere."

The clerk reappeared, carrying several sheets of paper. He set them on the desk and Paulding quickly perused them. Taking a pen offered by the clerk, he scratched his name onto the bottom of each sheet, and returned them to the clerk.

The clerk performed the ritual of sealing the reports into an envelope. All but one sheet was so treated and that sheet was neatly folded and handed to Richards.

"There you are, lieutenant," concluded Paulding, rising again to shake his hand. "Take care on your trip up the river."

The Washington Navy Yard along the Potomac was the result of a political convenience rather than a pressing national need. Whereas most considered Gosport the best yard in the country, Washington placed at the other end of the spectrum. Even so, it now assumed greater importance with the loss of Norfolk. And if Maryland changed allegiance, it could become the capitol's only link with the rest of the country.

The trip to the Navy Department was through the busy, clogged streets of the city. The people were agitated, even furtive in their actions. More than one man stood on a corner, openly pleading the case of the Confederacy to the ears of any who would listen. Richards also discovered it was a city cut off, the rail junctions in Baltimore under dispute. Regiments of infantry recently came from Baltimore and were barely able to make their way through the town without firing on hostile civilians. It was an unanswered question if the rail links would be opened without resorting to troops.

In the Navy department offices, a number of other officers waited to see Welles. Richards fretted nervously, struggling to contain his pent up frustrations with the delay. At length, he was ushered into the Secretary's office. Welles sat behind his desk while a squat, balding man stood next to him, collecting numerous papers.

"John!" Welles stood, his face etched in pleasure and surprise at Richards arrival. "It is good to see you." He took the younger man's hand warmly. "May I introduce my assistant, Gustavus Fox?"

"Sir," said Richards.

Fox examined him for a moment, nodding curtly. "Richards, eh?" His arms were full of paper, so he made no effort to shake hands with the officer. "Well, I have no time for pleasantries. We have a fleet to assemble." He was gone, barely bothering with a nod to Welles before leaving.

The secretary smiled after his assistant. "He takes some getting used to, but I would not replace him with a dozen others. He is all business at all times and cares nothing for the opinions of others. He is the most effective man in Washington, with the possible exception of Lincoln." He gestured towards a chair. "Now, what brings you to here?"

Richards handed the envelope containing the report on Norfolk to Welles. "Commodore Paulding's report. We arrived just in time to see the results." He shuddered involuntarily, recalling the sights of the previous night.

"Yes, it is all regrettable." Welles glanced quickly over the paper, and then set it aside. "We acted too slowly to accomplish anything and lost the MERRIMACK and several sailing sloops in the bargain."

"True, but it was better than letting them fall into the hands of the Secessionists."

"I suppose that is how we must look at it," returned the secretary, resigned to the inevitability of the situation. "What is to become of you?"

"We are to replenish and find a few more hands for the ship. Then it is along the coast somewhere for blockade duty." Richards smiled at the older man. "I should imagine you know more of that than I."

Welles returned the grin. "I should imagine you are right, lieutenant. It will be a few days at least before you manage to leave. I have plans to use you around here."

"My ship..." protested the officer.

"I have made arrangements for that, John. A captain requires a first lieutenant, someone to attend the day to day running of the vessel."

"RenError!..." protested Richards.

"RenError! is a fine man," interrupted Welles, "but as we both know, is deficient in experience. He was assigned in December for lack of a suitable officer of known loyalties. I am now able to remedy that situation." Richards opened his mouth to continue his protest, but Welles provided a stern glance. The fiery eyes of the Navy Secretary forced the young man into silence. "No! I need your assistance with this clutter." He waved his hand across the mass of paper on the desk. "I am weighted down with bureaucrats and could use someone who has actually seen a ship to help out."

The commander slumped in resignation. "Aye, sir."

Welles chuckled at the disappointment. "It is for the best. Lieutenant Burrows is an officer of character and knowledge. He will be a valuable aid for you." Welles smiled at the discomfort of his future son in law. "Besides, it will give you a chance to spend more time with Becky."

Richards brightened at the prospect. "I suppose there are some benefits to shore duty, Mr. Secretary."

"Then it is settled. Now I must get back to work. See to your ship, but I expect you for dinner this evening."

Stepping back into the anteroom, another officer brushed past him to speak with Welles. The Navy Department presented a show of busy determination. He stopped, for there was Rebecca standing near the scribe's desk and engaged in conversation with the man. It was a moment before she noticed him. Without a word, they stepped into each other's arms. The press of men about them might have been invisible as far as they were concerned.

"I have missed you so," she said. She kissed him and he pulled her tight.

"It was luck they sent me here." He released her, letting her back away to a more respectable distance.

"I have not heard from you for so long," she said, smiling. "It was perfectly wretched of you not to write!"

"But I did!" disputed Richards. "I sent a letter back just last month with John Worden."

Her face clouded. "You have not heard of Lt. Worden? The Secessionists have thrown him into prison!" Several eyes turned towards her at the fervor of her comment, but she continued without embarrassment. "He was passing through Alabama on his return from Pensacola when they arrested him. Father is still attempting to arrange his parole."

Richards thought of the worn, haggard man he had met in Florida. To be thrown into prison, or worse: it was not pleasant to conjure the possibilities. It occurred to him that Caldwell was in the Alabama Naval Militia. His friend might exert some influence to have Worden released. Richards resolved to write him a letter to secure Worden's release from the state of Alabama.

"Worden seems a good officer. I hope Mr. Welles is successful."

"Father shall be," she said, determined. "He sent him to Florida and will not be happy until they release him. But enough of that! How long will you be here?"

"That rests with the Navy Department. Your father wants me to help out here for a few days. We are to have dinner tonight."

Her smile widened. "Of course. Tonight then."

"All the damned rebels in the country could not keep me away."

He kissed her again and left the building. The return trip to the Navy Yard was more pleasant because of the brief encounter. He even found his sailors were in a better mood, finally recovering from the sights at Norfolk. Fire was always the seaman's enemy and the burning of so many ships had impressed the sailors in a way little else could.

"They are ready to coal us whenever we can get the ship warped across, John," explained LaForge.

"See to it." Richards took a deep breath. "There is more, RenError!."

"Yes?" LaForge was open, innocent. It was clear he had no idea what was coming.

There was nothing to lessen the blow that was coming. "I have a new lieutenant assigned as my first. You will continue as second."

"As second?" The words did not reflect the pain shown in the eyes. "I thought…"

"…you performed admirably," finished Richards. "And you have. Unfortunately, the Navy Department believes *COHOCTON* requires a first officer with more experience."

"As you say, captain." The voice now betrayed some of the disappointment previously shown by the eyes.

"I know, RenError!. I protested, but I, too, must follow orders." Richards did not wait for a reply. Instead, he changed the subject. "By the way, our letters did not reach the ladies. The rebel government saw fit to detain Lt. Worden."

LaForge shook his head. "Not very gentlemanly of them." He seemed to brighten slightly, overcoming the frustration of his demotion. "Will I be able to see Lorraine?"

"Certainly. We shall be a few days. Tomorrow, you must speak to the yard officers about getting some more hands. I will be tied up at the Navy Department for a while."

"And liberty for the men?"

Richards pondered the question. It was over three months since the crew was last allowed ashore. With the prospect of a blockade in the near future, it would be a long while before the opportunity presented itself again.

"Let them go, but maintain a strong anchor watch. If things in the city are any indication, Washington is not free of people who would wish to see COHOCTON crippled or destroyed."

"Eets good to see you ageen."

Lorraine was the first familiar face Richards encounter after a servant admitted him to Welles' residence. Though her English was improved, it was still difficult to understand her through the heavy accent.

"RenError! sends his regrets, Lorraine," said Richards, handing a servant his cap. "He will see you tomorrow."

Becky appeared and steered him to the dining room.

"Everyone runs about like mad dogs," she said. "It is a pleasant change to have someone who can be on time."

"Are things going well?"

She shook her head, dark curls jiggling to the motion. "These people have no idea where they are going and even less what they are doing."

"Including the Navy Department?"

"Especially the Navy Department!" She laughed at her thought. "John, I have never heard father swear as much nor as loudly as since we arrived here. But he, and that wonderful Mr. Fox, are making things better. Father would just be lost without him."

Her voice became serious. "Still, there is much doubt as to whether the government will stay in Washington. The rail lines to Baltimore are still disrupted and the Confederacy is making plans to attack the city as we speak."

Richards felt a sudden concern for her. "And you?"

"Father is sending me back to Hartford until the danger is past."

"A wise move."

She pouted. "Then I shall worry about him and you!"

Welles appeared and the four sat down at the dinner table. A conversation started about Hartford, as if they wished to avoid the very thought of the war. But the subject reared its head eventually, and the pleasant small talk faded. There was an awkward silence as the meal finished.

"Enough of this!" declared Welles. "We have reason to be happy tonight. John is here this evening and Lorraine will see her husband, also." He escorted the couple into the parlor. "You two spend some time together. I have work requiring my attention in the study."

Welles closed the doors behind him as he left them alone. The young couple spoke in low voices, sharing thoughts and making plans. But the coming war overshadowed all their efforts to ignore it. Finally, Richards bid her good night and returned to COHOCTON. He was glad for the short time of pleasure, wondering how long the moment could last.

Lieutenant Burrows appeared early the following morning, a younger officer accompanying him. Richards received the two men in his cabin, taking their orders and reviewing them in silence while he called for LaForge.

Burrows was a man in his mid-fifties, stout and balding. His prominent mustache was one with his equally long side whiskers. The hair was gray, his uniform worn and too tight about the waist. The orders explained that Burrows had come out of retirement to rejoin the Navy. With over forty years at sea, his knowledge and skill were exceptional.

The other officer was Edwin Nash, a former merchant officer serving as a volunteer lieutenant. He was another officer with several years of sea duty. His youthful face was topped by an unruly mop of brown hair.

"Lt. Burrows, Lt. Nash," said Richards. "Welcome aboard."

"Yes, sir," answered Burrows slowly. He pulled out a cigar and clamped it between his teeth. "I understand I am to serve as your first officer?"

A knock came clearly at the cabin door and LaForge entered. Richards made a quick round of introductions and had the officers gather around his desk.

"To answer your question, lieutenant," he responded to Burrows, "you will serve as first lieutenant. Lt. LaForge, you will remain as second with Lt. Nash as third."

"Given the previous experience of Lt. Nash," intruded Burrows, "would not he be better suited as second?"

LaForge opened his mouth to protest, but Richards held up a hand to prevent him.

"Lt. LaForge has shown himself to have sufficient experience to handle his duties," he said. He looked directly to Burrows. "He has been handling your duties for the past two months, I might add. You should also consider that Mr. LaForge is a skilled gunnery officer and those talents will be needed as well as sailing abilities."

"As you say," replied Burrows in a condescending tone.

"I do say!" snapped Richards. "I am required to serve ashore for several days, Lt. Burrows. You and my other officers are to prepare COHOCTON for extended sea duty."

"Immediately, lieutenant..." started Burrows.

"Captain," corrected Richards.

Burrows returned a hard look. "Captain," he corrected.

"Mr. LaForge," said Richards, standing and moving to the cabin door. "You will need to familiarize Mr. Nash with the guns and layout of the ship."

"Yes, sir."

"And Mr. Nash, you may aid Mr. LaForge in improving his skills in ship handling."

"Of course, captain," responded the new officer.

"Be on your way while I pass some final instructions to Lieutenant Burrows."

"Aye, sir." LaForge saluted and grabbed Nash's arm. "This way, lieutenant."

Nash wanted to say something else, but was drawn from the cabin by LaForge before the words emerged. Richards turned back to Burrows.

"A word, if you please, lieutenant."

"As you wish." Burrows was stiff and unyielding.

Richards returned to his desk, sitting on the edge where he could face the first lieutenant. He was suddenly aware of the vast different in their ages as he spoke.

"Have you ever held a command, lieutenant?"

Burrows eyed him carefully. "No, lieutenant, I have not. In my forty-three years in the Navy, I have not held a command."

Richards took a deep breath. "And you expected to get a command when you came out of retirement."

The new first lieutenant stood to face his superior officer. He was at least six inches shorter, but his eyes were unflinching.

"I did not expect to play first to a young pup such as yourself."

The young captain nodded, standing to face the older officer. "Well, sir, that is at least straight forward and honest. I expect you to maintain that honesty."

"Then I will see about my duties..."

Richards slammed his hand on the desk. "You will leave when you are dismissed, lieutenant, and not before!" The other officer turned to face him again, this time there was, perhaps, just a bit less defiance in his words.

"As you wish..."

"Captain," said Richards, harshly. "Captain," he said again, with less vehemence to the word. "And you must not forget that."

"No, captain." The response was slow and hesitant.

"We are to defend our country and this sloop must be ready for war, regardless of your personal feelings. I am in command of this ship and you will not confront me in front of my officers or crew again. Is that clear?"

Burrows nodded, the action coming with some reluctance.

"You know what needs to be done. You will prepare COHOCTON while I serve ashore. That is your duty and I expect it to be performed without question."

"Of course," said the first lieutenant, his last word added after a long moment. "Captain."

"Good. Then I leave the ship in you hands and will check with you this evening."

Burrows took a step back and saluted. Richards returned it.

"Then you are dismissed, lieutenant," concluded Richards.

Richards proceeded to the Navy Department and was assigned a small office. He shuffled through the clutter trying to make some sense of the stack of papers on the desk. He reviewed the papers with some boredom for a close to an hour before a senior officer appeared.

"Commodore Stringham!" he said, jumping to his feet. Richards had met the officer on two previous occasions and had developed a liking for him. The scuttlebutt in New York had Stringham preparing to retire, so it was a gratifying discovery to find him still on active duty.

"Sit down, captain," returned Stringham, a friendly smile on his lips. In good naval tradition, he referred to Richards by his position rather than his rank. "What has it been - two years?"

"Closer to three, sir, when COHOCTON left Boston for the Mediterranean." He was more than pleased Stringham remembered him.

"Hmpf, must be getting forgetful in my old age. I am to take over the Atlantic Squadron and set up the blockade. You will help with the ship assignments." A smile brightened Stringham's face. "And do not look so glum! We will have you back afloat in no time. Probably within the week, in fact."

"That would be good, sir."

The aged commodore laughed at the younger officer.

"Damned lieutenants anyway," said Stringham. "All full of sauce and ready to jump into the fray. I remember fighting pirates on the old CYANE when I was your age..." He let the comment trail off with a cough. "Well, I have more important things for you to do than listen to an old man reminiscing.

152

"The president has declared a blockade and we are to assure it is properly enforced. Most of the ships are outfitting in New York and Philadelphia. There are applications for officer positions and billings to fill. Match men to the ships, and then assign the ships to the stations. Refer them to me when finished. I shall figure out how to keep all those men, ships and guns supplied once they are afloat."

Knowing the importance of the task did not make it less boring. He struggled through the paper work. The list of ships grew daily, but the officers and men to man them were in short supply. More, the condition of the various vessels was unclear, his faith placed in the reports of the purchasing agents. Even then, many were ill-matched for the task.

The Navy purchased every ship available. Some were small and suitable only for inland waters. Many were old merchantmen and of little use. The sad part was there was no other choice in the matter. With three thousand miles of hostile coastline before them, the people controlling the Navy had no alternative than to expand it with all means available. It would take time to build proper warships.

"How is it proceeding?" asked Stringham, looking at the growing stack of papers marked as processed.

"I am finding some way to get this properly organized, commodore." He selected a billet placed to one side. "I might have a suggestion for this vessel, a man already assigned elsewhere." He handed the hastily scribbled sheet to the fleet commander.

"*MELFORD*, five guns, ex-merchantman. Fairly typical, I should think."

"Aye, sir, but in need of a captain. My new first lieutenant is a man of long practice. Such a vessel would be appropriate for him."

"You have had him barely a day. Is it someone I might know?"

"Lieutenant Roswell Burrows, commodore."

Stringham let out a long breath. "I see." He handed the sheet back to Richards. "No, I believe we need Lieutenant Burrows where he is." He prevented Richards from protesting further. "Assign *MELFORD* a suitable officer from your listings, commander," snapped Stringham.

The commodore turned and left without further comment and Richards returned the orders dealing with *MELFORD* to his stack to be processed.

That evening, he returned to *COHOCTON*, walking about the ship to inspect the work that had been done. He found Burrows on the quarterdeck. The first lieutenant saluted as he approached.

"Captain," he said pointedly.

"Mr. Burrows," answered Richards, returning the salute. "The vessel looks in good order, lieutenant. You have made good progress."

"Thank you." The answer was short. Burrows was uncommunicative.

"Roswell," he replied, using the man's Christian name. "I am assigning officers to ships at the Navy Department."

"Yes?"

"I offered you as captain to the commodore. It was turned down."

Burrows nodded. "Commodore Stringham?"

"Yes."

Nash appeared from below, walking back to the two officers. He saluted to Richards, and turned to the first officer. "The watch is aft, sir."

Burrows returned the salute. "Then I stand relieved, sir." He turned to leave the deck, but Richards followed and stopped him before he could go below.

"Lieutenant?"

The older man shook his head, declining to answer. "It is a long story, captain, and not worth the telling."

The tedium of the paperwork Richards processed was not diminished by the necessity of it. He ached for action, to have his ship at sea, and his discomfort did not go unnoticed by Stringham. The following Monday, the old commodore came in and placed a heavy canvas envelope before him.

"You are waiting for these, I am sure."

The lieutenant looked at the package, then opened it quickly. Stringham, after watching his reaction, walked over to the map on the wall. His finger rested on spot on the coast just north of Charleston.

"You will be here, at Georgetown. The station will be commanded by Captain Walter Michaels." His voice lowered to share a confidence. "I know Michaels. Not a bad officer, but with a tendency to be a bit stuffy and demanding. Nothing you cannot handle.

"He will command *DEFENCE*, a side-wheel sloop of ten guns. The third ship will be the *MARY JANE*, a converted merchantman. Only five guns and quite slow, I am afraid. She is all we have at the moment."

Richards nodded. He remembered the vessel, one like so many others being drafted into Federal service. "When will I leave, sir?"

"*We* leave the day after tomorrow. You will take me to the *MINNESOTA* so I can assume command afloat."

"It will be a pleasure," said Richards sincerely.

"I doubt it," returned Stringham with a laugh, "but you are stuck with me none the less."

The prospect of action was quickly replaced by thoughts of the ship. The next day would be filled with final preparations to leave. And he would have to entertain the fleet's flag officer and his staff, plus make accommodations for them. As he was considering that, he also remembered Burrows was aboard. Whatever stood between Burrows and Stringham could possibly surface. It would be impossible to keep them apart in the small confines of the sloop. He was obligated by tradition to host a dinner for the commodore, and tradition equally demanded the presence of the first lieutenant. It was short day's trip from Washington to Hampton Roads. He released a long breath. He would trust the brevity of the trip and the courtesy of the Navy to prevent any collision between Stringham and Burrows.

Completing the remaining work on his desk now became a driving force. He moved it past at a breathtaking pace so he might leave early to check on the state of his vessel. There was a brief meeting with Stringham to inquire on his needs and the amount of staff that would accompany him. The offer to dine aboard COHOCTON was extended and accepted, though the meal would doubtless take place at anchor in Hampton Roads and Richards was still unsure who aboard COHOCTON could prepare it.

It was not until he had completed his work and was in a cab on the way to the navy yard that the thought of Rebecca even entered his mind. That night would be there last together for the foreseeable future. The thought gave him pause and, for the moment at least, he thought about more than the sloop

That evening, he joined Rebecca for dinner. But even with her company, thoughts of the ship still plagued him.

"You seem distracted," she said, finishing her meal.

They sat in the dining room alone. Welles had sent a message that he would be in a cabinet meeting far into the night and would remain at the Navy Department. Lorraine had retired early and there were only one or two servants working in the kitchen.

"I leave the day after tomorrow." He felt a tightening in his chest as he said the words.

He stepped to her chair and held it for her. "I know. Father is returning me to Connecticut. He feels the capitol is in too great a danger for me to remain."

"He is right in that. Secessionists still talk openly on every street corner."

She nodded in reluctant agreement.

They strolled slowly from the dining room and sat in the parlor. She slipped her arm thru his and pressed herself closer.

When she spoke, it was a whisper, her voice low so no one would overhear. "I need to have you to myself this evening."

They sat in silence for a long time. He tried to think only of the young woman pressed close to him, his hand around her slim waist. Instead, his mind kept returning to COHOCTON.

The details of preparation tumbled through his brain. Provisions, training, trim - all jumbled together. There was the blockade, of the possibility of action and money to be made through the prize courts. And from the possibilities of profit, his thoughts came back to Becky and marriage. She was accustomed to the finer things in life and Richards had felt the fear he might not be able to provide them. Prize money would solve the problem. The cycle began again, but Becky broke into the thoughts.

"What is a battle like?" Her voice was low. "A ship battle?"

"I have never actually been in one," he admitted. He was too preoccupied by the thoughts of his ship to consider where the discussion was headed.

"You can guess. You have seen the results in foreign

navies."

He answered carefully. "Loud, painful, dangerous. Shell guns can destroy wooden ships very quickly." His words were calm, perhaps too calm for the moment.

"Why did they start this damned war?" She looked away from him, but he saw the tears on her cheeks.

"It is necessary..." He got no further as a look of horror formed on her face.

"You want this war!" she said, the realization striking her hard. "Like these damned generals and flag officers! You want to go out and fight!" She hit him hard on the chest, her balled fist striking painfully before he could stop her. Then she was crying, her face buried in his shoulder.

He tried to console her, to explain how he felt. But the words would not come. He could not really understand himself.

The morning of departure, he was up and shaving early. Even so, Burrows was already supervising the morning ritual of cleaning the decks. He saluted Richards when he emerged from below.

"Good morning, captain."

Richards returned the salute, wary. He had not seen Burrows in such an agreeable mood before. "Lieutenant," he said slowly.

"The ship is fully prepared to receive the Commodore, captain. If we make an early start, we should reach the fleet at Hampton Roads by night fall."

"Very good." The anticipation of the Commodore's presence was the overriding issue of the day and the thoughts of Burrows fell by the wayside. "Tonight's dinner?"

"I found a chef from a New York hotel among the new hands," replied Burrows. Before Richards could speak, the first lieutenant shook his head. "The reason for his presence is not open for discussion. Be satisfied he is here.

"The wardroom will serve as the location since it is larger than your cabin. I have also found a few hands with experience as servers in finer environments. I have seen to it they have new uniforms and will do COHOCTON proud, captain."

Richards' previous worries about the night's events faded. "You appear to have matters well in hand, lieutenant. My compliments and thanks."

Burrows yielded a brief nod of acceptance for the compliment. "The commodore shall find no fault with COHOCTON this day, captain, I assure you. I have threatened to re-institute flogging if there are any problems."

Richards returned a smile at the slight humor, and slowly paced the quarterdeck. He nodded to LaForge and Nash as they appeared on deck properly attired for the occasion. He had allowed them both to spend the final night in port ashore with their wives. Both returned very early in anticipation of the fleet commander.

A coach appeared along the quay and he felt tightness in his chest at its approach. He prepared to give the order to man the side as it stopped, but was puzzled as he noticed a woman's face in the window. There was a moment before recognition occurred as Becky stepped from the carriage. He was almost surprised at her appearance, for he had felt a barrier grow between them that night and he had not seen her since. A vague uneasiness appeared in their relationship, caused by his desire to serve afloat and hers to protect him. But he did not know how to mend it or even what the true problem was.

She walked proudly onto the deck, ignoring the stares from the seamen around her. The cabby followed her, carrying a large crate. Richards gave her a ritualistic kiss on the cheek, proper for daylight hours in the presence of strangers. That they would have engaged in something more passionate and personal only a couple days before was painfully obvious to him.

He took her hand. "Thank you for seeing me off."

She remained silent for a moment, walking to the stern. Her gaze wandered about the ship and avoided him. He followed close behind.

"I love you," she finally said, her eyes still directed across the harbor.

"And I do love you." He placed his hand on her shoulder. "No matter what, I shall always love you."

She shook her head sadly, a note of disbelief in her voice. "You will let the war, the thought of war, get the better of you. You shall get careless - hurt - killed..." A sob escaped her throat and she brought a fist to her mouth to stifle it. He slipped his hands around her waist.

"I will come back." It was a weak protest. He wanted to talk about the justness of their cause, of the need to preserve the Union and stand firm against the Secessionists, but he could not find the words in his heart. They would all sound hollow at this moment.

She leaned back, letting him support her weight. When she spoke, the words were barely audible.

"Be careful. For me."

He kissed her, finding the passion missing moments before. "Have a safe trip to Connecticut."

She nodded, tears pooling in her eyes. Then she noticed the cabby, waiting patiently next to the case he had carried aboard.

"A going away present," she explained. "Fresh food and some wine. Books to help pass the time. Some things to remember me."

She left the ship without a further goodbye, leaving the crate sitting on the deck. LaForge came from the dock, where Lorraine waited for Rebecca near the cab.

"Sims!" hollered Richards, staring at the crate. The sailor appeared from a hatchway, running quickly to the stern. The freshly scrubbed uniform and the polished buttons were clear in the bright daylight. "Get this to my cabin!"

He watched her leave the ship, the pounding of his heart replacing the anticipation he had experienced while awaiting Stringham. Now, as Rebecca's cab pulled away slowly, he had no thought of the Commodore. In fact, her presence had so distracted him he failed to note another coach approaching the ship. It was Burrows' order to man the side that drew his attention to Stringham stepping from the coach, followed by another officer. Richards sent some seamen over to take care of the luggage as Stringham came aboard and saluted the stern.

"Ah, Captain Richards," he said, smiling. "A fine day to up anchor! I would like to introduce Lt. Funston, who is serving as my flag lieutenant." Richards shook hands with the officer.

"A pleasure, sir," returned the youthful captain. By now, his officers had arranged themselves behind him for their introductions.

Richards watched as Stringham and Burrows shook hands. The older men's eyes met and held, but the words between them were filled with civility. Richards quickly introduced the other officers and the Commodore exchanged only a pleasant greeting with each. At the end of the brief reception line, Stringham stopped and looked about the ship before turning his attention back to Richards.

"Your ship appears fit for duty, captain."

"She is, commodore. And I would commend the actions of my first officer for seeing she is prepared."

Stringham gave a curt nod of acknowledgement, but made no comment. "Commodore, we will get under way as soon as your gear is stowed. We should be with the fleet by late afternoon."

Stringham glanced back across the city. "Whatever this war may bring, John, I shall be glad to rid myself of this place." He shook the lethargy from his manner. "Inform me when you are ready." He started below, the flag lieutenant close behind him.

As his feet touched the first stair, there was a commotion from below, followed by a rapid tattoo of steps coming up. Horrified, Richards watched as one of the ship's boys barreled into the Commodore, knocking him back into the quick arms of the flag lieutenant. Worse, as the boy stood up, he recognized Potter.

"Potter!" he snapped.

Hardy stepped forward, passing the commodore. "Your pardon, sir," he said, grabbing the youngster roughly. "I believe this one has a date with the gunner's daughter."

Stringham reacted with a chuckle, glancing to Richards as he spoke. "No harm done." He looked down at the boy and Potter seemed on the verge of tears. Stringham stared at Hardy as the old man relaxed his grip on the boy's arm. "My God, sir! Is that you, Elijah?"

Hardy smiled his gap-toothed grin and saluted. "It is indeed, commodore. It pleases me you remember an old gunner."

Stringham laughed and actually slapped Hardy on the shoulder. "You were bringing up boys when I was still a midshipman!"

"True, sir. Too true." Hardy pulled Potter from out of the hatchway so the Commodore could pass. "Salute the flag officer, boy."

Potter raised a hand in a poor salute and Stringham

returned, his chuckles still heard as he went below. Richards let out a long breath before turning to Nash.

"Mr. Nash, raise the Commodore's flag at the fore. Mr. Burrows, I will have the lines released. Signal the tugs we are ready to get under way."

The two officers worked quickly and a tug was already pulling them from the quay when the flag broke open forward, cracking crisply in the sharp breeze. As she turned her bow down the Potomac, COHOCTON was, at least for the day, flagship of the Atlantic Squadron.

Chasing a blockade runner

CHAPTER NINE

DEFENCE and *MARY JANE* set an easy pace for *COHOCTON* as the three ships headed south. The trip from Washington to the fleet anchorage beneath Ft. Monroe went smoothly. Stringham shifted his flag to the steam frigate *MINNESOTA* after dinner that evening. Burrows was good to his word and the former hotel chef prepared a fitting meal for the flag officer. And in spite of the obvious tension between Burrows and Stringham, the two were the picture of civility during the meal. Then *COHOCTON* had waited for the remainder of the squadron to arrive from fitting out at New York.

Richards' first meeting with Captain Michaels, the commodore commanding the small squadron, was not auspicious. The older man, round about the middle and constantly red faced, complained wearily of the efforts necessary to prepare the ships. Few of his complaints were justified considering the constraints under which they labored. Michaels still thought like a peacetime officer and the leisurely pace at which things could be approached as they cruised southward.

The set of *COHOCTON's* rigging was firm in the steady breeze. The two consorts were both paddle wheels and turned less than five knots while cruising, so he had all plain sail set to save coal. It was unknown how long it would be before relief was sent and the opportunity to refuel presented itself. It also gave the new hands obtained in Washington the opportunity to practice their drill aloft.

He eyed the two other ships in the squadron carefully, trying to judge their true capabilities. *MARY JANE* was a very old ship and someone had probably made too much money by selling her to the Navy. She was plagued by breakdowns and could only achieve six knots under full steam. Richards wondered if she could withstand the shock of firing one of the old eighteen pounders sighted along her upper deck.

DEFENCE, on the other hand, was a proper warship. A paddle wheel sloop built in the early forties; she was technically a more powerful ship than *COHOCTON*. But age was her problem too: the combination of an old boiler and engine with a weed encrusted bottom limited her speed to eight knots. It was clear most of the chase work would fall to *COHOCTON*.

For four days, the three vessels headed slowly south. The sea was smooth and the skies clear, even as they passed Hatterras. Richards noted the sun was low in the west. The southern coastline was out of sight in that direction, but they would arrive on station the following morning. Smoke and pleasant aromas rose from the galley stack and he breathed it in deeply. The New York chef became the ship's chief cook by acclamation after the Commodore's dinner. Richards smiled at the thought. It would be interesting to see how the chef performed with canned goods and salt pork later in the voyage.

The bells rang at the helm and he started below. He

was hosting a dinner for all his officers. Besides his four lieutenants, they had four midshipmen and over a hundred extra hands on board. He was hosting a dinner to get to know them all, and to assure they all knew each other. Depending on the sea traffic around Georgetown, the excess crew could be with them a long time or depart very quickly. It was all a matter of the number of prize crews to dispatch.

The table was being cleared and another round of wine was passed about. Richards noted each of the officers seated on either side before him.

Burrows, on his immediate right, was on his fourth glass of wine, and seemed barely affected by the alcohol. His eyes and speech were clear as he discussed a point with Nash to his right. For his part, Nash had only water before him as he had all evening. His strict New England background had rendered him a tea totaler and he remained true to his upbringing.

LaForge, on Richards' left, was only on his second glass, and barely into that. The captain had seen his officer drink more than that in an evening and remain level headed. The second lieutenant appeared determined to keep his wits about him in front of the two senior officers. Given the circumstances, it was a proper notion.

Wilson sat next to LaForge. He finished his wine and offered the glass to a passing steward for a refill. In truth, Richards paid no attention to his consumption. The engineer cared only for the machinery in the hold of the ship and nothing for the politics that dictated its use. There was no doubt in Richards mind about Wilson's concerns or competence.

Ambrose sat next to Wilson with MacDonald facing him. Both had imbibed continually and were red faced and rather noisy. They were discussing something of their experiences in various Mediterranean ports, their voices drowning out the chatter from the other guests. Their captain ignored it. As with the engineer, there was no doubt of their loyalty or focus. When needed, they would perform their duties to whatever level was demanded by the circumstance.

The four midshipmen sat at the end of the table, the most junior facing Richards at the end. They talked amongst themselves and all had already had two or three glasses. Richards smiled to himself, remembering a similar dinner with Commodore Perry in Tokyo Bay. He had not thought to match his intake of spirits to his experience with embarrassing results. These four young gentlemen were no different.

He struggled to remember their names correctly, finally placing Simpson, his face marked with a number of pimples, beside MacDonald. The unruly red hair contrasted with unusual blue eyes and helped sort him out from the others. The oldest of the group at eighteen, he was a senior at the Academy, called into active duty.

Asprey sat next to him, called from his junior year. Blonde hair and brown eyes made him blend with the other two midshipmen. He achieved high marks in navigation, as Richards remembered. Both he and Simpson were veterans of training cruises aboard the *CONSTITUTION* as well. It was a practical experience they would require in the coming weeks.

Miller, with general looks matching those of Asprey, was across from the senior midshipmen. A volunteer from New York, Miller's family owned a number merchantmen and he had served as third mate on a single cruise while learning the family business. He lacked experience, but his desire to volunteer when his family could easily buy his way out of the draft spoke to his motives and views of the war. Richards hoped those ideals would see the young man through the trying times before them.

Ryan was the youngest and sat at the far end of the table facing Richards. At sixteen, he was the least experienced officer and a mere freshman at the Annapolis with little real training and no experience. He also appeared to be nodding off, his wine consumption getting the better of his young body. It was time to address the issues of the evening before he fell asleep. Richards took a knife and tapped it on the side of his wine glass (his own carefully paced third) until he had everyone's attention.

"Gentlemen," he said, raising the glass. "To the Union."

They all raised their glasses and voiced similar opinions before taking a drink. Richards set his own glass down and carefully examined the men on both sides of the table.

"Tomorrow, we reach our station. By three bells in the forenoon watch, we shall begin our blockade of the Secessionist states." There was anticipation but no questions in the faces before him. He could not be sure of Ryan. "We search all vessels for contraband." He took a sip of wine, deliberately playing the drama of the moment. "Of course, contraband is anything destined for a southern port." There was the expected chuckle, Ambrose reacting too loudly to the weak humor. Richards ignored his response and continued.

"We stop *all* ships approaching Georgetown. We seize all ships going out." He took another sip of wine. "And we make bit prize money in the process."

There was a hearty round of approval at that incentive. Most raised their glasses in agreement. Ryan's eyes were barely open.

"Mr. Burrows," snapped Richards, his voice deliberately loud. All officers at the table straightened in their chairs at the following words. "Are we prepared for the blockade?"

Burrows did not hesitate. Richards wondered how much wine or spirits would be required to distract the senior lieutenant from his duties.

"Prize crews are detailed and boats assigned, captain." Burrows looked to the far end of the table at the woozy midshipmen. "Whether they will find their way back to New York is another question."

"Very good, lieutenant. I take you at your word." He turned to his left. "Lieutenant LaForge, are your gun crews properly trained?"

LaForge smiled his boyish features still predominant after the past three month's service. "I will keel haul the first one that hits a merchantman without my order, captain."

Richards had to return the infectious grin. LaForge was his friend and of all the men on board, the one he trusted the most. He reached over and grabbed his shoulder with enthusiasm.

"Mr. Simpson!" The youngster was suddenly stiff in his chair at the direct comment.

"Captain?"

"Is your prize crew ready for their first capture?"

"Yes, sir!'

Richards nodded. "I notice there are a number of freed men in your crew. Will that be an issue?"

Simpson was genuinely perplexed by the question. "Sir?"

Richards took a deep breath. While northerners voiced a ready support for freeing black men, that voice was not always upheld by behavior.

"Half your prize crew is black," returned the captain. The irritation was feigned, but it was designed to obtain an honest response from the young man. "Is that an issue?"

Taken aback, Simpson struggled for a brief second before responding. "I have spoken with the men, captain. They are all experienced seamen. I have no doubts on any of them, nor doubts on my own abilities to see us to a northern port."

Richard's head nodded in complete agreement. "That is what I needed to hear, Mr. Simpson." He looked to the other midshipmen. "All of you need to understand that as plainly as the sun rising in the morning. A crewman is just that, and it does not matter the color of his skin or the country of his origin. Is that clear enough?"

It was Miller that raised an objection. "But, captain! I have always heard the Negroes could not handle the complexities of serving aboard a ship."

Richards looked at the young man, his gaze deliberately harsh. "Look about this ship, midshipman. Almost a tenth of the crew are Negroes. It is sometimes hard to tell because of the men's tans, but it is true." He looked up and down the table at all his officers. "If black men could not handle their duties, we would find ourselves still sitting in the Brooklyn Navy Yard." He looked straight to Miller to emphasize the point. "Trust your men, Mr. Miller. Trained seamen can perform their duties, no matter their origins. Your job is to insure they are properly trained."

"Yes, captain." Miller's answer was properly subdued.

"Good." He looked to the far end of the table and Ryan appeared to be nodding off again. "Perhaps it is time to conclude the evening, gentlemen." He had learned what he needed on most of his officers. Nash was still an unknown quantity, but he would watch him closely the next few days. Ryan was even closer to sleep as these thoughts crossed his mind and he raised his voice to conclude.

"We need only the final toast of the evening!"

Asprey delivered a sharp elbow to Ryan's ribs that caused the young man to straighten. Miller grabbed his right arm while Asprey whispered furiously into his ear. An unsteady arm, supported by midshipman Miller, raised an empty wine glass. Richards noted the badly placed deck beam above his head and was grateful they drank the toast while seated.

"To President Lincoln." The words were slurred and as unsteady as the arm. "A long and successful term!"

The toast drunk, the three midshipmen helped their wobbling comrade from the cabin. Ambrose and MacDonald headed towards the deck to continue their discussion. The two junior lieutenants bid goodnight while Burrows finished another glass of wine.

"Lieutenant Burrows," said Richards, stopping the first officer before he could leave.

"Aye, sir," returned Burrows with a smile. "I will speak to the lads in the morning. Perhaps a run up to the crows nest before breakfast will teach them to control their intake of spirits."

Richards smiled. "An admirable thought, lieutenant."

Burrows saluted, his only unsteady act of the evening, and left Richards alone in his cabin. The youthful captain unbuttoned his coat, hoping the master mate could handle the ship until morning. Few of the officers would be able to address any problems until then.

On their fifth day out from Hampton Roads, the coast of South Carolina appeared to starboard. Soon after, the inlet to be guarded came into view. Of itself, Georgetown was a minor port. Opening to the southeast, the northern approaches were blocked by a long, low island. With only the single access, it would be easy for the small squadron to keep watch. But appearances were deceptive. As more blockaders appeared along the coast, the major ports would be denied to the south. Small ports like Georgetown would achieve new importance as their need increased.

"Signal from *DEFENCE*, captain," said Nash, holding the telescope to his eye as the ship rolled slowly in the gentle swell. "Inspect Harbor."

"Acknowledge." Sims stood at the helm and Richards nodded to him. "Four points starboard. Engine to one-third."

The ship closed the distance, slowing as it approached the inlet. Two small earthwork forts were visible on the opposite points of land. The sloop stayed outside possible cannon shot. Richards climbed into the ratlines and inspected the harbor through his telescope. Farther forward, Burrows followed his example.

"I count five, Mr. Burrows."

"Same here," replied the other lieutenant. "Three steam, two sail."

Richards returned to the deck. "Signal *DEFENCE*, Mr. Nash."

The ship angled away from the harbor and the masthead lookout shouted for their attention. "Ahoy the deck! Sail in sight, southeast. Two steamers to the south."

On the southern horizon, two smudges of smoke indicated the approaching ships. Whether they were coming to Georgetown, or simply leaving Charleston farther south, made no difference.

"All ahead, Mr. Sims. Steer due south!" The repeater rang out to indicate the new speed, followed in a few moments by an increase in the smoke from the stack.

"*DEFENCE* signaling again," said Nash. "Our number - 'General Chase, South'."

"Acknowledge! Go to quarters, Mr. Burrows. Have Lt. LaForge and Mr. Hardy supervise the forward pivot. Prepare to fire warning shots."

Burrows touched his cap. "Very good, captain."

He raised his speaking trumpet to his lips and sent the senior gunner and the gunnery lieutenant running towards the forward four inch gun. There was a flurry of activity across the deck and below as the ship cleared for action.

Meanwhile, the sailors brought aboard to serve as prize crews lined the side and the midshipmen grouped near the stern.

"Clear the starboard side!" ordered Richards as *COHOCTON* neared the first of the vessels. The idlers and young officers moved away from the occupied sailors. "God," muttered Richards under his breath. "I hope they do not fire at us with this crew scattered about our deck!" Nash grinned at the comment, but made no reply.

"Simpson!" The red-headed midshipmen jumped at his bark. "Get your prize crew together and be ready to lower the port quarter-boat! Check the first one!"

The reply, if any, was lost in the cheering as the first prize crew made for the boat. Simpson tackled his assignment with boyish enthusiasm. The long boat was swung up and hovering over the waiting sea as they neared their first catch of the day.

Forward, LaForge stood ready near the four inch rifle while Hardy supervised the loading. Potter stood nearby, jumping excitedly as they prepared the weapon for action. Hardy steadied the boy while continuing his task. The cannon trained across the beam at the first ship. The sailors stepped away when Hardy raised his hand to show he was ready to fire. Richards nodded at the gunner. He knew Hardy and LaForge needed no further instructions on the placement of the shot. The captain cupped his hands about his lips to be heard the length of the deck.

"You may fire when ready, Mr. Hardy."

The target held its course, oblivious to the warship rushing down upon it. Hardy jerked the lanyard and the gun hurled inboard. The single shell skipped across the water close off the bow of the steamer. A British flag fluttered to the gaff and the merchantman lost way, heaving to in the time honored tradition of the sea.

"All stop!" ordered Richards. The sloop lost way and he shouted to Simpson. "Over you go, lad. You know what you are looking for!"

The midshipman jumped into his boat and they lowered it from the davits. A yell indicated the boat was clear.

"All ahead, Mr. Sims. Steer for the other."

The first merchantman slipped astern. Though the colors were British, the contents of the slab-sided ship were all that concerned the Union inspection crew.

The second chase did not wish to be inspected, for it steered clear of the coast and headed out to sea. But COHOCTON had already worked up steam and easily overhauled the fleeing paddlewheel vessel. Hardy fired the forward gun again, and again the shell skipped past the target. The action failed to bring the merchantman to a halt.

"Aim high, Mr. Hardy. Fire with both guns!"

The pivot guns were both aimed by Hardy's expert eye and belched flame. Rigging parted as the shells flew between the masts to raise large water spouts on the far side. It was enough, for the ship slowed and ran up the Stars and Stripes.

"Mr. Asprey," said Richards, directing his attention to the junior midshipman. He ignored the crestfallen looks from Miller and Ryan. "Inspect the ship. I think we can guess what you will find."

The second quarter boat was lowered and pushed off. A quick glance showed the British ship, smoke again pouring from its stack, moving out to sea. The longboat was plying back towards the COHOCTON.

"Ahoy!" Asprey stood at the side of their second capture with a trumpet.

"Go ahead!"

"American registry, but the cargo is munitions. I found a Palmetto flag in the captain's cabin!"

Asprey's quick search confirmed Richards' suspicions. A Palmetto flag was the only way to gain entry ship into a South Carolina port without being fired upon. The lad may be young and inexperienced, but he did have his wits about him.

"Can you handle her north? You will need to get her to Baltimore."

"Aye, sir. There are only twenty in the crew and I have locked them in the hold. We will manage!"

The grin on the young man's face was visible even across the distance separating them. No doubt looking forward to his first command, thought Richards. "Very well, Asprey. I shall have a chart with a course plotted sent over directly!"

The second boat, minus the prize crew, returned during the brief conversation. Richards returned his speaking trumpet to its holder and waited while Burrows hastily prepared a chart with a course upon it for the youngster aboard the captured vessel. The boat took the chart across, then quickly returned and was hauled aboard.

The captured ship raised steam and the bow was pointed north. Richards followed it with his telescope for a while, noting the young officer at the stern by the wheel. He felt a slight tugging at his heart, as if he had lost one of his own. Yet the boy had been with the ship barely a month. He smiled and lowered the telescope. The other boat was still making its way back.

"Steer back to the squadron, Sims. Ahead slow. Perhaps we can save Mr. Simpson's crew a long pull back."

The first ship was unaware of the declaration of the blockade. Since the master agreed to honor it, Simpson released the vessel. Of course if the master had not agreed, his ship would have been seized on the spot. It was a wise, if simple, decision on the part of the British captain.

COHOCTON joined the *MARY JANE* at anchor outside the mouth of the harbor. The old ship lay there, a thin stream of smoke drifting lazily from the stack. *DEFENCE* rejoined the squadron later in the day after Michaels, too, had put a prize crew aboard a vessel.

Their anchor was dropped with a buoy attached to the cable so it could be slipped at a moment's notice. Additionally, the boilers remained lit in preparation for a chase. The precautions paid off when one of the sailing brigs tried to leave harbor by hugging the coast late in the afternoon.

For two weeks, the squadron busily prevented the swarm of merchant ships bent on reaching Georgetown. Two ships per day were captured, even the lowly *MARY JANE* taking her share of prizes. More prize crews were requested to prevent the warships from becoming unmanned. But by the end of the period, the effects of the blockade were felt. Fewer ships tested it and those which did took the blockaders seriously.

May gave way to June and the days of easy pickings ended. No longer were ships stopped during bold daylight runs for the port. As fewer captures were made, Richards came to realize how easy the first few weeks had been. He had actually lost track of the amount of prize money accumulated. Somewhere during that hectic period, he had fallen behind and never caught up.

Now he sat in his cabin, the ship rocking at anchor. His ears pricked at the sound of s sighting, then felt his heart sink as the watch officer announced *DEFENCE* as the ship called to the pursuit. He sighed and returned his attention to the book open on his desk.

Moby Dick was one of the parting presents from Rebecca. Yet after two months, he was barely five chapters into the novel. He wished it was only the demands of duty that slowed his progress, but he had to admit to himself he found the treatise heavy going. No doubt, his fiancé felt the nautical theme would appeal to him, as he, himself, supposed when he began the work. But the allegory of the novel was too heavy for his tastes. He closed the book with a self-promise to return to it.

He stood and straightened his shirt and pulled on his coat. He left his sword behind as he pulled on his cap and went out on deck.

"Captain on deck!"

Sims announced his arrival and Richards nodded in his direction. The other officers turned towards their captain.

"As you were. Where away?" he asked.

"East South East," replied Nash, serving as officer of the watch. He offered a telescope and Richards took it, spying the smoke smudge on the horizon.

He leveled the instrument and identified *DEFENCE* in the distance. The chase was unseen, already disappeared beyond the horizon. The paddle wheel sloop had already abandoned the pursuit and was returning to the small squadron. Richards closed the telescope and returned it to Nash.

"No prize today, Mr. Nash."

"Damn."

Richards smiled at the unaccustomed profanity from the usually devout New Englander. The slight curse raised the humor of the others on the deck. LaForge chuckled audibly and even the old first officer allowed a grin to touch his normally set features.

"We will have our chance, lieutenant," he said.

He examined the crew on the deck. The landsmen signed aboard in December were difficult to sort from the more experienced seamen. Potter frolicked with the other boys, taller and tanned. Like all the new hands, he now merged seamlessly into the crew, one more seaman aboard the sloop.

"Boredom can be as much an enemy as Secessionists, Ed," he continued, examining the rigging and looking into the sky. "You are a sailor. You are familiar with the dangers of inactivity." He turned to Burrows. "Drills to continue as planned, Mr. Burrows." His eyes returned to the sky. He felt the freshening wind on his face.

"Of course, captain." He gestured to the west. "Wind is backing. I fear a bit of a blow by morning."

"Then the men shall have something to keep them occupied at the dawn, Lieutenant."

The storm struck out of the south with surprising savagery early the following morning. First *MARY JANE* drug her anchor and the old ship fought to keep from being blown into the harbor or worse. With almost painful slowness, she worked clear of the land and towards the open sea.

Then Richards was forced to admit *COHOCTON* was also dragging anchor. At full steam, they labored around the point of the island and into open waters. Before losing sight of the flagship in the driving rain, *DEFENCE* was also seen to be moving.

It was two days before the storm abated and it was safe enough to return. *COHOCTON* was the first to reach the station, followed within hours by *DEFENCE*. It was not until late the following day that *MARY JANE*, forced to run before the storm, appeared.

Her rigging strewn with laundry, *COHOCTON* presented a decidedly unmilitary appearance while the crewmen attempted to dry their clothing. Richards stood on the deck, watching the harbor as *MARY JANE* went down to make the morning inspection. Michaels saw to it all ships shared the duty, both as a matter of fairness and to fight the dreary routine of blockade duty.

"I thought we lost that one," observed LaForge as MARY JANE slowly cruised across the mouth of the inlet, doubling back to examine it again.

Richards noted the circles beneath his eyes and the drawn features that bespoke of little sleep. LaForge was no longer the fresh faced boy he had met in December. He felt his own weariness and wondered that he did not appear much different.

"I was afraid we might lose this one, RenError!."

Nash was on watch and followed the old ship with his telescope. For one so junior, he learned quickly and was well liked by the men. It was a good combination.

"Something is happening, sir," he said, gesturing towards the mouth of the harbor. "There is smoke behind the headland."

Richards quickly climbed into the ratlines. The other ships became visible, moving around the point and heading boldly for the venerable blockader. A plume of smoke appeared at the bow of one, followed by the bark of a heavy gun. A column of spray lifted close alongside the Union ship.

"Gunboats, by God!" exclaimed LaForge.

Richards examined the four newcomers more closely, noting Burrows close beside doing the same. The other officers took note and joined them.

The rebel vessels appeared to be tugs, three with prominent stern wheels. Each had one or two ugly black snouts extending across the bow. Another gun fired, the results no more effective than the first.

"What do you make of them?"

LaForge had no doubts. "Obviously, they were converted from ships on hand by strengthening the forward deck to withstand the shock of the guns. They will not make very stable gun platforms. See?" He pointed as another of the boats fired.

The captain must have mistimed the roll of the ship for the shot went wild, striking the water several cables beyond *MARY JANE*. Faint cheers of derision drifted from the Union warship to reach their ears as the crew of the former merchantman taunted their would be adversaries.

"Certainly no long range shooting for them," concluded Burrows grimly.

There was an answering shot from *MARY JANE*, followed by a slow broadside down the length of the ship. The Union shooting was as ineffective as the Confederates, and no hits were scored by either party.

"What type of guns do you think?" asked Nash. The deep growl of the cannon reached over the sharper bark of *MARY JANE*'s ancient eighteen pounders.

"Thirty-two pounders," replied LaForge without hesitation. He shrugged at Richards glance. "I spent three years in gunnery, after all." Burrows titled his head in grudging acknowledgement.

"No doubt," agreed Richards. The firing from the ships became general and at least one shot struck the *MARY JANE*, sending up a geyser of splinters and debris.

LaForge continued with a sigh. "Besides, the rebels took three thousand of them at Norfolk."

The flagship made no signals for either Union warship to take any action in support of their squadron mate. Michaels was either too engrossed in the fight or felt *MARY JANE* could hold her own against the diminutive gunboats.

"There," said Nash. "She's hauling off!"

With a final broadside, *MARY JANE* steered clear, apparently satisfied with her showing. The distance opened and another sound reached across the sea to *COHOCTON*: the sound of men cheering. It was coming from the rebel gunboats.

"They think they scared her off!" Nash's voice was outraged at the prospect.

Richards stepped back down to the deck, returning his telescope to its holder. "Let them think that, lieutenant. A day will come when we shall take the time to show them otherwise."

Flags broke into the wind aboard *MARY JANE* reporting the day's find. Two new merchantmen had entered overnight and another had escaped. It was becoming a familiar story.

The harbor at Georgetown was shallow; too shallow in fact, for either the *DEFENCE* or *MARY JANE*. The blockade runners took advantage by waiting in a convenient inlet to the south. They ran in during the night or bad weather, remaining close inshore where the heavier Union warships could not reach. The storm had provided just such an opportunity.

COHOCTON possessed a much lighter draught than the other two ships in the squadron. It was a point to ponder over a breakfast of tinned pork and hardtack. Something had to be done to make the blockade more effective. With armed gunboats available, it would become even harder to enforce. A plan crystallized, one to provide the action Richard's wanted and to prove to the rebels it was no longer a paper blockade. After finishing the plain meal, Richards called for his clerk.

It was a dark night, with little wind and no moon. The feel of the air foretold fog by dawn. They were ideal conditions for a runner attempting to reach the port.

Michaels had approved the plan with some hesitation, and Richards now took the opportunity to put it into effect. The lights were blacked out and, engine turning slowly, *COHOCTON* edged closure to the shore. A leadsman was forward, a human chain quietly passing the depths as they coasted through the shoally waters.

"Quarter less five!" came the whispered comment.

"Hold her steady." Richards tried to keep a clear image of the chart in his mind.

"It will be a long night," observed Burrows drily.

"And a quarter four"

"Point port," said Richards.

"Sparks to seaward, captain!" It was Asprey, returned from his trip north.

"Shall we close?" asked Burrows. He licked his lips nervously.

Richards shook his head. "Stand clear. The rebels are sending one through to report. If she makes it, they will release others."

"But we lose this prize!" protested the first lieutenant.

"Aye, in an attempt to gain others!" Richards turned to the older man, his features nearly invisible in the night. "Further, if they do not send out any more ships, we will return to deep water before dawn so we do not give the plan away. It will be of use to us yet!"

Burrows did not reply as the depth was called.

"Deep six!"

He nodded to Richards and walked forward to inspect the gun crews yet again.

The night wore on, Richards pacing tirelessly on the quarterdeck. The ship continued in a slow ellipse along the coast, but no other sightings were made. Richards began to doubt the wisdom of letting the first through when the fog settled in, cloaking the ship in gray and making the whole adventure assume a surrealistic air. The fog brightened and the forms of the men standing about could be discerned. LaForge came from the gun deck.

"Well?"

"We will hold her here for a bit longer, RenError!."

LaForge stopped, ears straining into the blank wall of fog as Burrows rejoined them aft. "Do you hear something?" *COHOCTON* was on a northerly course and pointed towards shore. "Engines!" hissed LaForge.

Richards stopped pacing and concentrated his hearing. There was a dull throb reaching them from forward. "Helm, a point port. Prepare to fire to port!" He looked at his two lieutenants. "RenError!, back to the gun deck. Mr. Burrows, prepare to fire a warning shot on my order!" The two officers left, LaForge at a trot and Burrows at a dignified pace.

"Quarter less four!" The men still passed the calls from the leadsman back.

"Mr. Nash, get forward. Tell the leadsman to call clearly as soon as we open fire."

The sound of the other engine grew louder. And then, looming darkly through the fog directly abeam, there was a low, black shape.

"Mr. Burrows!" shouted Richards. The pivot gun roared, shattering the carefully preserved silence. A crash of wood followed as the shot struck home.

"Ship to starboard!" shouted Asprey, pointing to another shape hardening to the right. The crew of the rear pivot reacted quickly, swinging the gun and running out. They fired, striking the vessel amidships.

Both ships heaved to, an almost panicked reaction at meeting the well armed and prepared warship. A third runner stumbled across them, colliding with one of the halted ships. Prize crews were told off and they got under way. Turning south, two more vessels were surprised and taken. Their course reversed again, the leadsman still calling from the bow.

"A quarter four!"

"The fog is thinning," noted Burrows. For all his doubts earlier, he now grinned broadly at their success. "Perhaps we should head on out."

Richards felt the call of the excitement, pleased with their results. "Just a bit longer. Finish this turn to the north, and we can call it a day."

The gray wall surrounding them brightened with the dawn. The visibility, though poor, gradually improved. The fog burned off and Richard's found the ship moving through separating patches of mist still clinging to the surface of the water.

"Ship on port beam!" This call came from the masthead. "I caught a glimpse of her heading this way through the fog!" Richards did not appear to hear. "Heading towards us?" He found his own question disquieting. What purpose would a blockade runner have in pursuing the sloop? He looked in the direction of the approaching vessel and cast a glance at the compass. "Helm, two points port." Richards strained into the mist, groping for a hint of the other vessel.

"A half three!"

"Shoaling, Sir," pointed out Nash

The slowly idling ship crept forward, passing through a clear patch before the fog closed tightly about them again. There was the sudden crash of two guns from astern. The air was torn by the sound of shells passing overhead. The misty, dark shape of a gunboat faded into the fog astern.

Burrows gaped in surprise at the apparition lost in the murkiness aft. "Are they all out?"

The question was answered by another gun firing off the starboard bow. A shot struck forward, accompanied by the angry screech of splinters and screams from injured crewmen. The sailors jabbered, shifting nervously at their stations.

"Steady!" called Richards, his mind working furiously.

"By the mark three!"

"God!" The comment was wrenched from Nash, either by the presence of the gunboats or the depth of the water. There was less than six feet of water beneath the keel.

"Starboard a point! Mr. Burrows, run out port and starboard and be ready."

"Sir!" He was gone, shouting commands and restoring a semblance of order to the deck. The wounded men were carried below and others stepped from their sailing duties to take the places of the injured.

Richards turned slowly all the way around, straining into the mist for the merest hint of the rebel gunboats. He had to plan on all four enemy boats surrounding him. So far, they had been attacked from the starboard aft and the port bow. To his right, he thought he saw the slightest darkening of the fog. He made his decision.

"Pivots to starboard! Fire on my order." Richards' mind race and he was amazed at how easily the decisions came. It was his first time under fire, but it might have been only an exercise. "Sims, ready to come about to starboard. When I give the order, ring up half speed."

"And a half three!"

"Now, Sims!"

"Roundly to starboard, up to half speed!" Sims repeated.

Nerve wracking seconds ticked by, punctuated only by the calls from the leadsman and whimpering sounds from the injured. Richards concentrated on the blank wall of gray about them, alert for the first signs of another gunboat. Then it was there, a growing thickening of the fog.

"Pivots, fire as you bear!"

The sloop continued its turn and the shape of the

gunboat solidified. The flash of its guns lit up the fog, but the sound was lost when a shell struck somewhere beneath. Together, the two deck guns fired, thick smoke clinging to the deck and sweeping about the men as the vessel accelerated. The Union shells exploded in the structure of the gunboat and it was immediately engulfed in a cloud of white steam as its boiler burst.

Richards ignored it, as he ignored the screams and shouts of the scalded men aboard the luckless rebel. Instead, he twisted to Sims.

"Hold starboard, ahead two-thirds." He shouted down to LaForge on the gun deck. "Prepare to engage with both broadsides!"

The ship forged ahead as the cry of "a quarter less four" came from the leadsman. Then, on either beam, lay two more gunboats, stalking jackals suddenly confronted by the charging lion.

The starboard battery fired, the four shells striking and falling about their target. The small ship exploded in a cloud of debris. The port battery followed suit, but with less results. One shell hit, but failed to disable the warship. The other three shells only lifted a shower of spray around the rebel craft. The close call was sufficient to force the gunboat to seek the shelter of the fog and it disappeared into the haze.

"Are we going to chase?" asked Nash, anticipation heavy in his voice.

"A quarter four!" *COHOCTON* moved into deeper water.

Richards resisted the impulse to pursue the rebel. He shook his head. "No, there are two of them left. They can hurt us badly if they catch us at the wrong moment. Let them run and we will see if we can salvage the first one." To confirm the decision, he faced Sims.

"Steer south, Sims. Slow to one quarter."

"Aye, Sir. Slowing to one quarter."

"Have Lt. Burrows and Lt. LaForge secure the guns, Mr. Nash. Tell Lt. Burrows to prepare a damage report."

"Yes, sir." Disappointment replaced the heady excitement in the young officer's voice.

As Nash left to carry the orders, Burrows returned from the forward gun, a bloody white bandage tied about his upper left arm.

"Mr. Burrows!" exclaimed Richards, unable to keep the concern from his voice. "Are you badly injured?"

Burrows smiled weakly, but winced when he tried to gesture with the wounded arm. "I have experienced worse, captain. I shall consult the surgeon when the ship is secured."

"If you are sure, lieutenant," replied Richards. He watched the first lieutenant go about his duties. He wondered about the older man, his dedication to duty and his apparent lack of advancement.

Burrows was in his small cabin, his arm now properly bandaged by the ships surgeon. Richards watched him struggle back into his coat. LaForge was supervising the recovery of the damaged gunboat and the other officers were engaged on deck. For the moment, he could speak with his first officer without interruption.

"How is the arm?" he asked.

Burrows winced as his injured limb slipped down the sleeve of the coat.

"It has been better," he replied.

Richards confirmed they were by themselves. "I need to ask a question, lieutenant. I would appreciate an answer."

Burrows straightened at the words and was cautious

when he spoke. "I shall try to give the response you are seeking, sir."

Richards took a deep breath, and spoke what was preying on his thoughts. "Why are you here, lieutenant? Why don't you have a command of your own?"

Burrows looked small and beaten as he sat on the bunk in the cramped space of his quarters. After resisting explorations of his past for the few weeks since joining the sloop, the older man relented.

"You are a young man, Richards. You have yet to make a mistake that will haunt you the remainder of your life." He looked up, his eyes earnest. The craggy face was sad, but he did not stop once he had begun.

"It was during the Mexican War, Richards. I commanded a party assaulting a battery guarding Vera Cruz. It was a simple plan, the type of operation sailors carry out every day in times of war. We ran afoul a nest of Mexicans that were more determined than most. They held us up, scattered my men. We were forced to withdraw, pull back to reorganize and treat the wounded before making an attempt on the battery. By then, it was too late."

"Such things happen, Mr. Burrows. There is nothing sure in war, regardless of one's valor and intentions."

Burrows let out his breath and the sound could only be considered a sigh.

"As I said, we were delayed. Commander Stringham he was back then, brought his ship into the inlet to land the troops. The battery opened fire and cut up the sloop very badly before we could launch our attack and silence the guns. A lot of good men died that day." The sad eyes considered him more closely. "Your father was one of the men killed on that deck, lieutenant."

Richards had been unsure what to expect from the other man. It certainly was not what had just been told. Burrows stood, somewhat unsteadily. Richards stood back to allow him to pass into the wardroom. Burrows grabbed a deck beam to steady himself as he finished the tale.

"Stringham has never forgiven me. He always felt I should have succeeded as if we had not encountered the Mexican patrol. Stringham was close to your father, lieutenant. His loss affected him deeply and he blamed me." The voice grew bitter as he concluded. "He blamed me then and he blames me still." He faced Richards, angry at the thought. "Do not take me wrong, lieutenant. I try - *the lord knows I try* - not to blame you for my misfortune. Your father was my friend as well and I certainly have felt a sense of guilt on my part in his death. But this!" His eyes swept about him, taking in the ship. "This is almost more than I can bear. To serve *under* you rather than command a ship of my own…"

Burrows let the words trail off. He took a deep breath and his voice was calmer as he finished.

"This is the Commodore's last punishment, Lieutenant Richards. I shall serve here as long as he thinks necessary before being retired without ever having a ship of my own. I am resigned to it." He pulled on his cap and touched the brim. "I shall see how the repairs are progressing, captain."

Richards watched the first officer climb the ladder clumsily to the deck above. This was certainly more detail than he had ever heard regarding his father's death. If anything, the revelation made the situation with Burrows even more uncomfortable than it had been. In fact, the situation was becoming intolerable. Before, he felt the command of COHOCTON would function more smoothly without Burrows. Now he knew it.

Photo # NH 55257   Confederate blockade runner Colonel Lamb

A typical blockade runner

CHAPTER TEN

COHOCTON drifted in the swell next to the damaged gunboat. The rebel lay, slightly down at the head. The surgeon's report listed five dead and seven wounded three seriously. Not too bad. *Considering*, he corrected.

There was no danger from the remaining gunboats once the fog had lifted. It allowed Richards to indulge his curiosity. "Mr. Burrows, continue the repairs. I am going to inspect the prize with Lt. LaForge."

LaForge waited on the gunboat, covered with dirt and soot. He tried unsuccessfully to brush it from his uniform.

"She is called *REPRISAL*," he said, "though the original name of *PENELOPE* is around here somewhere. Three dead aboard her, no other crew around. That last shot broke the steam head, and she is in no danger of sinking." He lifted his hand from a railing and it was covered in grime. "What a mess!"

The little tug turned gunboat was not pretty. It was a cramped ship with a smelly interior. The whole vessel was badly in need of a coat of paint. The fires were hauled and, once the boiler had cooled sufficiently, men started repairs on the steam head.

The forward deck was reinforced, as suggested by LaForge. Two thirty-two pounders, U.S. Navy 1819 pattern, occupied the area created there. A small powder room existed, but most charges lay about in ready use piles. It was a careless way to handle something so dangerous and explained the disastrous end of its sister earlier in the day. Satisfied with the inspection, Richards prepared to leave until LaForge called his attention back to the guns.

"Did you look at these closely, John?"

Richards examined the guns again. This time he noted the heavy reinforcing bands around the breeches.

"Banded thirty-two's? Where the devil did these come from?"

"Not just banded," added LaForge. "They are also rifled." He continued his explanation. "It was an idea Lt. Brooke put forward once, but it met with little acceptance. He must be reworking those Norfolk guns. These will probably fire twice the charge of our thirty-two's. With the rifling, they are much more accurate." He regarded the gunboat with disgust. "If put on a proper ship, that is!"

Richards had learned enough of LaForge's character to see where he was going. "New toys, lieutenant? I think not..."

"But, John, it would be almost like having two additional rifles! And they use the same ammunition as our standard thirty-two's."

"Regulations..." started Richards in a half-hearted protest. Michaels would never approve the trade. That thought alone made him reconsider the proposal. "We would have to keep the two guns we have now. Lower them into the hold..."

"Of course," interrupted LaForge. "We cannot lose Navy property. We need an explanation for this ship's guns."

"Was she taking water when you boarded her?" Richards warmed to the idea.

"A little. Some boards were sprung by the boiler explosion."

Richards shrugged. "There is your answer. Note in your report you thought it best to put the guns overboard to keep the ship afloat. Since we are taking the guns, we might as well transfer the powder and shot, too. With luck, we could end this engagement with more supplies than we started!"

Once the theft was completed, a tow line was passed to the gunboat. *COHOCTON* returned to the squadron, the captured runners still waiting to be sent north. Captain Michaels came across himself to receive the report on the operation.

The commodore was piped aboard with due ceremony, and Richards invited him to lunch, preferring to make the report over a meal. They were served pork and beans, the standard to which *COHOCTON* was reduced for every other meal. Richards saw fit to cap it with a glass of the wine Becky had given him.

"There is not much to tell, Commodore." Richards refilled his commanding officer's glass. "It went according to the plan and the results lie out there." He raised his glass, toasting in the direction of the prizes. "It was a little exciting when the gunboats appeared. There was a bit of fancy dancing, but we sank one, captured another and the rest ran for home."

Nash interrupted, a combination of wine and excitement overcoming caution. "It was much better than that, sir! The ship handling was magnificent! It was as though he could see right through the fog and tell where they were going to appear next..."

Richards gave Nash a stern glance and the exuberance died away. Michaels was unaffected by the flowery praise, as well he should be. He spoke in a quiet voice after sipping the wine.

"How badly were you damaged?"

"A shell strike forward and a single shot in the stern quarter. The carpenter will have both to rights by nightfall."

"Casualties?"

"Five dead, three wounded." Richards hesitated before finishing the report. "The surgeon does not expect one of those to make it through the night."

"I see," said Michaels. He took another long drink from his glass. "You made a good catch, lieutenant. However, I doubt if we can risk any more exploits of this kind."

Richards did not try to hide the disappointment in his reply. "Certainly not on a *regular* basis, captain, but at least on occasional. We need to keep the rebels respectful!"

"No." The answer was flat and definite. "This is the only ship I have to catch most of these runners. I cannot afford to lose her on such chancy propositions, no matter the gain."

Richards wanted to protest further. But the futility of his complaints to Michaels was obvious and he meekly agreed. Besides, he had another issue to address with his commander.

"This is really excellent wine, Mr. Richards," noted Michaels, raising his glass to inspect it more closely. The shift in subjects served to close the question of inshore raids. "Where did you get it?" he asked, finishing the contents of the glass and setting it on the table.

"A gift from my fiancé."

"Excellent, Richards. Truly excellent."

Michaels stood and walked to the cabin door with Richards behind. But an idea came, fighting its way through the resentment Michaels created. He ordered Sims to fetch another bottle of the wine before joining the commodore on deck.

"They should bring a pretty penny in the courts," pointed out Richards, indicating the prizes preparing to sail. "But the blockade comes first, of course. I should not wonder a few will be purchased by the navy for use on the blockade."

"I am glad you can see it my way." There was a glint of prize money in Michael's eyes even so. "And a few new vessels to replace some of our old tubs would be most welcome."

Sims appeared from below as Michael's paused at the entry port. The seaman held back until Richards waived him forward.

"By the way, sir," he continued. "I would like to make you a present of a bottle of wine."

Michaels was surprised by the offer, but stared hungrily at the bottle. "Well, I really shouldn't," he said, reaching over to take it gently from Sims. "But if you are sure you can spare it..."

"With my best wishes, commodore."

Richards helped him over the side. The boat was barely out of earshot when LaForge approached, his anger uncontained.

"Why did you do that?" he demanded. "Give him a bottle of wine indeed! I should think you would smash it across his head!"

Richards understood the fury. "We cannot do this sort of thing everyday, RenError!. The next time we want a bit prize money, we shall invite the good captain over for dinner and a few glasses of wine. Then, we casually mention the success of this venture. He will be more amenable then."

"Maybe you are right..."

"Ahoy the deck! Sail to northeast!"

Nash was already at the side, waiting for the flags from *DEFENCE*. "Our number!"

It was to be a busy day. "Slip the cable and ahead two-thirds. Steer northeast!"

"Warship, sir!" came the report from the lookout. "Steam frigate. British by the cut o' her!"

The ship was sighted from the deck. The rigging, rake of the masts and cut of the bow were obvious. She was indeed British.

"Pardon me, cap'n." A sailor stood nearby, cap in hand. His English accent was plain.

"Yes?" said Richards.

"She be *DAUNTLESS*, sir, thirty-two. I served in her for a while back in fifty-three."

"Thank you," said Richards. The navies of the world were a close knit lot. It would have seemed more unusual to have no one recognize the newcomer.

"What is a British frigate doing here?" questioned LaForge, checking the newcomer more closely with his telescope.

"Checking the blockade, I imagine," said Burrows. "Assuring the empire we are maintaining the proper protocols."

The British warship altered course slightly to close with them.

"All hands," instructed Richards. "Prepare to render honors."

The crew rushed into the rigging to man the yards. Similar activity took place aboard the other vessel. The frigate passed on the opposite course, and Richards felt vaguely proud of the two obvious wounds on the ship's side.

The colors on both vessels dipped in salute. The British warship continued south along the coast while *COHOCTON* reversed course to rejoin the squadron.

"I would not want to fight her," commented LaForge absently.

"It might prove interesting," mused Richards aloud. He regarded his crew, still at their stations. "Stand down," he ordered.

*   *   *   *   *   *   *

Another month passed of the dull routine of blockade duty. After the fight in the fog, the remaining two gunboats were content to confine their activities within the harbor. For the ship's crews, it was a trying time of boredom. The British frigate was seen occasionally but little else of interest happened. With the short summer nights, conditions were generally unfavorable for running the blockade so few ships tried. Richards in particular found the inactivity maddening.

Ships appeared from the north. Instead of replacements, however, they were store ships. Water was replenished and food brought aboard. One trying day was spent lying in a heavy swell with a coal ship banging alongside. If the dirty business of loading coal was difficult ashore, it was next to impossible at sea. But the sailors managed and the warships maintained their station.

In mid-July, two new ships arrived with *BUOYANT* and *DAPHNE* joining the little squadron. They were smaller even than *COHOCTON*, but they were Union Navy vessels. Both were one time blockade runners, now pressed into service against their former masters. Each mounted only three or four guns, but they were sufficient to deal with an unarmed runner. They were better suited to their task than either the *DEFENCE* or *MARY JANE*. And as Michaels was careful to explain, with five ships available, extended chases could be permitted.

"Smoke, captain."

Nash's words were a routine report, indicating a vessel on the move within the harbor. It usually heralded a brief glimpse of one of the remaining gunboats maneuvering the restricted confines of the small bay.

"Ship standing out of the harbor!" Excitement crept into Nash's voice. This was something unusual. A low, gray shape moved rapidly against the shore. There were two funnels, raked sharply back, and a large wheel house amidships.

"She is a saucy one!" Burrows moved over to better observe the runner, following it with his telescope. "Very cheeky to try to run past us in broad daylight."

"Stand ready!" ordered Richards. They were closest to the fleeing runner and would be most likely to be dispatched. Nash confirmed it within seconds.

"Our number!"

The sailors ran to their stations in a rush, glad to shed the routine of watching the port. When the orders came, they were able to respond with unusual swiftness and enthusiasm.

"Slip the cable!" shouted Richards. "General quarters. Steer south, southwest. Ahead full." The ship picked up speed as they moved to cut off the rebel's escape. Richards bent to the speaking tube. "Wilson!"

The tinny voice quickly replied. "Aye, sir!"

"We will need all you have got today. This is a fast one!"

"Yes, sir."

The ship pulsed harder with the engineer's reply. By

now, the runner was directly abeam of the *COHOCTON*, staying close inshore.

"She is quick," commented LaForge. "Shall I load?"

Richards pondered the question. The target was out of range and pulling ahead slightly on the parallel course. They could not change course to close the range without falling even farther behind.

"Wait and see how this goes. We might not get the chance to fire."

Paddle wheels and a flat bottom left the runner with a shallow draught, even under full load. There could be little doubt she was laden, either. After a stay in a Confederate port, she could be expected to be stuffed with cotton and turpentine. Even so, she was still capable of running closer to shore than the *COHOCTON*.

"What do they hope to gain by this?" Burrows asked the question aloud. "If she keeps going at this rate, she will run into the blockaders around Charleston."

LaForge agreed. "Then she must try to get past us and out to sea."

"We will catch her for sure if she does," stated the young captain.

"Squadron out of sight, sir," reported Nash.

"Thank you, lieutenant," returned Richards. Georgetown left behind and Charleston not yet in sight ahead. There were few possibilities open to the enemy Captain. "You are right, RenError!. It is either try to get past us, or go to ground somewhere along the coast."

The chase continued, the twin lines of black smoke from the ships thinned and fanned by the breeze astern. The runner slowed slightly. But before *COHOCTON* could get within range, it slowed still further and headed for an inlet, coasting into a lagoon opening onto the ocean.

"We can get in there after her," observed Burrows as

COHOCTON slowly cruising past the opening. "The inlet must be five hundred yards across."

A bright splash marked the runner's anchor hitting the water. The black smoke tapered to a thin line from the two stacks.

"This is too easy," returned Richards. There was a disquieting feel about the place, an indication all was not what it appeared. The sloop reached the southern headland of the lagoon. "Port your helm and steer north."

Nothing was apparent. Both headlands were marked by dunes, but this was nothing unusual along the coast. They reached the northern headland before Richards announced a decision.

"Dead slow, Mr. Sims. Lt. LaForge, you may load the pivots with shell. Let's have a lead in the chains."

They moved towards the opening, Richards strained to the limit by the ease of their approach. There was a plume of smoke from the southern headland, followed closely by the sound of a cannon. The shell skipped towards the ship, barely a cable clear. He nodded with new understanding.

"You may return fire, Mr. LaForge."

The forward rifle fired, the shell splashing into the water short of the target. Three more guns fired from the rebel position, shell splashes rising close to the hull.

"By the mark five!" The leadsman's call was all but lost in the crash of a gun.

A steady fire was started by the guns to the south, but all went wide of their mark. The deck guns replied rapidly.

"Shoals to port!"

"Starboard two points," said Richards. "RenError!, you can engage with your main battery." LaForge grinned, going below to take charge of his guns. "Lt. Burrows, take charge of the pivot guns."

"A quarter four!"

The approach will be tricky, thought Richards. The ship edged further north.

"The headland, sir!"

Nash's words were lost in the roar of guns; four bright tongues of flame licked out along the northern shore. Shock went through the hull when one struck home.

"A quarter less four!"

The starboard battery fired in reply, followed shortly by the port battery. Their position worsened by the second.

"Hard starboard, Sims. Full about!"

Shell splashes rose next to the ship, drenching the deck. The Union guns sent up geysers of sand as their shells sought out the hidden batteries. The Confederate fire did not slacken, and another shot hit them before they withdrew out of range.

LaForge returned to the quarterdeck, his face dirty from the powder smoke. Richards stood quietly examining the two batteries.

"An interesting game," commented Richards without taking his eyes from the shore.

"Hard to get at their batteries," said Burrows as he examined one closely. "The earthworks are deep, but that means their fields of fire are limited, too."

"And all the while, the prize just sits there as bait. We could always close and engage the batteries," LaForge ventured.

The lieutenant commanding dismissed it. "Risky. They have at least two ten-inch guns in that northern battery. And if we engage one battery, the other can fire at us unmolested."

"Tonight then," offered Burrows. "A cutting out expedition. The inlet is wide enough to slip past with small boats and not be seen by either battery. The runner will not have any guns."

"Still too risky. They will expect it and would cut a party to ribbons in the middle of the inlet. We could lose the ship if we moved in for support."

"All cutting out expeditions are risky," countered Burrows. But he was not looking at Richards. Instead, he stared at the anchored blockade runner. "That is a well found ship and will bring a good bit of prize money. They will be getting her ready to leave in the morning, so the boilers will be ready once we seize her."

"I am not thinking about the prize money." But while the words left his mouth, Richards appraised the worth of the vessel.

"We cannot let it escape; turn our tail and run!" LaForge's words held a note of frustration. "We cannot sit here until they decide to leave. We have to rejoin the squadron eventually and they know it. They will just wait us out!"

LaForge was right. The runner could not be allowed to escape, nor could it be guarded forever. Nor could he take COHOCTON in with the batteries in place. That left only Burrows' expedition. But attempting to take a ship by storm at night was extremely dangerous. His men would be exposed to enemy fire for a long time before reaching the anchored vessel. Yet the runner was too valuable to set free.

"You will lead the party, Mr. Burrows," decided Richards. Like it or not, that was the first lieutenant's duty. And for all his improvement in ship handling, he could not trust LaForge with the command under such conditions. "Tell off boarding crews to each of the three boats. Asprey and Simpson can lead the other two. RenError! will take charge of the main battery, Nash at the pivots. COHOCTON will need enough men for one broadside and the pivots. Leave me a good leadsman, too."

"Immediately, captain!"

Burrows, enthusiasm marking every feature and move, called the men together. It was the most animated Richards had seen him since he joined the ship. There could be no doubt of the man's bravery or commitment to this new enterprise. The man's girth and age did nothing to diminish the senior lieutenant's zeal for the attempt.

A patrol course was set for the ship and they moved slowly back and forth across the mouth of the inlet. Throughout, they remained outside the range of the shore batteries.

Richards disliked staying aboard while Burrows led the party, but the ship's captain could not be killed on some fool expedition. Instead, he would insure *COHOCTON* was in the best place to help if needed.

The rebels could not be sure what action the Union warship would take. The uncertainty would keep the runner in the harbor for the night. After dark, *COHOCTON* continued north, a stern light showing as if carelessly left burning. Once it was extinguished, the ship circled back. It was an old trick, but hopefully it would give the rebels pause and they would wait until dawn to be sure the sloop had departed. At the same time, the sight of the ship leaving might be enough for them to slacken their vigilance.

The engine barely turned over enough to fight the flood tide. Without sighting the land, they were as near as Richards dared come for fear of giving the whole operation away. They drew close enough so the boats could make the trip with a minimum of strain, the rush of the tide aiding the effort.

"All set!" Burrows' features were a dark blur on the deck.

"Be careful, lieutenant. At the first sign of trouble, get

the hell out of there."

There was a dull gleam of his teeth, dim against his dark face. "You can be sure, captain." Then he went over the side and the three boats faded into the blackness.

"Ahead slow. Steer south, southwest," instructed Richards.

The ship was cleared for action, the remaining seamen standing nervously at their stations. Only half the crew remained aboard, the rest struggled with the boats in the water. He issued a silent prayer they would not have to set any sails this night.

The leadsman stood in the chains, drenched with spray and waiting for the order to begin casting. The gun crews lolled about, voices hushed and discussing their prospects of monetary advancement from the night's activities. Hardy waited by the forward pivot; a smaller, darker form stood next to him that might have been Potter. The boys brought several ready charges up to the guns. Richard's felt a general dread at leaving the powder lying about, but it would allow the guns to be worked faster in an emergency.

He stood quietly as they cruised near the southern rebel battery. Occasional glances at his watch by the compass light gave an indication of how far the boats progressed. Richards let out an involuntary sigh of relief when he knew the boats were past the guns guarding the entrance.

The inlet was lit by the flash of a gun announcing that his feeling of relief came too soon. The boats lay starkly outlined in the flare and still several hundred feet from their objective. While the sound of the first gun rolled over the ship, another gun fired from the rebel ship. In the brief light provided by the flashes, the boats maneuvered frantically, drawing away from the withering fire put out by their adversary.

Blockade runners did not carry guns. The tonnage

was more profitably used for cargo. Their quarry was not a blockade running commerce ship. She was a would be raider trying to escape to prey on Union commerce. The realization came too late to help the men on the boats in the inlet.

"Man the port guns, pivot guns to port!" he shouted. The gun trucks rumbled while the hidden batteries added to the attack against the boats. Richards took a step forward, as if to rush his crew's aid. He stopped short at the uselessness of the gesture. His thoughts raced ahead, deciding what was needed to save his men. "Leadsman, start casting! Helm, four points to port and ahead one-third!"

The ship accelerated, closing the southern headland. The raiding party was in bad trouble, the boats desperately trying to get past the batteries and out of the lagoon.

"A quarter less four!" It was quickly followed by another shout. "A half three!"

"Starboard your helm. Roundly now!" The southern battery was clearly marked by the bright muzzle flares.

"A quarter three!"

"Damn!" The oath escaped Sims, impressing on Richards' consciousness. There were only six feet of water beneath the keel.

"Starboard another point! RenError!! Aim for the flashes and prepare to fire!"

"By the mark three!"

The crewmen struggled to align the guns; the boats were lit by the Confederate cannon. Only two boats were apparent. The pieces of the third intermingled with the forms of men suspended in mid-air was shown by the brief light. The horrible tableau was frozen in Richards' mind before darkness again closed on the inlet.

COHOCTON reached the southern headland, the

hidden battery close abeam. The sloop's six guns fired as one. Their shells struck in and around the hidden guns. Secondary explosions erupted, caused by the enemy's powder.

"Reload! Hold your course."

"By the mark four!"

They were now in the center of the inlet, running towards the northern battery. The southern guns were silent, flames flickering around their location.

"A quarter four!"

The northern battery was no longer firing. Richards guessed they were retraining the guns to engage the sloop. Nash called for the pivots to run out, the rumble of the carriages lost in a ragged salvo firing from ashore. One shot hit the ship forward, but the others disappeared into the night.

"Fire!" The two pivots fired, but the broadside guns could not be brought to bear on the northern earthwork.

"A quarter less four!"

"Hard starboard, full circle!" ordered Richards to keep the ship off the northern shoals.

Only two guns fired from the battery when they drove around to re-engage. A broadside crashed out as the guns came to bear. The northern battery fell silent.

"Dead slow," said Richards. "Steer south to meet the boats!"

After the roar of the cannon, the night was very still. The dull throb of the engine and the sluice of the water along the hull were the only indications the ship was moving at all.

"There they are!" A lantern swung slowly close to the water to mark the boats' position.

"All stop," said Richards.

Burrows came aboard, drenched in water and blood. The boat was damaged and had barely made it back. A blast of grape had blasted along the side and wounded most of the men. The first officer held his thigh where a piece of shot clipped him. It was hard to imagine the effort the wounded men put into working themselves clear.

"Mr. Simpson is relatively unscathed," said Burrows, gripping his wound. "They hit Asprey with canister when were still too far out to rush them. I moved in to pick up Mr. Asprey and his men, but a shell hit them full before I could reach them."

"You should have pulled clear," replied Richards.

Burrows shook his head. "I was late to an engagement once before. It was not going to happen again."

The young captain nodded, feeling new sympathy for his older first lieutenant.

"Stand easy," said Richards. Once the extra hands for the boarding party were removed, Simpson's boat was ordered to stand ready to search for survivors. He spoke to Burrows, his concern obvious. "Your leg?"

The wounded man struggled to grin. "Not too bad."

Richards nodded lips tight. "Now we take care of that damned raider!"

"What are you going to do?"

Richards ignored the question. "Ahead slow. Another man to the chains."

The ship moved slowly, the twin chants guiding them through the tight waters of the inlet. COHOCTON approached the runner bow on and only the forward pivot gun could maintain a slow return fire.

The rebel raider replied. The shots were widely spaced, for apparently only two guns were mounted. The first shot splashed down close to port, the second to starboard. A third shell hit the forward pivot, knocking the gun from its mount. The crew was reduced to a heap of struggling figures.

"All stop!" It looked as if they would run the ship down before the order was given. "Rudder starboard!"

The ship slowed, losing further way as the bow turned to the right. They swung broadside, the runner less than a cable abeam.

"Fire!"

The shells from the remaining five guns tore into the slim shape of the southerner. The order to fire at will was given and the guns were worked with vengeance. Though two more shots were returned, the ship was aflame from bow to stern within minutes.

The rebel settled in the water. Crewmen jumped over the side to swim for shore. Cease fire was ordered as water rushed across the vessel's deck to extinguish the flames. Only the upper works and light masts were above the surface, still wreathed in flames.

"All ahead slow, hard starboard when you have steerage. Secure the guns. LaForge! Hardy! Get a crew working to remount that forward gun." The words came of their own volition, for Richards' thoughts and eyes stayed fixed on the remains of the would-be raider.

The Hatteras Expedition with *USS COHOCTON* on the far right

CHAPTER ELEVEN

COHOCTON returned to the squadron, the depleted crew still working to repair the damage caused in the brief fight. Burrows stood the watch, a makeshift cane held in one hand to take the weight from his wounded leg. Richards waited in his best uniform, staring across at the *DEFENCE* for the summons that must come.

He pictured the morning after the attempted cutting out. The burnt remains of the runner thrust from the water to mark its burial spot. Moans and groans drifted from below. With so many wounded, Ambrose extended his sickbay onto the gun deck. The sounds were punctuated by an occasional scream as the surgeon continued to operate on the injured.

Simpson found only three more survivors from Asprey's boat. Joshua, the slave taken aboard in Pensacola, was gone too. Three canvas wrapped forms lay at the side awaiting a brief service before being dropped over the side. It was the thought of Joshua which preyed on Richards most, however: the man who sought freedom only to die in a meaningless boat action.

"Did you indicate my part in your report?" asked Burrows, breaking into his thoughts.

"You had no part." The words were flat, emotionless. "I am the captain."

"We do not expect you to take all the responsibility!" protested LaForge.

"I did that when I took command, RenError!." He regarded the other officer, his pants still holed and bloodstained from his wound. Simpson broke into the conversation.

"Our signal, Sir. 'Captain Repair On Board'."

"Call my barge," instructed Richards. He faced LaForge, a fury in his eyes. "I did it for the money - the goddamn money!" He waved his hand across the deck. "All this because I could only think about the prize money that ship would have brought. It damned well was not worth it!"

"John, I was after the prize money, too." LaForge's voice was calmer, supportive. "We all were."

"But it was not your decision. It was mine. And I am responsible for not seeing she was an armed raider and not a runner."

Sims moved into Richards' view before going over the side to the boat. On his way to the flagship, the thoughts continued to assail him. It was not only the money that had driven him to try the cutting out expedition. It was the thirst for action, the inner spoiling for a fight which had grown over the dull weeks since the action against the gunboats. He tried to ignore it, but the urge was there, pressing.

It took only a moment to be shown to the captain's quarters aboard the *DEFENCE*. There he stood in the uncomfortable heat of the afternoon while waiting for

Michaels to read the report. When finished, the commodore tossed the paper onto the desk in disgust.

"What are your casualties?"

Richards took a deep breath. "Thirty killed and missing. Another thirty-five wounded."

"Sixty-five men, lieutenant. One third of your crew!" Michaels stood to face him. "It was a foolhardy expedition, Mr. Richards, and you paid the price for it. Damn, but I ought to relieve you of command!"

"Yes, sir." There was enough internal guilt so Michaels' words had little effect.

"This casualty report will not go well when it reaches Commodore Stringham; I can assure you of that! Do you have enough men left to effectively handle the ship?"

"No, sir. We will need replacements, and some of the wounded should be sent north for better care."

Michaels was close to exploding. "And the ship, man? What about the ship?"

"We took a bad hit below the waterline, sir. She is seaworthy, but definitely in need of more work than we can do on her at sea."

"So now I have to write orders for you to report back to the Roads?" Michaels' voice made the whole affair a deliberate attempt to cause him discomfort. "Mr. Richards, I was very happy with your performance until now. But this sort of..." he struggled, searching for the right word, "...recklessness cannot go on. Is that clear?"

"Very clear, sir."

Michaels sat back down, deliberately facing away from Richards. "You shall have orders to proceed north by the end of the day. Now get out of my sight!" No mention was made that he could not have known the ship was armed.

"Aye, sir." Richards saluted and left the cabin.

The return to Hampton Roads took three days. The report was filed with Stringham and the ship received orders to proceed north to Philadelphia for refit. Another day was spent reaching that city. There, almost a week after the fight, the wounded were removed to shore.

It did not take long to get the ship into the hands of the dockyard, but then progress slowed considerably. The anchorage was filled with other ships outfitting for the Navy, all vying for the limited resources available. New hands were signed aboard and the repairs began as best they could with their own resources.

Richards sat in his cabin, musing over the watch bills. COHOCTON was still close to thirty hands short, even with the replacements. A light tapping on the door sounded through the small space.

"Enter."

Burrows came in, sitting down without waiting for an invitation. LaForge waited in the doorway.

"The foremast is repaired and the new rigging tarred," he reported

"Good. How are the new hands working out?"

Burrows chuckled. "The Americans are all landsmen, trying to stay out of the army. The seamen are all foreign and they are still learning the language!"

Richards was unaware of the slight humor. He looked to LaForge and held up a letter. "I got a reply from Washington. Both the ladies are still in Hartford."

"Thank God." LaForge's phrase was a prayer instead of a curse.

"Indeed," agreed Richards. "According to Mr. Welles, the loss at Bull Run has left the capitol in a very tenuous position. Mr. Lincoln is considering shifting it farther north, away from the threat of rebel forces."

"If that happens," observed Burrows slowly, "we might as well admit the war is lost."

Richards studied LaForge more closely. The lieutenant, though four years his junior, was tired and haggard from his exertions. "Have you been sleeping?"

"Well enough when I can." LaForge smiled, his eyes going over the other man. "Better than you, I should think."

Richards did not feel like discussing his own health. "Let me know when the carpenter is finished with the shot hole in the hold."

LaForge nodded. Richards watched him go, and looked to the stern windows and the crowded shipping. He felt impotent, tied to the shore when the ship should be at sea where it could aid in the struggle.

"You need to take care, captain."

He turned back to the first lieutenant. The older officer stood and leaned on the desk to match his gaze.

"I have seen it. A single bad action has ended more than one officer's career."

"You are worried about me?"

"Do not attach more to this than your brother officers." Burrows turned to leave, but stopped at the door. "You have a promising career in front of you, John. Remember the men you saved and get past this."

"Thank you for your concern, Mr. Burrows."

The other man's words had little effect on the lieutenant commander. No sooner was the first officer gone than his thoughts returned to the cutting out attempt. The lost lives continually preyed on his thoughts. There was evidence everywhere on the ship. Now the nation teetered on the brink of destruction, and he could do nothing to prevent it because of the damage received.

He concentrated on his work. Tours and inspections were the order of the day, constantly checking and rechecking the progress of the repairs. Trips ashore to plea and argue with the dockyard officials. For two weeks it continued, on the move from the early hours of dawn until well after dark, leaving him worn and fatigued.

Through the haze of exhaustion, he found Sims often at his side, as well as LaForge and Burrows. Hovering there, the three were always willing to take a job from his shoulders. Sims saw he ate at regular intervals, scolding him when a meal was untouched. Burrows took papers from him at night to work on them himself. LaForge would share a glass of wine and pleasant talk. Sims would magically appear to get him to bed. The fatigue ebbed away, and with it, the worst of the depression.

Then one morning, refreshed from a good night's sleep, Richards was able to look at the ship and see she was ready for action. The wounds were at least outwardly covered. The new crewmen were rough, but they needed the experience to be gained at sea instead of the harbor.

There was a last trip ashore. He posted two letters, one each to Gideon Welles and Becky. Then a telegram to Stringham stating the ship would leave that afternoon. With the sun high on a bright summer's day, the ship weighed and started south.

The anchorage below Ft. Monroe was a clutter of shipping, a forest of masts and close pressed hulls that were difficult to maneuver through. A major expedition of some sort was plainly under way, rousing the curiosity of all hands when the COHOCTON dropped anchor.

The MINNESOTA, along with two other steam frigates, dominated the scene; the commodore's flag at the fore showed she retained the role of flagship. COHOCTON's anchor had barely broken water before the signal was raised for her captain to come aboard.

Even at sea, Stringham's desk was deluged with the paper work of the squadron. He barely lifted his eyes when he waved Richards to a seat.

"I read your report on the attempt against the blockade runner last month."

The mental anguish reawakened at the reference to the ill fated operation. He expected Stringham to pick up where Michaels had left off in July.

"Your commanding officer agreed with everything you said and more." Sympathy and understanding were etched on Stringham's face. "*I say you were too hard on yourself.*" His words were quiet, soothing. "It is difficult to send men to their deaths, but all operations hold the prospect of failure. It was a reasonable gamble. Unfortunately, this time you lost. You could not have guess a blockade runner was fitted out as a raider with cannon."

"But the men..." protested Richards.

"What do you expect? This is a war and you are going to lose men whether you like it or not. If you lay your ship alongside an enemy to trade broadsides, your men will die just as surely as those in the boats. Now straighten up, John!" Stringham brought a fist crashing onto the desk for emphasis. "You are one of the best ship captains in the Atlantic Squadron and I will not lose you to misplaced feelings of self-pity."

"Aye, sir." He managed to put some force behind the two words.

"Now, I want to hear no more about it. Damn it, you and your men did your best. This was not the first unsuccessful ship action in the history of the Navy. We all have more to worry about than a failed cutting out expedition!"

Richards smiled, feeling some of the weight lifted from his shoulders. The guilt was still there, the questioning whether the decision had been correct. But Stringham's words placed it in perspective, making the failure something he could live with. The comments also echoed those made by Burrows the week before.

"If that is true, sir, may I be allowed to make a recommendation?"

The commodore's eyes narrowed.

"Proceed."

"If that view applies to me as a ship's captain, does it not also apply equally to junior officers?" Stringham nodded and Richards continued. "Then surely it must also apply to Lt. Burrows."

He was pressing his luck with the commodore, but Richards pressed ahead with barely a pause.

"I have much cause to harbor ill will to Burrows, commodore, but I do not. He has been wounded twice in my service and has worked as hard as anyone could want to keep *COHOCTON* at best efficiency. He has served his penance, commodore, and he owes me no debt."

The anger that darkened Stringham's brow eased. He nodded slowly and looked through the papers on the overloaded desk. He dipped pen in ink and it scratched across the sheet. With a quick signature, he sanded the page and handed it to Richards.

"He may have *KATAHDIN*. She is only 690 tons, but I am sure she will see much service as the blockade continues. You will keep your second as first lieutenant?"

"Lt. LaForge will make a fine first, commodore." He took the signed order from Stringham. "Lt. Burrows will be pleased to see this."

"Very well. Now to the situation at hand," continued the commodore with barely a break. "We are going to take Hatteras and close down Pamlico Bay to the blockade runners. *COHOCTON* will be part of the fleet."

The offer of action had the desired affect. In spite of himself, Richards leaned forward in anticipation. Stringham chuckled softly.

"That's more like it, boy!" He cleared the papers from the map on his desk. "I command the operation. With *COHOCTON*, we have eight warships and three army transports with troops. You know about Hatteras; we need the lighthouse re-established before the weather turns. And if we succeed in closing the bay down, we will slow the blockade running business considerably."

"But the frigates, Sir?" questioned Richards. "*MINNESOTA* and *WABASH* cannot get into the bay. The bars are too shallow."

"Which is one reason for *COHOCTON* and *PAWNEE* to be along. You two will do the work in the bay until we get the heavy ships inside."

Richards nodded still unconvinced. "That will take time."

"At least a week," agreed Stringham. "Maybe two. You will take care of things until then. There are many places the frigates cannot go in the bay. I will manage to keep you busy for a while."

Richards sat back, the thought of action sweeping any lingering doubts from his mind. "When do we weigh?"

"Three days, lieutenant. We are waiting on the last transport now. Be ready the morning of the twenty-sixth."

The afternoon of the twenty-seventh of August found *COHOCTON* slowly cruising past the fleet assigned to capture Hatteras. The frigates and transports were anchored, and the sloop moved to inspect the two forts guarding the entrance to the bay. The commodore's orders were to proceed as near as seemed prudent and determine their armament and structure.

Richards found it strange he was so calm. The forts stood on opposite lips of the narrow inlet. The ship had been badly damaged by two much smaller batteries, but he did not hesitate at closing the range. True, the heart was pounding in his chest, but it was not fear. It was anticipation.

The southern fort was the smaller of the two, and it opened a slow but steady fire upon the sloop during the approach. Several men murmured at a large waterspout alongside, but were quickly silenced by the petty officers.

Richards climbed into the ratlines to observe as much detail as possible. LaForge performed an identical task from a bit below him. A shell whined between the masts, parting a stay with a loud crack. Top men moved immediately to repair the damage, and the young captain spared it only a momentary glance.

"That was close!" observed LaForge drily. "I make only eight emplacements." His pencil scratched across a bit of paper. "Thirty-two pounders again. Maybe a couple smaller."

"Damned thirty-two's," Richards returned. "We shall never see the end of them. Let's take a look at the other."

The ship steered north, the firing falling away behind them before ceasing all together. The second fort remained silent while the COHOCTON closed the distance. Without the guns firing, it was impossible to tell exactly what the Confederate forces had available. While trying to estimate what guns were mounted from the number and size of embrasures, the COHOCTON moved well within range.

"He does not want to reveal his strength," said LaForge, his eye glued to the telescope. "Still..." The words died as the fort passed slowly abeam.

Richards toyed with the idea of firing a broadside into the small fortress to raise a response. Instead, he finished LaForge's thought. "Still, we should not provide him too good an opportunity."

Their observations completed, the ship moved away. The larger fort stayed silent behind them, its capabilities hidden. The officers watched it fall astern.

"Damn fine show, John," LaForge said, his lips tight. "I was scared spitless. You did not even flinch!"

Richards wondered how to reply. How could he explain the thought of fear had not occurred to him? Instead, he remained non-committal.

"Cannot let the men see us quaking now, can we?"

LaForge smiled, the action forced. "Give them an example like that, and they will follow you into the mouth of hell!"

"Flagship, captain! 'Repair On Board'."

While going across to the frigate, he mulled the action over in his mind. He had not been afraid when the fort opened fire. The thought itself was amazing. Less than two months before, the ship was in an action with the loss of close to half the crew. He had walked a deck raked by shell and wood splinters, emerging unharmed. Was this guilt he kept in his mind merely a front to hide his desire for action; a salve to his conscious for getting other men killed?

The thoughts kept him busy on the long pull, for the COHOCTON was the most distant vessel from the flagship. By the time he reached MINNESOTA, the other captains were already gathered in Stringham's cabin.

"Well, lieutenant," began Stringham as he was shown to his chair, "what have you found out for us?"

"Much as expected, commodore." Richards made his report, conscious of the eyes of the other captains around him.

"I see nothing to change my plans," the commodore concluded. "Captain Mercer, WABASH will tow the CUMBERLAND. Captain Van Brunt," he continued, looking to the commander of the MINNESOTA, "we will follow. Captain Chauncey shall trail in SUSQUEHANNA. We will engage the larger fort first, gentlemen. The southern fort is small enough to overlook for the moment." He smiled suddenly. "Of course if you find him in your sights, you may remind him of your allegiance!"

Stringham paused, inspecting the captains. "*PAWNEE, COHOCTON* and *MONTICELLO* will remain anchored with the transports." When the three younger men opened their mouths to protest, Stringham raised his hands for silence. "These ships I have detailed are sufficient for our purposes and more would hamper the operation. I want your ships ready to be under way and move to any position I might require you."

Richards agreed with the plan, even while disliking his part in it. Each of Stringham's ships carried four times the number of guns of any of the sloops. They faced a combined force of no more than twenty-five guns in the two small forts. The large frigates should pound them into submission rapidly.

"The ships will stay in motion," explained Stringham further. When Mercer of the WABASH began to speak, the commodore stopped him, also. "I know it will spoil our aim, but it will also spoil the aim of the rebel gunners. I am not interested in speed. We need to capture the forts and gain entrance to the bay with the minimum of damage to our vessels. We are too short of ships at present to risk them for no end."

He eyed each captain while concluding his statement. "The Army will land when either the forts surrender or are reduced and unable to withstand an assault." General Butler, commanding the army forces, nodded in agreement. "Are there any other questions?" The response to the question was silence. "Very well, gentlemen. In the morning, we shall sound reveille for these misguided rebels!"

COHOCTON was roused at dawn, with the men fed

and the routine of scrubbing the decks completed early. Afterwards, though the ship was to play no part in the day's events, they cleared for action. By then, the bombardment ships closed the fort, black gun barrels spaced evenly along their sides.

It was an unusual experience for Richards to be only an observer. The gunfire began and the ships received an occasional reply from the rebels. The area around the fort was covered with the explosions of shells pouring from the ships.

Richards followed the proceedings, acutely aware of his desire to join them. The previous day, he had been ready to engage this same fort with his little sloop. Now, he would be more than happy to participate in the general bombardment. He was unaware of his angry pacing back and forth along the quarterdeck. He saw only the firing ships, smelled the pungent odor of the powder, felt the anchored ship roll and dip to the combined action of the ships' wakes and the sea.

As the firing continued, the surface of the sea became hazy with the smoke from stacks and guns. After two hours of the continual roar of cannon, neither of the forts made any effort to reply to the broadsides. Even so, rebel flags continued to fly over the hard-pressed batteries.

The transports moved down the coast, landing their troops below the southern fort. The sloops stood by, little more than interested bystanders. Thus far, the expedition was simply a drill with live ammunition. All the same, Richards wished to be a participant instead of a spectator.

Stringham kept the ships moving in their elliptical course, maintaining the level of gunfire. By mid-afternoon, the men from the southern battery quitted the structure, running to boats anchored within the sound. The Union troops quickly took possession. The flag raising brought a half-hearted cheer from the sloop's crewmen. Dusk approached and the frigates finally pulled away to anchor with the rest of the vessels. Their sides were stained from the smoke, but there was no indication any of the ships had been struck by so much as a single shell.

The next day, Stringham changed tactics. Now confident in the inability of the rebels to damage his ships, the bombardment force anchored within range of the fort. This time, most of the shells hit the bastion and its faces turned into masses of flying sand and debris. *PAWNEE* and *COHOCTON* were at last ordered out, cruising slowly back and forth to await further instructions.

The fort was quickly silenced by the volume of fire. The Confederate soldiers were driven from their guns by the exploding Union shells, but nothing else happened until shortly after noon.

"Ships in the sound, captain," reported Nash. The crew stood lazily about, their eyes fixed on the anchored frigates. The lieutenant was the only one alert enough to keep an eye in the other direction.

Dark smoke lay low against the western horizon. Richards barely kept his voice even when he spoke. "Signal the flag. 'Enemy in Sight to West'!"

The approaching vessels were mostly small transports. Whether to remove the troops or to reinforce them was unknown. Either way, it was *COHOCTON*'s job to stop them.

"Get these idlers to their stations, Mr. Nash. RenError!, get down to your guns. We will need them shortly, if I am any judge."

The signal flags snapped out in the breeze, followed in moments by a similar signal from PAWNEE. The return signal was a welcome order to engage.

"Three points to starboard!" Richards' maneuver would bring them astern of PAWNEE. She would lead their entrance into the bay. "Prepare to engage to starboard!"

A cable astern, *COHOCTON* was wrapped in smoke from *PAWNEE*'s stack as they followed her into the mouth of the inlet. Passing through the narrow strip of water, the starboard guns fired at the fort but received no answering shots. Considering the slight distance between them, it was a further indication of the effectiveness of the shelling.

"PAWNEE signaling," reported Nash. "'Form Line of Battle'!"

"Keep us in position, Sims." Captain Rowan was making the most of his momentary freedom. Two sloops could hardly be considered a battle line.

The Confederate ships, seeing their approach, reversed course and retired northwards, scurrying for the sounds from which they appeared. A defiant group of gunboats moved to cover the retreat. They were unfit to fight either of the sloops, much less both together.

"Shoals ahead!" The lookout was watching for more than enemy ships.

"Slow to one third. Bring her up a point!"

Rowan led directly towards the rebels, firing while at extreme range. Shells splashed among the makeshift warships, but no hits were obvious. Richards held his fire, waiting for a suitable target. The gunboats continued to close their larger antagonists. Potter appeared, breathing heavily after running from the gun deck.

"Mr. LaForge's respects and he would like to open fire!"

Clean and tanned, the youth was so much different from the telegram boy in New York. Richards replied with equal formality to the excited boy's message. "My respects to the lieutenant and he may fire when ready."

"Aye aye, sir!" Potter was gone at a run, disappearing down the companion.

Brave men crewed the small warships, men as brave as any of their own. Still, it would be a one-sided battle and there was not the slightest hesitation in the decision to engage.

The broadside guns fired, interrupting the thought. They were followed by the sharper crack of the deck rifles. Unlike the PAWNEE, which had fired at the gunboats as a general target, LaForge singled out one as an aiming point. The shells struck the hapless vessel and it disintegrated in a flying cloud of splinters under the heavy hits.

The gunboats returned fire, raising splashes around the sloops. A bright orange flash blossomed along the hull of PAWNEE as she was hit. The smoke cleared, blown away by the speed of the ship, leaving an ugly black hole with small tongues of flames licking at the splintered edges.

The pivots fired again, one shell striking another gunboat. Discouraged by the damage, the rebel pulled clear and retired up the sound. Only a few more shots were exchanged before the gunboats scattered, moving in all directions to escape the fire of the two warships. It was impossible for the Union vessels to pursue them as they made for shallow waters where neither COHOCTON nor PAWNEE could follow.

The fort fell before they returned to the fleet. The Union troops took possession, herding a small group of prisoners onto the beach. The Union fleet had triumphed over this small portion of the Rebel army.

Ships of the Port Royal Expedition

CHAPTER TWELVE

The action at Hatteras Inlet was a mixed blessing.

With the main entrance to Pamlico Sound closed, blockade runners were forced to use other, more treacherous inlets. Despite the control of the forts, boldly handled runners still gained access at the price of losing some of their numbers to natural hazards.

Meanwhile, *PAWNEE* and *COHOCTON* were the only Union ships within the sound, waiting for their larger consorts to carve their way through the inlet. It was over a week before *MINNESOTA* gained an entrance. And even then, the appearance of the larger ships was more hindrance than help to the two sloops.

The frigates, drawing nearly thirty feet, were much too large for the shallow waters. They proceeded through the shoals with great caution. Groundings were a daily occurrence and *COHOCTON* was continually called to either undertake the back breaking task of towing the larger ship free or to protect it from the rebel gunboats until floating off on the next tide.

The rebels maintained an active presence in the sound undeterred by the overpowering naval force. Their boats were small and could not fight the larger Union ships, but they were always close. They stood ready to fire a shot or to take advantage of an opportunity where they could attack without suffering the consequences.

During the third week in September, PAWNEE frustrated a final attempt by the rebels to retake the forts. Stringham decided to no longer risk the frigates and withdrew them from the sound. The operation, at first so successful, fast became a burden to the victors.

COHOCTON reported to the flagship. Gratefully, Richards watched the waters of Pamlico Sound fall behind. A single soldier stood the ramparts of the northern fort, waving his hat as the ship slipped past. One of the sailors returned the solitary action.

Stringham appeared much older, the life drained from his face and his skin a pale pallor. "We are getting ready to launch an assault on Port Royal, lieutenant. I am sending COHOCTON back to the Roads to participate." The words were drawn out, emphasizing the exhaustion evident in the man's manner.

"You do not feel well, sir?" asked Richards, concerned for the commodore's welfare.

"Feel well?" Stringham let out a low, tired chuckle. "I have not felt well since this whole damned war began." He sighed, straightening slightly. "This is my last command, John. The Atlantic Squadron is being turned over to Flag Officer DuPont when I reach the Roads. I am more than glad to give up the command and step aside."

"I will be sorry to see you leave."

"Thank you for that, Richards." Stringham smiled, the old fire returning to his eyes. "But now to your orders. You will proceed north and arrange the transport convoy. Port Royal will be a larger expedition than this. We shall gain control of a port that all our ships can use. Blockaders will not have to go all the way to Philadelphia or New York to refuel and refit if we are successful."

"That would be an advantage, commodore." A memory of the coal ship banging alongside in a heavy swell came clearly.

Stringham handed him the written orders. "I will see you in Maryland when the commands change. And do not look so glum, John," he continued. "You will hear from me occasionally. I shall be working in the Navy department as long as I am fit."

Richards smiled at the fatherly old man. "I trust that will be a long time."

At the side, he waited for Sims to appear with the boat. It would not be the same without the commodore in charge of the fleet.

"North again, cap'n?" asked Sims, his eyes looking across the water.

It seemed all but impossible to keep any information from the men it concerned most. "Aye," returned Richards, mulling over the prospects.

Sims eyed the young captain. "Still worried about that run in down south?" he ventured. The protectiveness was still there.

"No, just thinking. The commodore is stepping down."

Sims shook his head sadly. "Grand old man, sir. 'Twas a pleasure serving under 'im."

"It bothers him too, you know," continued Richards absently. "Letting men die."

"It happens." The coxswain shrugged. "It's our way of life."

"Our way." There was a need to explain further. "I know you accept it, but I feel sorry for the others. Like the slave, Joshua." He kept on in answer to the questioning glance. "He did not ask for this. After escaping slavery, we should have set him free, given him a life to lead."

"He didn't feel that way," said Sims. "He weren't much for talking, but there was one thing clear. Joshua stayed with us because he chose to. For him, it were the best he could do. It made him happy."

"You think so?" queried Richards.

"Cap'n, I know so."

The third week in October found *COHOCTON* sitting at anchor beneath the guns of Fortress Monroe in Hampton Roads. The size of the expedition was staggering with over three thousand troops to be transported - an entire Army Corps. Richards repeated his earlier efforts of coordinating transport, writing orders for vessels and assigning the troops to go aboard them.

There were thirty-four transports to move the troops and sixteen warships to guard them. Grouped around this growing fleet were twenty-five coal ships which would be sent ahead to meet the fleet at Port Royal. With coal available, fleet operations would begin immediately upon the capture of the harbor.

Flag Officer DuPont took command of the squadron with little ceremony. In an act calculated to make the change of commanders more apparent, *WABASH* was detailed as flagship. Unlike Stringham, who enjoyed the company of all the officers in the fleet, DuPont rarely brought the men together. Richards had to be content with the dispatches received from the flag officer for information.

The fleet grew daily and it appeared they must eventually choke off the entrance to the Chesapeake. And the expedition, supposedly a closely guarded secret, advertised its presence. Every morning, there were observers on the southern shore, the sunlight glinting from their telescopes while they examined any new additions to the force.

On the twenty-sixth of October, a longboat arrived from the flagship carrying sailing orders. Richards took the weighted envelope below, noticing the scurrying activity aboard the coal ships. While he sat near the stern window reading the carefully written pages, the coal fleet loosed sails and slipped from the anchorage. Three days later, the signal appeared at the masthead of WABASH and they were finally under way.

"A bit of a storm brewing!" commented LaForge, his hand tightly gripping the rail against the deep plunging of the ship.

"More than a *bit* I fear," returned Richards. They were dampened by the spray bursting across the bow and sweeping the length of the deck.

On the first day, the fleet moved down the coast in good order, following the carefully detailed sailing order laid out by the flag officer. But that morning, before the calling of the first watch, it became obvious the weather was turning. Richards became grim and determined. Hatteras was not much farther ahead and he stilled carried strong memories from earlier in the year.

"Another man on the helm I think, Mr. LaForge." The ship carried plain sail, but the wind was rising from abeam. The pennant cracked stiffly from the mast, its motions blurred by the force.

"We shall not make it through the forenoon watch, captain," ventured Nash. For having so little experience, he showed a keen weather sense.

"You are probably correct. Take in main courses, Mr. Nash, and a reef in the topsails. Get the t'gallants off her, too."

The seamen climbed into the rigging, gripping the ratlines against the pressing wind. The canvas was brailed up and the motion eased with the lighter pressure aloft.

The fleet already had problems in the increasing storm. The disparity in the ships separated them, blowing ships to windward. The transports, starting from orderly lines, soon spread from horizon to horizon.

"Flagship signaling!" Richards waited expectantly for Simpson to finish the report. "'Make for Fleet Rendezvous'!"

Richards nodded with apprehension. Many of the troop transports were old ships hurriedly pressed into their new calling. Over half the warships were little gunboats unsuited to facing heavy weather. And as the force of the storm grew, COHOCTON asserted her cantankerous nature, calling four men to the helm and requiring the pumps to be started. As the fleet scattered before the storm's strength, an old transport lay close abeam.

"Keep station on the transport!" There was a large letter strung between the stacks on the vessel - 'K'. A check of the signal book showed her to be the ST. ELIZABETH.

"What do you think?" LaForge's voice was a shout, barely audible in the growing roar.

"She is an old New York ferry," explained Richards, recalling the facts from his efforts at organizing the transport fleet. "We will stick close. She was not built for this type of weather!"

For the next day, COHOCTON lay to windward of the struggling transport. Every hour gave some new sign of the strain aboard the old steamer. Deck fittings were carried away; paint was stripped by the force of the water, leaving large bare spots on the hull and upper works. A series of planks were ripped from the prominent wheel house amidships. By the evening of the first, it was doubtful the transport could survive. Richards retired to a restless sleep, fearing the worst for the occupants of the vessel.

"Captain!" Sims voice was almost lost in the sound of the storm, but the touch of his hand roused Richards from his light sleep.

"What is it?" He struggled into a sitting position, bracing himself against the heaving motion of the sloop.

"Rockets from the transport!   Mr. Nash says they are distress signals."

Richards nodded, standing on the unsteady deck. He bundled himself back into the oilskins which were discarded just moments before. He winced as the heavy material rasped along a salt sore on his neck. The captain followed the treacherous path of guidelines to the wildly pitching deck.

There was not enough light to see the transport, but periodically a white rocket streaked into the low clouds, leaving a brief trail to be quickly dissipated in the wind. The helm was put over and the sloop crept down towards the position.

The ship slowed, Richards repeating the order twice to be heard through the speaking tube. All sail had disappeared the previous day, closely brailed to the yards to await more favorable conditions. They approached the stricken transport under steam while still maintaining enough headway to keep from floundering.

A dim light came with dawn and the dark shape of the *ST. ELIZABETH* appeared close abeam. The transport lay in desperate trouble, low in the water and listing to port. The paddle wheels barely turned and waves crashed across the entire length of the ship.

"Boats with pumps?" suggested LaForge.

"They would never be able to transfer them."

"What then?"

The transports' movements were slowed by the load of

water within her hull. *COHOCTON* pitched violently in the heavy seas. There was only one choice in the matter.

"We will close with *ST. ELIZABETH*. Launch our boats to remove the soldiers."

The orders were followed but the evolution of lowering a boat into the seething waters was no simple task. They soon made their difficult way to the sinking ship. Soldiers along the deck of the transport crowded into the small boats and headed back. The remaining boats from *ST. ELIZABETH* were put to use, but they were even smaller, if possible, than the sloop's. The first man up the side was the first officer from the *ST. ELIZABETH*.

"She is finished for sure!" he yelled without bothering to introduce himself. "We must have sprung some boards below the water line. No surprise with the pounding these last two days! The pumps cannot even slow the water she is taking and the fires will be awash within the hour! You must move closer and take the troops off directly!"

It was a desperate thought. *COHOCTON* was skittish under much better than the prevailing conditions, yet there were almost three hundred troops aboard the transport.

"Keep the boats working from your starboard side! I shall try to close with the port. Maybe if we stay in your lee, we can drop lines for the soldiers to climb up!"

The transport officer nodded in agreement. "I know it will be difficult, but we must do something!" He did not bother to salute but walked back to the entry port and dropped into a boat returning to the other ship.

Richards wondered about the man. The sea was ready to claim his ship, but he returned to her without hesitation. *Brave*. A bravery akin to standing under the fire of the forts at Hatteras. Maybe even better, for here the actions were directed towards saving lives.

"Dead slow!" he ordered. "Drop astern and bring us up along the port side!"

Sims and Healey, two permanent fixtures at the wheel, nodded to acknowledge the command. If it could be done, the two expert helmsmen would manage it.

The maneuver was dangerous, and Richards was well aware of the risks. COHOCTON could easily end on top of the lower transport, sinking the unfortunate vessel immediately. The action would result in equally fatal damage to COHOCTON.

The storm worsened, sheets of spray clouding the sight of the other ship close off the bow. Richards had never considered such a death before. If both ships were sunk, no one would have a chance of survival in the small boats. They would just disappear from the face of the earth, the waters closing above the vessels to hide their resting places.

ST. ELIZABETH sank noticeably lower with each hour. The paddle wheels stopped their anemic motions and the thin trail of smoke from the stacks died. COHOCTON was quickly overrun with wet and weary soldiers filling the hold to capacity. But still more soldiers came, braving the weather to crawl into a small boat or to attempt the treacherous climb up one of the lines trailing over the side of the ship.

Sometimes the ships separated, soldiers clinging to the lines desperately until hauled up by the sailors, or until swept away by the foaming sea. In one horrifying instance, a soldier mistimed his jump to be crushed when the boat smashed against the side of the ship. Of the soldiers huddled on the deck of the sinking transport, more were washed away with each wave to thrash and struggle in the water until finally swept out of sight.

"We cannot stay here much longer!" shouted LaForge. Hardly any freeboard separated ST. ELIZABETH's deck from the surface of the water. "If she goes down, we will be caught in the suction and pulled into the wreck!"

It was a hard decision, but the order was necessary.

The lines withdrawn, COHOCTON drifted to a safer distance.

Soon the gun deck, too, was filled. Troops were forced to COHOCTON's main deck, pressing close to one another for warmth in the freezing rain. The officers' cabins were opened to the men, but it made little difference. COHOCTON was not large enough to carry all the soldiers aboard the transport.

The boat crews, though changed at regular intervals, were exhausted from their efforts. One boat was hurled against ST. ELIZABETH by a rouge wave, causing it to capsize. The boat, crew and men aboard disappeared beneath the water and were not seen again.

When the deck of the transport was awash, the boats could no longer risk approaching it. The remaining men swam for the boats. Another boat sank when swamped by frantic soldiers. Then, in a brief instant, the ST. ELIZABETH was gone, taking with her a large portion of her crew and officers. In the premature dusk caused by the storm, the small boats were recalled. They had scoured the area for swimmers, but could not be allowed to become lost in the darkness.

Soldiers littered the deck of the ship, making it almost impossible for the weary sailors to go about their tasks. The bow pointed towards Port Royal and the ship's speed increased. Richards thought back to ST. ELIZABETH's first officer. He was not among the survivors. Such a man would not be. He would stay with his ship until all others were removed.

The next morning, the driving rain first eased, then quit. The sea settled though the ship still pitched violently. Burial services were held for several soldiers who died from exposure during the night. Richards read the words quietly from the Bible as body after body went over the side, a thirty-two pound shot tied to their feet to speed them to the bottom. It was noon the following day before Port Royal was in view, ships from the fleet already anchored around the entrance of the harbor.

It was an exhausted group of sailors who moved the soldiers to other transports. Crews were changed after only two trips; the men were incapable of any more. Boats arrived from the transports and other ships in the fleet, allowing the men of the *COHOCTON* time to recover from their exertions.

The storm completely abated on the morning of the fifth. *COHOCTON's* crew was given an easy day cleaning up. Only light work was ordered, and they deserved much more before facing the enemy. They received a note from DuPont, congratulating the ship for their efforts. The sailors received it with a riotous cheer.

That evening, Richards reread the letter before placing it in the logbook. The officer from *ST. ELIZABETH* was in his thoughts, even with the assault set for the next day. He determined to find out the man's identity and write a letter to his relatives, wondering if he had a wife or children. The praise seemed more appropriate for the dead sailor. He closed the logbook and returned it to the desk. He hoped the battle would remove the memory of the past four days.

The attack began early, the major warships forming a line to bombard the fort on the southern point of the harbor entrance. *COHOCTON* supported a flotilla of gunboats guarding the northern flank.

The roar of cannon fire grew with the bombardment. The Confederate gunboats gathered across the harbor, but kept their distance from the more powerful Union warships. What they hoped to accomplish against a fleet led by several fifty gun frigates was unclear, but sloop was on station to spoil any attempt.

Five gunboats huddled around *COHOCTON*, all very like their Confederate counterparts. If the ship was small and steam driven, it had been bought and had at least one gun mounted. Possibly useful against ships of equal size, there was no hope for them in open waters where full size warships could maneuver. On the rivers and tributaries, they were in their element and could give a good account as they were doing along the Potomac.

Like Hatteras, the Confederates underestimated the effects of naval shell fire. It was barely an hour before the last gun in the main fort ceased to reply, the troops deserting their posts to seek shelter from the bombardment. Common teaching held one gun ashore was worth five afloat but they were proving that untrue. Shells transformed shore bombardment in the same manner as ship battles. The guns of the fort had not harmed the fleet, whereas the ships forced the rebel gunners to flee for their lives.

Then the enemy gunboats drew his attention. In a brief instant, the water churned around their sterns and they moved forward.

"Stand ready!" ordered Richards, looking at the expectant faces of his own gun crews. "Order our gunboats forward," he said to Simpson, watching as the flags were bent on. It was a useless gesture, for the gunboats forged ahead to engage their opposite numbers without awaiting orders.

"Are we just going to lie back here?" asked Hardy, his eyes focused on the prospective targets.

"I do not wish to run over our own ships," snapped Richards, irritated by the question. He wanted to bring the ship into battle as badly as anyone.

The two squadrons of gunboats were hotly engaged, dancing in and around each other in a fashion COHOCTON could never match. But though the shells were flying between the little ships with ferocity, neither side did much damage to the other. Three rebel boats broke from the melee to head for the main fleet.

"Here is your chance, Mr. Hardy," said Richards. "Ahead one-third. Run out to port and prepare to fire!"

The sloop rushed upon the three gunboats. If the Rebels felt any hesitation in their course of action, it was too late to reconsider. Bravely, they pressed forward with their attacks.

A wolf amongst sheep, COHOCTON scattered the rebels. One angled in from the port as the main guns erupted. The deck guns joined in, two shells exploding in bright flashes on the target. There was a bigger flash and explosion as the waiting ammunition ignited. Covered with flame and smoke, it drifted clear of the battle before disappearing in an explosion of debris and steam.

The other two gunboats approached, their crews clearly reloading their guns though Richards did not recall hearing the shells pass. COHOCTON shook as her guns fired again, the smoke blowing inboard to hide their assailants. When it cleared, one was but a shower of pieces falling into the still waters. The boiler exploded in a white cloud which hung above the water for a few minutes before dispersing.

Richards felt admiration for the commander of the third, who pressed the attack alone. Both its guns fired. A shell struck near the midship pivot, filling the air with screaming wood and metal splinters. When the smoke cleared, it was as if the gun crew had never existed. The broadside fired again, two shells piercing the doomed gunboat. It settled rapidly, firing one last, defiant shot before the water closed across the deck.

Hardy returned from the bow, stopping momentarily to examine the wreckage around the damaged pivot. His face was smeared with powder, but his teeth shown white in the sun.

"We'll have her fixed in no time, Captain." He let his eyes drift to the gunboats. "A lot like swatting flies, Cap'n!"

Richards felt a sudden irritation at being reminded how

easy it was. "Too much so for my tastes! Simpson!" he hollered. "Take the launch and search for survivors!"

All the Federal gunboats appeared undamaged after the wild skirmish. The rebels retreated into the river, rushing out of sight behind the intervening land. Discarding the idea of sending the gunboats in pursuit, Richards signaled a withdrawal. There was no way to tell what the rebels had waiting at the mouth of the river.

The main fort struck and troops boarded boats and moved to the shore. Other boats left the warships but headed north. The fort there had also struck the soldiers there apparently wishing to avoid the shelling which had befallen their larger companion. A signal from WABASH called for all ships to dispatch their Marines to take charge of the structure. MacDonald left with his small contingent. For all the pain of the trip, it was a short day's work.

It was the last week in November when Richards was called to *WABASH*. It was his first opportunity to meet with the new flag officer commanding the Atlantic Squadron, but he was mistaken in the notion. He met only the flag lieutenant and was entrusted with a weighted canvas envelope containing the dispatches detailing the success of their operation.

The lieutenant made it clear the *COHOCTON* was entrusted with this duty, not because of the skill of her crew or commander, but simply because she was a small ship and available. But Richards was not disappointed at the assignment. The messages were to go directly to Washington.

Washington was still the closest active Navy Yard to the scene of operations. It was a more difficult place to reach than in the spring for the rebels were seizing control of the southern bank of the Potomac, making the approach tricky and dangerous. Of course, soon it would no longer be necessary to use the northern port. The capture of Port

Royal eliminated the problem. Upon entering the Roads, *COHOCTON* made directly for the mouth of the Potomac. The ship moved slowly, finding the tight channel with leadsmen forward and aft. It was necessary to keep the crew at quarters during the trip up the river. A badly damaged gunboat greeted their arrival, a sure sign things were still in doubt along this route to the capitol.

"Damn but this is nerve wracking," commented LaForge, scanning the bare trees along the southern bank for some sight of rebel forces.

"A point port," instructed Richards before answering. "Caution always is, RenError!." He pointed down the relatively straight stretch of river to the next prominent bend. "Those are the danger points. We are moving the slowest and are in their sights longer when we make the turn."

LaForge smiled drily. "I shall keep it in mind."

So it continued for several hours, the ship working up river against the current, the occasional piece of ice banging against the side to make everyone start at the sound. When the attack did come, it was not the sudden onslaught of a heavy gun. Instead, a crewman gripped his chest and staggered backwards, his action closely followed by the crack of a musket.

The wounded man fell to the deck, his chest an expanding mass of red as other crewmen bent to aid him. Before the attacker was spotted, another shot snapped in the cold air, followed by a grunt and a seaman falling with a hand pressing to his shoulder.

"Do you see the smoke?" asked LaForge.

"Not yet," returned Richards. A musket ball struck the deck rail, ripping out a splinter less than a foot from the two officers. "Get to the guns, RenError!. Load with canister and prepare to fire."

LaForge disappeared below. Another shot struck,

glancing off the side of the midship deck rifle.

"Everyone down!" ordered Richards, waving for the crewmen to lie down on the deck. While they sought the safety of the bulwarks, MacDonald lined his Marines against the side and shot back at the hidden sniper. A marine fell, his face destroyed by the minne ball.

"Have you marked their position, lieutenant?" asked Richards as he ducked involuntarily at the whine of a ball close overhead.

"Just forward there, captain!" shouted MacDonald, his excited voice addressed as if Richards was on the other end of the ship instead of within feet of him. "That dense stand of trees!"

Richards nodded towards LaForge's expectant face looking up from the hatch coaming. "Fire singly as you bear, RenError!!"

The four guns fired in turn, each one roaring out and closely followed by the next. The smoke swept across the deck, temporarily blinding and choking. When it cleared, all attention was on the trees.

The larger trees still stood but were scarred and marked by the heavy pieces of canister. Smaller trees and saplings lay about, cut and broken by the passage of flying metal. No further shots came from the grove.

"Rest easy." Richards was loathe to dismiss the men from quarters. It was still a long way to Washington. The sailors rose slowly, peering over the side to the southern shore.

Whether they succeeded in killing the sniper or merely forcing a cease fire, they would never know. It made little difference, for the war and chance of death continued. But for whatever reason, the sloop was unmolested for the remainder of the trip.

Evening was a strange interruption to the course of Richards' and LaForge's lives of the past twelve months Both were ashore, Nash standing the night watch. Rebecca and Lorraine had returned from Hartford and prepared a large meal for them at Welles' residence. But compared to Lorraine's enthusiastic greetings in French, Rebecca remained calm and distant.

When the meal was completed, RenError! took Lorraine on his arm and led her to a quiet corner of the drawing room. Their voices were hushed, the couple ignoring the other two in the room. Richards sat with Becky, a discreet distance between them while the conversed.

"How was Hartford?" he asked. He was glad to see her after their long separation, but still felt the presence of the barrier between them.

"Quiet." Her voice was low, her eyes directed towards their reflections in the window. "Like another world." He nodded, unsure. She continued speaking. "I am sorry I was not here to see you in July."

The mention brought back the turmoil and depression of that month, followed closely by the memories of the night action.

"I wish you had been here." He touched her hand. "I missed you; no, I *needed* you."

"In spite of your war?" The words were sharp, bitter.

"My war?" He drew his hand back. "I did not start it."

"But you love it, don't you?" Her eyes stared into his, unflinching, her voice colder than he could imagine.

He was assailed by emotions and did not know the answer. With her beside him, his love of Becky was foremost in his mind. But the thrill of action, the wild rush of battle, was there also, undeniably strong in his feelings.

"Rebecca, I love you," he pleaded, reaching for her

hand again. She pulled in away without answering and his pent up anger burst forth. "Damn it! What do you want from me?" he demanded.

She rose from the couch. "Say you love me more than your cursed war!"

He stood to face her, their eyes locked. "I cannot," he responded, his mind twisted in confusion. "I cannot because I do not know. Rebecca, when I am with you, nothing else matters. Nothing! But the war, the battles...I exist for them." He struggled with the words, forcing them out. "It is like being away for years and suddenly returning home."

She gaped. "You consider *that* home?"

"No, not home," he answered. "My life."

She turned from him, her eyes on the dark glass of the window. "I don't understand."

"Neither do I. But that's the way I am; that is what I feel."

She did not answer. Her eyes were cast down, and he waited for a reply that was not forthcoming. He touched her shoulder, but while she did not resist, neither did she yield. He dropped his hand and left the room. She started to follow, but he did not see her. And when her mouth opened to speak, no sound came out.

Richards stood the late watch aboard *COHOCTON*, leaning against the aft rail on the weather side. He drew slowly on his pipe, the sharp taste of the tobacco a pleasant sensation in the chill night air. He did not smoke often, just in the few quiet times. With the war, tobacco was a valued commodity, but he barely gave it a thought. Instead, he fixed his eyes on the far shore. Across the short stretch of dark, ice choked water lay Virginia.

He did not want the war. He felt rather than knew the

fact. He did not wish for it to occur. There, so close, was his home state and he could not go over there. His uncle was somewhere in Virginia, probably at the farm. And his friend, Caldwell, was in Alabama the last he had heard. He wondered about Jud. Perhaps the next gunboat with a rebel flag would be commanded by the senior lieutenant from Alabama. No, he did not pray for war.

For ten months, he had seen more men killed and maimed, more suffering than he thought possible. It could happen to Jud: it could happen to him. But when the shells were flying, none of it mattered; none of it crossed his mind. Not the fear, not the pain, not the death. But with it all, he *had* to be there. He *had* to be involved. The side of his mouth turned up at the thought, unconsciously knocking the dottle from the pipe into the cold water. A moth reacted the same way to flame, drawn into the light until the creature was destroyed by the fire.

He replaced the pipe in his pocket. It would be the same with him. The realization arrived with calm certainty. When all about were torn apart and killed, it could not be long before he, too, was caught in the destruction. And who else might go with him? He looked inboard, examining the dim outlines of his ship in the night. One hundred, sixty men shared this home, this life.

The following night found Richards ashore. Gideon and Rebecca had collected him and their coach was heading back into the city. The dim gaslights struggled feebly against the dark night air but the driver steered along the narrow streets with practiced ease. For a while, the only sounds were the clatter of the wheels and hooves on the cobblestones.

"Well," pronounced Welles, after examining the silent couple at length. "When are you two going to set a date?"

The quiet was even more pronounced when neither Rebecca nor Richards attempted to answer. Welles looked from one to the other before letting out an indecipherable rumble.

"I see." The coach stopped in front of the house. "I don't know what the problem is, but I expect you two can work it out." He opened the door and stepped down, making one last comment before closing it. "Just don't behave like children over it!"

They sat in embarrassed silence for a moment before Becky spoke. "He is right. I am behaving like a child."

"No, you are not," said Richards, trying to defend her feelings. "You just do not understand. I cannot blame you for that."

"I do not understand," she answered, the words almost a plea. "John, I do not want to be a widow at the age of twenty!"

His mind filled with rushing thoughts, unsure what to say or do. But she moved closer and lay her head on his shoulder.

"I have seen so many widows these past few months. It is barely a year and so many have died already." She sighed and continued. "I love you," she said, her voice soft and smooth. "I love you for the way you *are*."

Richards slipped his arm around her waist and she pressed even closer. "We shall make arrangements for the marriage next time I am in port. I promise."

He kissed her, and the uncertainties of the past months vanished. "I love you more than anything," he said. He did not notice his voice grew softer. "That is all that matters."

New orders awaited his return to the ship. LaForge was allowed only one more day and night with his wife before they were forced to weigh. Washington was left astern, the two women on the dock gradually diminishing until lost behind the land of the first bend in the river.

Richards examined his command. All the men were rested and happy. LaForge was detached, suffering from the euphoria of his time with Lorraine. But he was not thinking as a captain while regarding his first officer and friend. *What was worse?* To leave a young widow behind, or to never give marriage a chance?

He let out a sigh, a sound that Sims did not miss. Richards saw the look the helmsman was giving him. He misunderstood, of course. He knew Sims was thinking of the pretty young woman on the dock. Richards' thoughts turned to the river ahead.

USS SAN JACINTO stopping the *SS TRENT*

CHAPTER THIRTEEN

"Christ Almighty!"

LaForge shouted the oath; it was all but lost in the roar of cannon and the crash of rigging. The rebel gun lay directly ahead, mounted high on a bluff overlooking the river. The first shot screamed above, cleaving the topmast to drop on the crowded deck below.

"Clear away that rigging!" yelled Richards, pointing at the mess lying across the aft pivot gun. The more experienced of the hands were already there, axes swing at the rigging and splintered wood. "Hardy, damn your eyes! Get on the forward rifle! Marines to quarters!"

The ship was a hornets' nest of activity, men rushing madly about as water spout rose alongside with another crash of the rebel gun. There was little need for the orders: the men were running to stations thoroughly prodded by rebels. But the rebel gun was well sighted, and there was a long stretch of river to traverse before they passed it.

"It's too high!" announced Hardy from forward. The pivot gun could not be brought to bear.

"Well do something, for god's sake!" It was LaForge. There was an unpleasant note of panic in the voice.

"Get below and see what you can do," ordered Richards. "We will be broadside in a bit and maybe you can elevate one of the thirty-two's enough." He waved down a protest. "You heard me!"

There was no time for argument. A shell struck the forward rail, bursting in a shower of steel and wood that cut down some of Hardy's gun crew. Men rushed to their aid and to take their places, shouting all the while. But it did little good to curse. Richards rang the repeater.

"Half speed!"

Wilson was a good officer, as Paulding had noted so many months before. He did not question the wisdom of the order; his only response was an increase in revolutions to the screw.

"Leadsman, sir?" ventured Nash as they gathered way.

Richards laughed. "We have little time for that!" He looked to the helm. "Sims! Steer closer to the northern shore."

It was dangerous. If the ship grounded, the rebels would destroy her at their leisure. It was the very situation they were attempting to create.

"By the mark five!" Nash had not waited for permission, but taken it upon himself. Richards mentally noted it for the action report.

Simpson shouted from the port side. "Captain! Something in the water over here!" Richards ducked involuntarily when another shell struck the water and drenched the aft deck. Still, he quickly reached the side to see where the midshipman was pointing. "There!"

Whatever the object might be, it was fairly large and just beneath the surface of the water. There was a bulge where the river swept across it and left a wake trailing downstream. At the increased speed, they were coming on it quickly.

"Point starboard!" Its purpose was unclear, but there was no advantage in risking a collision. At the same instant, another shell exploded above them, wounding two crewmen forward. One of the thirty-two's fired from below, but Richards spotted the shell exploding well below the Rebel position.

The object came abeam, and even the roar of Hardy's rifle firing a futile reply was dwarfed by the sound of the explosion to port. A massive column of water rose, carrying with it chunks of ice and mud from the bottom of the river. It rained across *COHOCTON*, drenching everything from the topmast down.

"What the hell was that!?" Simpson gripped the rail, staring at the seething waters in shock.

"Keep a sharp eye for more, Simpson!"

COHOCTON came upon the bend in a rush, steering more towards the center than the outside of the curve. It would be safer on the inside, to move the ship where the Confederate gun could not be sufficiently depressed to fire at them. But the inside bend was shallow and they faced enough risks.

Once east of the bend, they drew out of range of the Rebel piece in short order and with no additional damage. No more of the underwater weapons were sighted or detonated. LaForge re-emerged as the crew secured from quarters and labored to repair the damage.

"What was the big explosion?" The words showed deep concern, not the professional interest usually displayed by the officer.

"Some sort of explosive device under the water. I do not know how they detonated it," replied Richards, regarding his officer carefully.

"I have heard talk of such. Electrically detonated by wires from a position ashore." LaForge glanced astern, then to the damage about the ship. "Back in the Crimean, I think."

"We are past it now," returned Richards.

If LaForge was not actually afraid, he was at least displaying an uncharacteristic caution. *Is that what marriage did to a person?* Richards considered mentioning the fact, but let it pass. A short few hours before, the man was lying in a hotel room with his bride at his side. Certainly the past few minutes represented a tremendous change from those peaceful surroundings

"When you are ready, run an inspection below the waterline. That charge was fairly close when it exploded."

LaForge stared blankly for a moment, then recalled his duties. "Aye, sir."

Richards watched him leave. *Marriage.* It might be a bigger step than he thought.

COHOCTON returned to Georgetown. In the weeks the ship was absent, the MARY JANE was assigned north to serve as a troop transport. Michaels received promotion to commodore and flew his flag from *TICONDEROGA*, a recently commissioned ten gun sloop. The small fleet now included two new four-gun blockade steamers which appeared in growing numbers from northern shipyards.

Richards eyed the new array of sea power with mixed emotions. Now, any ship in the squadron was capable of fulfilling all the tasks required. This relieved *COHOCTON* of the burden forced upon her previously. On the other hand, fewer ships were testing the better equipped blockading squadron. This, plus Michaels' prejudiced command, might keep him from seeing any action at all. As it was, a cutter had stopped the previous day and sent dispatches to *TICONDEROGA*. So far, Michaels followed his usual pattern of not relaying any information to his subordinates until it was absolutely necessary.

The only excitement to stir their days was oft received reports from Georgetown. Escaping slaves, either daring the swim from shore or stealing small boats, brought word that a privateer was fitting out. The men had worked aboard the vessel and gave a complete description. The next time *COHOCTON* performed the morning inspection duty, Richards paid particular attention to the raider.

She was a slim paddle wheel capable of a good turn of speed. But the narrow lines suitable for blockade running would work against the vessel on the open sea. Her armament would be small and endurance short. That much could be surmised from their distant, tantalizing views. She would be deadly enough against unarmed merchantmen and the Navy, stretched to the limit by the needs of the blockade, and did not have ships to spare to search for her.

Richards closed his telescope and climbed the ratlines. Speculation mattered little, for he doubted any opportunity to get her under his guns would present itself. Nash, standing the watch, walked across to greet him.

"I can hardly wait to take that one," he commented, the gleam of prize money in his eyes.

Richards followed his gaze ashore. "Not much chance if she stays in port, Mr. Nash."

He felt reluctant to engage in conversation and turned away to begin his morning ritual of pacing the deck. Nash was oblivious to his wishes and fell into step beside him.

"All the same, it might be worth a try. Perhaps a cutting out expedition with other ships in the squadron?"

The mention of such an operation instantly brought forth a flood of memories. Richards managed a controlled reply.

"I think not. We have tried that before."

The young officer realized the subject was dead. Nash turned his attention to the flagship and more general topics. "I wonder if we shall hear any news?" he queried. "The last Boston paper mentioned the Rebels were working on an ironclad. I wish the commodore were more forthcoming."

The irritation over the interruption of his daily routine and the suggestion of a cutting out expedition had grown as Richards paced. The continued chatter proved too much for his endurance.

"I am sure the commodore will be interested in your opinions, Lieutenant Nash! I shall relay them to him at the first possible occasion!" He regretted the comment as soon as he spoke, the hurt look on Nash's face a sign of how deeply it cut.

"I am sorry, Ed," said Richards, touching the other man's arm. "It is just this damned blockade." He forced a grin. "If we do not see some action soon, I shall go completely mad!"

Nash returned a weak smile, but the words had not healed the wound. "Aye, sir", he replied, his voice even.

Richards turned away, wondering what was prepared for breakfast but knowing the answer. Pork and beans were the standard meal aboard any of the warships, and *COHOCTON* was no exception. He expected it for two of every three meals.

"Sir," interrupted Nash again. "Signal from the flag. 'All Captains'!"

Richards returned to the junior lieutenant. "Now this makes a change!"

Nash nodded. "You shall have your chance to relay my suggestions to the commodore sooner than you thought."

Richards chuckled at the retort. "So it seems. At least it will save me from those damned beans for breakfast!"

The commodore's cabin was crowded, for *TICONDEROGA* was little larger than *COHOCTON*. Michaels, short and rotund, sat behind his desk while the others managed to seat themselves in the small space remaining. His face, normally plump and cheerful, was grave. He fingered a dispatch nervously before clearing his throat.

"Gentlemen," he said, his voice strained "I have received news of a dire situation." He stopped, mopping his brow with a large kerchief before continuing.

"On the eighth instant, the frigate *SAN JACINTO* stopped the British steamer *TRENT* in the Bahamas. The captain removed two Confederate emissaries and their assistants." He halted, letting the words register. "If you do not see the importance of this act, the British vessel was stopped and searched on the high seas and had no connection with a Confederate port of call. That damned sea lawyer of a captain has tried some legalistic double talk to justify his actions, but the British will not have it."

Richards leaned forward. "Will it be war then?" he asked. Oddly, the possibility did not frighten him.

"Hmpf!" grunted Michaels. "At least one of you sees where this can lead. Not yet, Richards, but that is the talk up north. Nor should I have to tell you we cannot fight a war with England while we are dealing with this damned rebellion!"

"So were does that leave us?" asked Allen of the *DEFENCE*.

"Proceeding very carefully," returned Michaels. "We

see the British almost weekly, inspecting the blockade, waiting for us to make a mistake. That mistake must not happen! Abide by the letter of the law. You know the international requirements for a blockade. We must live up to them." Michaels was adamant, his words clear and concise. For the first time, Richards could appreciate how the commodore rose to his position.

"And if the British start something, commodore? Then what?" he asked.

Michaels let out a long sigh. "Then, my hot-blooded friend, we had best be ready to fight!"

He paused, looking to each in turn before continuing. "Use extreme care whenever dealing with the British. No further provocations will be made." He eyed Richards carefully. "I will personally flay any man in this squadron who causes one!"

The threat of another war put a damper on the morale of the tiny squadron, even with the approach of Christmas. The men were kept busy with drills, working constantly on handling the sails and guns. Watches were changed regularly, breaking the habitual rut of day to day existence as often as feasible. It was all they could do to overcome the dreary routine of the blockade.

The holiday passed with little celebration, though an extra tot of whiskey was allowed for the crew. There was a bit of singing and dancing to help break the boredom. The next day, the wind picked up from the west, foreboding worse to come: another winter storm to add to the misery of blockade duty.

"Shake out the tops'ls!" instructed Richards to LaForge and Nash. "We shall move her further out to sea."

"What about the boilers?" LaForge gestured towards the thin stream of smoke trailing from the stack.

"Keep them going for the pumps," Richards answered,

"but we will not waste coal fighting this damned storm."

The other two officers nodded, calling hands to carry out their instructions. The rigging filled with seamen scurrying aloft. As they reached their positions, Richards gestured to one of the men forward. The winch started and the anchor pulled free from the seabed.

Immediately, *COHOCTON* paid off, her head pointing east at the pressure of wind and rudder. The sails cracked open over head, flapping wildly for a few moments before sheeted home against the growing storm.

"Don't look good, does it, captain?" commented Sims, leaning hard against the force of the wheel.

Richards examined the clouds and the set of the sail. "It could be worse, Sims," he replied. "At least we have plenty of sea room."

The ship pitched in the growing waves, the vessel as close to the wind as they dared. They could not allow themselves to be blown too far away, so the order was to tack, to wear back and forth across the wind to make up for distance lost to the storm.

They were not facing the fury of a storm such as claimed the *ST. ELIZABETH.* But for four days, *COHOCTON* was tossed about, blown east and south in spite of their best efforts. Crewmen, so recently proclaiming their wish for some excitement, were given that and more. They worked constantly during those days, fighting salt hardened canvas, sea and storm to keep their ship afloat. An exhausted crew greeted the brightening dawn on smooth seas when the storm abated.

LaForge yawned widely, the stubble on his chin and cheeks a testimony to his efforts. "Where are we?" he asked.

Richards leaned across the chart table, shaking his head. "Somewhere out here, I would imagine." He tapped the chart, indicating the open ocean well over a hundred miles southeast of the coast line.

"What about the rest of the squadron?" asked Nash. His eyes were puffy and there were salt sores along the jaw line where his oilskins had rubbed.

Richards shrugged. "Scattered, I am sure. Set a course west north west for now. The noon sighting will fix our position." Nash nodded and went on deck. Richards looked to LaForge. "Good ship handling, RenError!. One might think you were a sailor."

LaForge smiled weakly at the off hand compliment. "I had a good instructor," he answered.

Richards nodded. "And I a good student." He tried to stifle a yawn, but was unsuccessful. "I wanted just about any sort of action to get us away from that damned station. I am not sure this was preferable."

"You were the one who said it could be worse."

"Sail ho!" The muffled shout from the masthead was startling to the two officers.

"One of the squadron?" ventured LaForge as Richards led the way to the deck.

"Could be anything out here."

"A steamer, sir," said Nash when the two officers emerged onto the deck. "There, just about due north."

Richards took the offered telescope and quickly picked out the smudge on the horizon which marked the location of the other ship.

"No likely one of ours," he said, returning the instrument to Nash. "She is heading out to sea." He thought for a moment, rubbing his rough chin. "Give chase, Mr. Nash. Full speed ahead."

"Aye aye, sir!" The enthusiastic reply did more to wipe away the young man's exhaustion than any amount of sleep. The bells of the engine room repeater rang out while Nash fairly shouted into the speaking tube.

"Why bother?" asked LaForge, a telescope trained on the distant ship. "This far from shore, she could be anything."

"Very true." Richards examined the ship again, and still made out little more than the dark stain of smoke. He lowered the telescope and gave LaForge a conspirator's wink. "When was the last time we gave COHOCTON her head and let her run?"

LaForge chuckled.

Richards closed the telescope with a snap. "I think I will go below for a shave and something hot to eat."

By midmorning, their quarry was growing closer at an agonizingly slow rate. Richards, refreshed from a shave and the first hot meal in days, waited for some word from aloft. LaForge appeared, also revived by a meal and razor.

"Anything new?"

Richards shook his head. "I sent our young Mr. Simpson aloft with a glass. If he does not see something worthwhile, I am afraid we shall have to call this off."

The thick smoke pouring from the funnel was testimony to the expenditure of coal invested by COHOCTON. The arduous task of coaling at sea was an unpleasant job and Richards determined not to use any more of the precious fuel than necessary.

"Ahoy the deck!" Simpson's voice was thin and distance, coming from the topmast.

Richards raised his trumpet. "Go ahead."

"A slim steamer, cap'n," shouted the midshipman. "Raked funnels and wheels amidships, brig rig."

"Sounds like the privateer," observed Sims.

Richards looked at the seaman in awe. "So it does, Mr. Sims." LaForge shrugged, but Richards continued the line of thought. "The winds went from westerly to northerly. If the squadron was scattered by the storm, it would make the perfect opportunity to run. Given the winds and seas, she might end up around here."

"That is a small ship, John," said LaForge. "She would be unpleasant in heavy weather."

"*Unpleasant* does not stop sailors, RenError!." Richards turned towards the hatch. "Nash!" he shouted.

The young lieutenant's face appeared, one side still covered with shaving soap. "Sir?"

"Get to the masthead. You have been lusting after that privateer for the past month. Tell me if our chase is the one!"

Nash did not bother with shirt or coat. He wiped his face quickly, tossed the towel to a surprised sailor, and rushed for the maintop. Richards paced expectantly, his gaze fixed on the fleeing vessel.

Nash's voice shot the length of the ship. "It's her!"

Richards called back. "Are you positive?"

"Aye! It is the same rake of funnels and masts for sure!" Nash did not waste time climbing back down the ratlines. Instead, he slid down a backstay like a top man. Out of breath in his excitement, his bare chest stained black with tar, he ran up to Richards.

"I am positive, captain! Like you say, I have been watching her for a month!"

"If you are wrong, I will take the cost of the coal out of your pay!" chided Richards. He bent to the speaking tube. "Engine room!"

Wilson's voice replied immediately. The engineer had already heard the news. "*COHOCTON* will catch her, captain!"

Richards examined Nash's wild appearance. "Mr. Nash, it will be a while before we run this beggar down.

Perhaps you can see fit to dress for the occasion?"

The lieutenant laughed aloud. "Yes, sir!" He was gone.

To LaForge, Richards took on a more serious note. "We cannot let this one get away, RenError!. The Navy has no spare ships to track her down."

Morning passed into the afternoon; the pursuit wore on. They closed, but ever so slowly. Richards paced the quarterdeck in impatience, gauging the shortening distance. The early winter evening could end it, for the privateer would lose them in the darkness.

"Long cannon shot within the hour," said Hardy, his expert eye the final judge on such matters.

The captain nodded. "Very good, Mr. Hardy. Clear for action, gentlemen!"

LaForge and Nash needed no further urging. The drums beat and the sailors, grouped forward to watch the progress of the grim race, rushed to quarters. Richards felt satisfied. Storm or no storm, tired or not, the men were ready and responded to the call to action in record time.

"Load?" asked LaForge. Richards answered with a nod. He spoke to Hardy.

"Get on the forward rifle," he instructed. "I want a ranging shot as soon as you are ready."

A powder boy rushed past, the bag slung over one arm. He was all but unrecognizable as the homeless Potter from the year before. Everyone had changed, mused Richards, including himself. *Come of age.* Sims and Healey stood to the wheel, easy but firm. Ready for anything. The whole ship was.

"Sail to the northeast!"

The new sighting came as a surprise to the waiting men. Richards looked in the indicated direction, picking out the pyramid of canvas against the horizon. And while he was looking at the newcomer, Hardy reported.

"Ready, cap'n."

"Fire, Mr. Hardy."

The roar of the gun made Richards wince, but he was pleased by the sight of a waterspout just ahead of the fleeing privateer. A flag broke out at the stern of the ship, a small dot of blue and red.

"Showing her colors," said Nash.

"British, damn it!" Richards could not contain the words.

"Chase changin' course, captain!" said Hardy.

Richards had little time for thoughts. "Lookout! Anything else on the sail?"

"Warship, sir! Takin' in sail now. She's making steam!"

"One of ours?" asked LaForge.

"Not bloody likely," cursed Richards. Their chase headed for the newcomer. The blue flag with the red and white crosses proudly declared neutrality. "Give her another warning, Mr. Hardy. Make the bastard heave to!"

The shot was fired and the shell landed close alongside their quarry. This time, it had the desired effect. The flag lowered and the ship slowed.

"More on the sail, sir," said Nash, indicating one of the lookouts who had come to the deck.

"Yes?" snapped Richards.

"It is the DAUNTLESS again, cap'n, the frigate we saw last summer."

The young captain gritted his teeth. He saw it coming the moment the British flag broke out on the privateer. There was little doubt the ship's master had papers to support his claim.

"All stop," said Richards. "Heave to within easy

cannon shot of the chase. And run up some colors of our own!"

A British warship: *was the meeting an accident or deliberate?* There was no way to tell. What had the sailor said last summer? Thirty-two guns. Richards knew something of British ships from his time in the Mediterranean. They would be eight or ten inch guns, possibly with a mixture of thirty-two pounders. They would smash his little sloop with a single broadside.

"Frigate heaving to!" announced Nash.

COHOCTON sat with the privateer to port and the warship to starboard. The British stood to quarters though her gun ports were closed. Richards took a deep breath and lifted the speaking trumpet.

"Ahoy, *DAUNTLESS! USS COHOCTON.* This is Lt. Commanding Richards. I would like to invite your captain aboard to discuss the situation!"

There were several nerve wracking seconds while the British weighed his proposal. "This is Captain Harrington. I will accept your invitation!"

An involuntary sigh of relief escaped. At least the English captain was willing to talk. Unfortunately, Richards had no idea what he was going to say.

"Sims!"

"Sir?" the helmsman questioned.

"Straighten my cabin for our visitor." Sims turned to leave, but Richards stopped him. "And open a bottle of wine!"

He tried to present a calm picture for his crew while the British boat approached. Crewmen presented appropriate honors for the visitor, but it was equally clear to the British captain all guns were fully manned.

Richards gripped the railing, his fingers aching from the pressure. His insides knotted at the prospects before him. If necessary, he would fight the British frigate, but they stood no chance of winning. He did not want the responsibility of starting a war with England. Richards eyed the rebel ship, a picture of innocence and the cause of all his troubles. The English officer, followed closely by another, approached the quarterdeck. Richards saluted.

"Captain Harrington, I am Lt. Commanding John Richards. My officers, Lieutenants LaForge and Nash."

Harrington acknowledged the presentations with a minimum of recognition. He introduced his aide in a similar fashion. But his eyes were busy, darting about the deck and resting briefly on the two rifles.

"Would you like to step into my cabin?" continued Richards, remaining the cordial host.

The trip below was short, but Richards did not rush it. He gave the frigate captain sufficient time to note the crews standing at the ready. Once in his cabin, he allowed the officers to sit while he poured them each a glass of wine.

"A glass first, I think," he said, pouring carefully. "This is very good wine; a gift from my fiancé, the daughter of our Secretary of Navy." Richards hoped the connection would make an impression, but Harrington pointedly ignored it.

"You are chasing a ship flying a British flag," he said, taking a glass but leaving it untasted. "You fired upon her. I am in these waters to protect the interests of the Empire."

"As well you should," returned Richards, handing both the aide and LaForge a glass before taking one himself. "But that ship did not show any colors until you appeared. And I have seen her before, lying trapped in a blockaded port."

"Did you actually see the ship leave the harbor?" Harrington finally sipped the wine, but kept his eyes riveted on the young commander.

"No." The word came slowly. "We were blown away from the port by the storm. We intercepted the vessel on our way back to the station."

The corner of Harrington's lips turned up. "Then you cannot swear it is the same ship."

LaForge leaned forward, unable to contain himself. "The ship is armed, captain. We believe her to be a raider - a privateer."

Harrington waved off the comment with a free hand. He did not acknowledge the comment as coming from LaForge. "Armed? It is hardly unusual for merchantmen to arm themselves." He took a healthy drink from his glass. "And I believe our governments have had previous discussions on the free use of the seas!"

The realization on how to continue struck him so suddenly, Richards' conversation faltered. He took a long sip of wine to cover the hesitation.

"Captain," he said, setting the glass on his desk, "would you like to inspect my ship while we discuss this? I am sure you will find it interesting."

"Why not?" returned Harrington. The British captain was unable to disguise his eagerness to inspect his potential opponent. While the two junior officers returned to the main deck, Richards led his visitor along the gun deck.

"Here are two nine inch Dahlgrens," said Richards at the rearmost guns. "They are some of the newest and heaviest guns in our Navy. We have mounted them on pivots, so we can use them on either broadside." Harrington examined the weapons in silence, not failing to notice both were trained on his ship. "Of course," Richards continued, "we do not want to use them against you. Our countries have always tried to work out their differences without hostilities.

"We have four thirty-two pounders." Richards spoke casually as they strolled amidships. "Two on either broadside. These are very similar to the guns on your ship, I believe."

Harrington coughed nervously. "Uh, yes," he stammered.

"I feel you are a fair man," stressed Richards, mixing the discussion with his lecture. "I propose we both inspect the ship. If you are convinced she is nothing more than a merchantman, I will abide by your decision and return to my other duties."

They reached the forward end of the gun deck, where LaForge had mounted the captured rebel guns, one on either broadside. Richards rested a hand on the cold iron breech of one of the cannon.

"These are interesting pieces. We captured them from a gunboat this past summer. The same day you made an inspection of our station, if memory serves." Richards saw the light of recognition in Harrington's eyes and kept speaking. "Notice they are standard thirty-two's, but the breech has been banded and the barrel rifled. Unfortunately, the rebels captured over three thousand of these guns when they overran our Gosport Navy Yard."

"These rebels seem damned clever," noted Harrington.

Richards nodded. "They make due with what is available. But what of my suggestion, Captain? We both inspect the ship; the final decision is yours."

Harrington rubbed his chin thoughtfully. "It seems fair enough." He eyed Richards, their gazes meeting. "I have the force to make my decision stand."

Richards ignored the open threat. "Shall we use your boat?"

As the British captain and his aide climbed down to their boat, Richards passed quick instructions to LaForge. He did not believe the rebels would submit meekly to capture.

"I saw your ship earlier this year," noted Harrington, friendlier on the short trip. "As I recall, she was damaged slightly."

"A slight argument with the gunboats I mentioned. We sank one and captured another," Richards answered simply.

"Have you seen much action?" probed Harrington.

"Enough."

The conversation ended as they bumped the side of the rebel. They were greeted by the ship's master.

"I am Captain Wendell," he said, introducing himself in a definite British accent. "What can I do for you gentlemen?"

"Your papers, if you please, sir." Harrington displayed more courtesy than he had aboard the Union warship. "There seems to be a disagreement as to your purpose in these waters." He glanced to Richards. "We shall straighten this out and have you on your way."

Wendell produced the requested papers immediately. "Damned nuisance, in my opinion!" He took a deep breath. "It's gettin' so you can't make a decent livin' no more, if you catch my meanin'."

"I do indeed, captain." Harrington studied the pages carefully before handing them to Richards. "Plain as day, lieutenant," he said, stressing Richards rank instead of position. He tapped the pages meaningfully. "Clearly English registry and cargo. Nothing to do with your war."

Richards ignored the papers. "You agreed to a dual inspection of the ship, Captain Harrington. There is only one thing I wish to see before you render a decision." He did not wait for a reply, but started towards the bow of the ship.

"And what is that?" The Englishman's footsteps were a bit behind the Union officer.

"Their guns, Captain. Let us see where they got their guns!"

All four of the vessel's weapons were mounted near the bow, a pair on either side. The first was an English model and Richards heard a grunt from the British officer as they passed it. The next was what he expected.

"A thirty-two pounder, captain," he said, standing over the gun. "Banded and rifled; a twin to the ones aboard my ship." He faced the English captain. "The only place they could have gotten this is in a rebel port. Their only use is for raiding."

"Yes, you are right," admitted Harrington. But when he turned to confront Wendell, he faced a group of armed seamen.

"We can't let you take us, captain," Wendell said, the smooth British accent disappearing. "We have a letter of marque from the Confederate government. We are a legal privateer."

"You cannot be serious!" Harrington gestured at the pistol. "DAUNTLESS will blow you out of the water!"

"Not with her captain aboard." Wendell gave a smug smile.

"*COHOCTON* will not be deterred by the presence of an English officer," interjected Richards. Wendell and Harrington faced him and he slowly withdrew his watch. "In exactly five minutes, my ship will open fire."

"Not with you hostage..."

Richards cut the Confederate captain off. "If I do not tell them differently, they will consider me dead."

Harrington protested. "But the *DAUNTLESS*! If you fire on this ship, she shall sink yours."

Richards shook his head. "Probably, yet we cannot have twenty ships tied up looking for this one. What will it be, Wendell? The prize courts or the shells?"

Wendell was visibly torn by the indecision. He searched Richards closely, hoping for a sign of a bluff. He lowered his pistol slowly and handed it to Harrington.

Richards closed the face of his watch. "With your permission, Captain Harrington, I shall have a prize crew sent over."

Harrington nodded his agreement.

COHOCTON's boats were in the water moving towards them. Harrington came up beside Richards, inspecting the Union sloop.

"That was a bold bluff, Captain."

"Bluff? I am afraid not." Harrington faced Richards in surprise. "I could not allow this ship to escape, captain. I passed the word to my first before coming across."

Harrington shook his head, smiling. "You may not have been as easy to fight as I thought."

Richards smiled back. "I hope not."

The prize crew from COHOCTON climbed noisily aboard and stripped the privateer's crew of their arms. Nash was there, giving orders and taking charge of the captured vessel.

"Everything in hand here, Mr. Nash?"

"Aye aye, captain!" he replied jauntily.

Richards laughed, releasing some of his pent up emotion. "I suppose I must let you take her north."

"Yes, sir!" If Nash still harbored ill feelings over Richards' earlier irritation, he failed to show it. "If I might suggest Mr. Simpson for acting lieutenant..." he ventured.

"Based on your vast experience, no doubt," chided Richards. "But Simpson it is. Take care, captain."

Richards went over the side. It was only a few minutes

before he was on his own ship and watching the prize make steam.

"A good New Year's present," commented LaForge.

"That she is, RenError!. I am reliably informed Mr. Simpson is ready for a lieutenant's duties."

"Already done, sir," returned LaForge.

Richards let out a long sigh. "Now all we have to do is explain everything to the commodore."

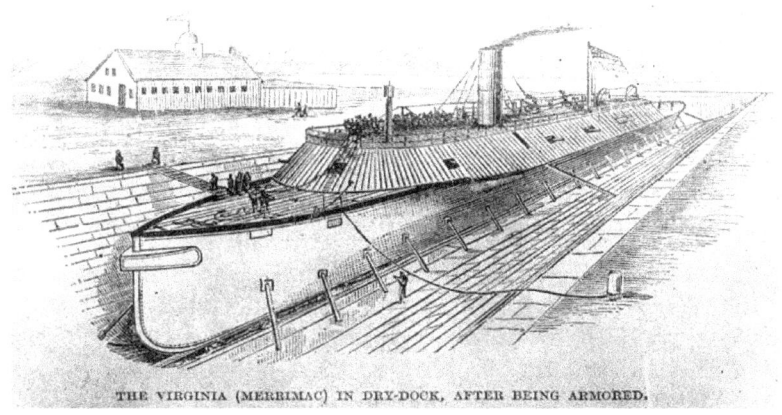

CSS VIRGINIA in dry dock

CHAPTER FOURTEEN

The new year began with no sign of an end to the hostilities. For the north, the constant string of defeats on the ground was balanced only by the constant string of victories afloat. For *COHOCTON*, it meant constantly plying the waters around Georgetown, a port rapidly losing significance because of the effectiveness of the blockade.

After the capture of the privateer, few ships tried to enter or leave. Richards frequently found himself walking the quarterdeck, yearning for action, any action, to break the monotony. But January progressed and it was only the struggles against nature which caused excitement in the squadron. February arrived and one of the new blockaders was transferred to join the forces around Charleston.

The men of *COHOCTON* had settled into a fine working crew. Orders were executed quickly and efficiently. Richards was willing to put their ability to reef or deploy sail against any ship in the fleet. Now they lolled about the deck, any number of conversations taking place as the sloop rolled gently at anchor.

Potter and Jigs were rough housing while the other boys egged them on. Hardy sat to the side smoking his pipe, like a grandfather watching them. Simpson was now a seasoned officer, pointing out rigging and directing two new midshipmen in their studies. Others sat about reading letters from home or composing them. It was an idyllic scene, one that would make most captains happy. For Richards, it only added to his growing sense of boredom.

He turned his attention outboard and watched the *TICONDEROGA*. A dispatch cutter had stopped briefly before continuing south. Perhaps something would come of this visit, but he doubted it. In a peacetime navy, he expected nothing better. But the longer the war continued, the more he craved action to spice the dull routine.

He toyed with the idea of requesting a transfer to the river forces serving on the Mississippi. Their exploits filled the northern press and there seemed no end of fighting on the western waterways. Yet he remembered the cramped, smelly gunboat from the previous summer and could not imagine himself commanding one. By the time the signal flags broke out on the command ship, Richards had lost interest. The war was bypassing him and his command. He started when Simpson called his attention to the signal.

"Our number, captain."

The words were calm and simple but Richards' heart leapt at the prospect. Before the young officer could continue, he had grabbed his own telescope and read the flags faster than Simpson could decode them.

"Sims, my boat!" he ordered. Even seeing Michaels was a welcome change from the boring existence his life had become. "Simpson, inform Lt. LaForge of my departure!"

He did not wait for an answer from the acting lieutenant. Instead, he climbed down after the sailors, hardly giving them time to settle before ordering them to shove off.

His rush was not worth the effort. Michaels was his curt and formal self, taking his time before revealing the reason for the summons. The commodore reviewed Richards' past performance in detail before getting to the point. It occurred to the young captain that if the commodore followed this process with all officers in all interviews, he would soon spend the rest of the war on a single, interminable sitting with some hapless subordinate.

"You are being transferred to Hampton Roads. Admiral DuPont feels the need of a ship with less draft in those waters."

Richards leaned forward, unsuccessful in containing his curiosity. "When do we leave?"

Michaels was matter-of-fact. "Immediately." He shuffled the papers on his desk. "Here are your orders." He handed the lieutenant a second sheet, an apparent afterthought. "This came in the same group of dispatches."

It was a promotions list. Towards the bottom was his name, raised to the grade of commander. He returned the paper to Michaels.

"Heaven knows why they should promote you," replied the commodore. "After that fiasco last summer, I am surprised they did not court martial you. Oh well..." He let the comment fade. "Congratulations on your promotion," he said flatly. "That is all." He returned to his cluttered desk without waiting for an answer.

The announcement was received with a wild shout by the men. Being so close to northern ports meant shore leave would be available and the fact was not lost on the sailors. They responded with unaccustomed energy readying the ship. LaForge's reaction was different, however. Instead of pleasure at the prospect of having his wife nearby, he grew agitated at the change. It was the night watch, with the ship cruising north under easy sail, before Richards confronted him.

"You do not want to go north?" He leaned on the rail next to the other man.

LaForge hesitated, a long pause before he replied. "Have you read a Baltimore paper within the last month?"

"I am not much for newspapers. I prefer official dispatches," responded Richards.

LaForge continued with a change of subjects. "The *MERRIMACK* was burned at Gosport. We saw her sink." Richards acknowledged the fact. "The rebels have raised her and are converting her to an armored ram."

"I have seen armored ships before," Richards pointed out. "The French had them in the Mediterranean last winter."

"But this is not a French ship!" LaForge's voice rose, attracting the attention of the duty watch. He lowered it before continuing. "This is a rebel ship and we are being sent to guard her."

The new commander digested the information slowly. LaForge was no coward. He was also one of the best ordnance officers in the Navy.

"Can it be that bad..." he started.

"Yes, it can!" The words were an intense hiss. "There is not a ship in the fleet able to stop a well-built and handled ironclad! And as you are always pointing out, these are not landsmen building this ship. They are sailors. Men we know. Men as dedicated, well trained and experienced as ourselves."

Richards swallowed. It was strange to have his own words echoed back in such a fashion. "How do we fight it?"

"I do not know," returned LaForge.

"We will need more, RenError!." Richards thought aloud, contemplating the possibility. A ship armored against their best guns was not a pleasant thought. "Consider it. Give me a plan and I shall follow it to the letter."

LaForge forced a weak smile. "I do not like being a prophet of doom."

Richards laid a hand on the man's shoulder. "Then do not be, RenError!. Now this is your watch; I am going to bed."

Sims brought a mug of coffee to his cabin. Richards sat, feet thrust out and deep in thought. The coxswain opened his mouth to speak, but did not. Instead, he wished his captain a quiet goodnight and left the room.

Richards took a drink of the thin coffee, then stood to pace. LaForge's comments made sleep impossible. Iron ships, shell guns, wooden hulls - all spun through his mind. The thoughts were appalling when the implications struck home. One iron sheathed ship could, quite literally, engage the entire fleet without fear of damage. What could his sloop do if presented with such a threat? He forced himself to undress and lie down, but the thoughts would not leave him. It was a shallow, troubled sleep.

COHOCTON entered Hampton Roads the last week of February. It was one of the most peaceful and tranquil scene Richards had witnessed since the beginning of the war. Three large frigates lay beneath the guns of Ft. Monroe. Further west, near Newport News, a sailing frigate and sloop stood a quiet watch.

The weather had moderated and the winter chill was gone from the air. Few opportunities for battle were apparent, even given the close proximity of LaForge's iron monster. Though he had developed a strong trust in LaForge, Richards suspected the officer might be wrong in this instance. And if things remained as peaceful as they appeared, he might be able to contact Welles and arrange for his wedding.

A commodore's pennant flew at the stern of

MINNESOTA. Richards ordered out his boat and reported there. He was met by Captain Henry Van Brunt, commanding in the admiral's absence. He remembered the balding, slightly rotund figure from the Hatteras expedition.

"Good to see you again, commander," said Van Brunt, smiling at the new insignia on Richards' shoulders.

"Thank you, sir." He handed him the orders.

"You are just in time for dinner," said Van Brunt, giving the paper a cursory inspection before passing them to a clerk. "Why not join us? I am sure you could do with some fresh food after such a long time on the blockade."

One did not refuse invitations from senior officers, particularly when he offered food that did not come from a tin.

It took but a moment to be seated. Captains from the other ships were also present and little mention was made of the war as they waited for the food to be brought forward. It was finally Van Brunt who broached the subject of *COHOCTON*'s transfer as the servers withdrew after setting several plates along the dinner table.

"We are glad you arrived, Commander Richards." The elderly captain passed a platter of steaming chicken. "These waters are too shallow to make effective use of the frigates. We need a ship to follow the rebels back into their base."

Richards sipped his wine. "And what of *MERRIMACK*?" He watched Van Brunt for a reaction and was surprised at the cavalier response.

The commodore dismissed the ironclad with a wave of his hand. "She will not be ready for months! Within two weeks, our own ironclad will be here to deal with her if the rebels choose to bring her out." He leaned towards Richards as though conveying a great confidence. "Personally, I feel all this bother is unnecessary.

MERRIMACK always was a poor steamer before she was sunk. I would be surprised if her engine worked at all!"

John Marston, captain of the ROANOKE, joined the commodore. "If she does appear, we have four frigates. We shall drive her to roost quickly enough, if we do not sink her outright. You will see."

In spite of his endearment for action, Richards felt dismay at the expectation of following the ironclad back to its home port. The scheme was foolhardy, though he could not express such an opinion openly to Van Brunt.

"And what action will we take?" he asked, phrasing the words carefully, striving not to offend his host. "If she should appear, of course."

"There is only one real worry, Richards." Van Brunt winked at Marston.

"Sir?" Richards' curiosity peaked.

"MERRIMACK might withdraw before we can sink her!"

The officers around the table laughed heartily at the joke. Richards forced a few chuckles but remained unconvinced by the easy talk. Their lack of concern was based on ignorance and he placed his trust in the knowledge shown by his senior lieutenant. He left the meal with more disquiet than he held before his arrival.

Aboard COHOCTON, Richards turned his attention to preparing for a battle he did not wish to fight. For two days, he drilled his crew, bringing forth a flurry of gripes and com- plaints at the effort. But if fight they must, he was determined they would be ready.

"Captain!" Midshipman Weeks stood the watch, but was gesturing away from the other ships in the squadron. Instead, he indicated the rebel shore to the south. "Boat putting off!"

Richards took the offered telescope. The dingy held a single passenger. It headed for *COHOCTON*, the closest ship to the southern edge of the bay. When it finally bumped along side, the occupant slumped across the oars, exhausted by his efforts. Two crewmen helped the man aboard.

"Who are you?" asked Richards.

The man gasped for breath, supported by sailors on either side. He finally managed to force out an answer.

"Jarret, sir. Carson Jarret. I am an ironworker." The man gulped for more air. "I have been working on the *VIRGINIA* - the old *MERRIMACK*."

"Take him to my cabin," instructed Richards with only a bare pause. He continued to LaForge. "Get the surgeon and meet us there."

Richards found Jarret sitting in a chair, still breathing convulsively after his exertions. Two sailors stood watch with Sims over him.

"You can leave, Sims. Have MacDonald post a sentry and only allow Lt. LaForge and the surgeon to enter."

"Are you sure it is safe?"

Richards regarded the exhausted man. "I believe I can handle him," he replied, amused at Sims' protectiveness.

The seamen left. When the door shut, Jarret spoke quietly while they waited for LaForge and Ambrose.

"I never thought one way or the other 'bout slavery, captain, but those poor devils they have working on the VIRGINIA..." He paused, the memory too much for him. Strength grew in his words he continued. "Black or not, pack animals are treated better!"

Ambrose and LaForge entered and there was a lull in the conversation while the surgeon quickly examined Jarret. The prescription was the usual dose of ship's whiskey. Jarret took the cup in both hands, the spirits returning life to his face.

After dismissing the doctor, Richards returned to the discussion. "Now, Jarret, what of *MERRIMACK*?"

"She is ready to come out," he said, his eyes and voice steady. "The chief engineer told me himself. And Lt. Caldwell has the gunboats ready..."

The name was like a slap of cold water. Richards hardly recognized his own voice when he spoke. "Caldwell? Judson Caldwell?"

"Yes," returned Jarret, surprise at the recognition on his face. "With Buchanan and Brooke busy with the ironclad, he is preparing the smaller boats."

Caldwell. Of all the places.

"A friend?" LaForge's words made little impression.

"He was first officer before resigning his commission," said Richards. He felt the pressure of LaForge's hand on his shoulder.

"I spent two years working with John Brooke before the war." The words were quiet, sympathetic.

"When will they attack?" asked Richards, dismissing Caldwell from his thoughts.

"Any day," returned Jarret. "They are ready for their trial run within the week."

Richards shook his head. "Within a week! RenError!, ask him about the ship. You know more of such things than I."

LaForge, questions already prepared, spoke quickly and with no hesitation. If the ironworker did not provide a satisfactory response, the lieutenant probed until contented with the answer.

On many points, such as the numbers and types of guns, Jarret was completely ignorant. But when it came to the ship's structure and the type of armor plate, Jarret was a well of information and was more than happy to pass his knowledge to the Union officers. He sketched a layout of the vessel for the two men, pointing out some of the weaker aspects of the design.

After two hours of questioning, Richards was convinced of the man's knowledge and sincerity. Ordering his boat, he escorted Jarret, along with copies of the sketches and LaForge's notes, to the *MINNESOTA*.

Van Brunt listened to Jarret's story in quiet tolerance, asking few questions. When the man finished, he examined the drawings for only a few moments before returning them.

"Is this a ploy to scare the officers and men of this fleet?" he demanded angrily. "You do not expect me to believe this nonsense, do you?"

"It is the truth, captain. I swear it is," replied Jarret.

Van Brunt laughed aloud. "What mindless drivel, Richards! Four inches of iron indeed. The thing would capsize when it hit the water! Commander, see this man ashore and into the custody of the Army."

"Yes, sir." His voice sounded hollow in his ears as he spoke. After risking capture, the ironworker deserved more than to become a prisoner.

"And, commander," continued Van Brunt. "I received this note just before you arrived. It seems Miss Rebecca Welles and Mrs. Lorraine LaForge have come to Ft. Monroe."

"My fiancé, sir," explained Richards, "and my first officer's wife. Would it be possible..."

"Of course, man!" Van Brunt looked at Jarret in disgust. "You have nothing to fear from *this*. Make what arrangements you can after you take the prisoner ashore."

Jarret sat in silence, broken, unable to speak.

Richards finally interrupted his thoughts when they neared the dock.

"Are you telling the truth?"

"I swear!" The voice pleaded. "It is God's truth. All of it!"

The officer considered the man. He felt an obligation, a debt to the man who risked his life to bring them the information. "I have some influence with the Secretary of Navy. If this proves true, I will see you are released."

Jarret's spirits rose with the words. "Thank you!"

Soldiers were waiting for the prisoner when they reached the dock. Richards watched him escorted away; wondering what was to become of him. Then other thoughts intruded themselves and he prevailed upon an Army officer for the use of a horse.

It was over a year since riding last and it took several minutes to adjust to the sensation. Fortunately, the trip to the fort was short and he was quickly admitted. Becky came running to him before he could hand the reins to a soldier.

Their arms were around each other, and he pulled her close, or at least as close as her wide skirt allowed. It was a dream for her to be there, so far from Washington. He held her for a long time before he could speak his thoughts only of her.

"You should not have come," he said continuing to hold her. "It is very dangerous."

"Oh, John," she chided. "Even father said it was all right. He hired the yacht to bring us down from Baltimore."

Richards shook his head, forcing the unpleasant words out. "You must leave tomorrow."

"Tomorrow? But we plan to stay the week!" protested Rebecca. "The commandant's wife has found rooms for us."

He kissed her. "I would like nothing better than to have you so close, but you do not understand. The Confederates have finished their ironclad. We can expect it any day."

"Finished? Father said it would be months..."

"That is what they wanted us to think." He took her hand and kissed it. "You must return to Washington. Convince your father. I am told we are building an ironclad, too. He must see it gets here as soon as possible."

She looked down, her words low. "I can at least stay the night."

"Yes, you can," he answered. "I will have dinner with you, but RenError! will want to see Lorraine. One of us must be aboard the ship at all times."

"Will you see me off in the morning?"

"Becky, my duty..."

"Yes. Your *duty*." The words carried a world of hurt. They also accepted the facts.

The time passed quickly. The meal was short and she stood with him at the gate.

"You fear this ironclad, don't you?" she asked. The question was rhetorical, but he answered.

"If it should escape..." He stopped himself in mid-thought. "The fleet, the entire eastern seaboard, could be at its mercy."

"And you plan to fight it." The fact was obvious.

"If necessary."

"You will be killed!" The protest was a whisper, tears welling up.

"Perhaps." The thought was not far from his mind. "I must do what I can to stop it."

The true horror of the situation became clear. "You cannot!"

She was in his arms, crying. He held her, held her while his heart cried to never let go.

"I love you, Becky. No matter what happens, I need you to know that."

He kissed her and mounted the horse. That night, he stood LaForge's watch while the officer spent the night ashore. The extra watch made no difference, for he would sleep little. His eyes were always to the southwest on Sewell's Point, even though the land was hidden in darkness. Over there lay Norfolk.

CONGRESS engages the *VIRGINIA*

CHAPTER FIFTEEN

LaForge stood at the stern, watching the small yacht spread its sails and head into the Chesapeake. Richards did not look. There was the chance he might catch a glimpse of dark hair; see a pale face turned in his direction. At the moment, he could bear neither. His attention was to the southwest, towards the jutting land blocking his view of Norfolk.

He placed a hand on LaForge's shoulder and the man started at the touch. "The rest are gathered in my cabin, RenError!. It is time we join them."

LaForge stared north, though the yacht had disappeared minutes before. "Lorraine is frightened, John. I did not know what to tell her."

Richards nodded, the conversation with Becky still stark in his memory. "Nor did I to Rebecca." The officer turned to the companionway. He did not have to look, for LaForge would be close behind.

"Seats," said Richards when he entered the room. The assembled men started to rise to greet him, but he waved them back. There was little time for formalities.

The gathered officers waited expectantly and his gaze went to each in turn. Hardy, old and gruff; Simpson, young and excited. Richards would have preferred Nash, but he had received a command of his own on taking the raider north. Wilson, pale from his time beneath deck; grimy from his work. MacDonald, stiff and erect in his Marine uniform, ready to go on parade. LaForge, suddenly mature and competent. Weeks, looking for a chance to follow Nash and Simpson. A new midshipman. Richards suddenly realized he could not remember the young man's name.

"Wine first," said Richards, glancing to Sims. The seaman was there as deliberately as the officers. The connection to the men forward: if the officers showed no concern, the word would be passed.

Sims presented the wine bottle carefully. "'Tis the last one, Captain."

Richards nodded. They had hoarded them carefully over the last months. "Pour it, Sims. I cannot think of a better group to drink with. And take a glass for yourself."

Sims smiled broadly. "Well, thank 'ee, cap'n!"

Some of the tension evaporated with the exchange. Richards felt vaguely guilty at the success of so obvious a ploy.

"To business." He took his seat while Sims poured the wine. "RenError!, you had a day to review Jarret's comments. What have you determined?"

LaForge rolled out the sketch made by the ironworker on the table. Expectantly, the officers leaned forward to examine it.

"I am no naval constructor." LaForge's voice was clear and sure. "I cannot vouch for everything I say, but I know a thing about our artillery. There is not a gun aboard to go through this."

"Not even the Dahlgrens?" asked Hardy.

"Not even with double charges. She is covered by four inches of iron, backed with twelve inches of oak." Everyone caught their breath, but LaForge did not wait for more comments. "*MERRIMACK*, or *VIRGINIA* if you prefer, will have a deep draft. She is a sister to our frigates out there, and draws as much. She will probably draw even more with the extra weight of iron."

"And what will that gain us?" asked Simpson. There was no fear or doubt in his voice. LaForge and Nash were correct. The boy was ready for the position.

"We might be able to force her aground and board her."

MacDonald nodded. "Carry her by storm? How will we get inside?"

LaForge looked to the Marine. "Notice," he said, tapping the gun ports on the drawing. "Jarret was very clear on this point. There are no shutters fitted. We can enter there. Those are also the aiming points for our guns, Hardy! We use shell instead of shot and try to injure the crew with splinters."

"*If* we are lucky enough to place one through a port," added Richards.

"*If*," LaForge agreed. "Of course, that is Mr. Hardy's department." Everyone laughed at the weak joke. "*MERRIMACK* was a poor steamer before. The submersion will not have done her machinery any good. With the extra weight of armor, she will be slow and difficult to handle. The rebels are counting on invulnerability to counter balance it."

The young commander judged how best to present the picture presented to his men. He considered what few advantages they might have.

"We are faster and more maneuverable," Richards stated firmly. "We can escape into shallow water if necessary." He looked to each of the officers in turn while placing a finger on the drawing. "This thing is impervious to anything we throw against it. If we must engage, we aim for the gun ports. If the opportunity presents itself, we board and storm. Questions?"

"When can we expect her?"

The voice was nervous and hesitant: the new midshipman.

"Within the week, boy," returned Richards. There was a touch of amusement at the thought. The boy was probably five years his junior.

"One final comment," he continued. "When you speak with the other ships, do not broach the subject of the MERRIMACK. They assume they are safe and there is nothing you can say to change their opinion. Captain Van Brunt will not be happy if he catches us spreading scary rumors about the fleet!" He managed just the right inflection to bring a chuckle from his officers. He looked for the helmsman.

"Let us have the rest of the bottle, Sims!" he said, raising his glass. The seaman came forward, carefully apportioning the remainder amongst the officers while not forgetting his own glass. "To victory, my friends. And good fortune to us all!"

Three days passed and no sign of the dreaded Confederate ship was seen. The warship was expected to round Sewell's Point and head for the anchored fleet at any moment, but each succeeding day passed without the MERRIMACK.

A short note arrived from Becky, announcing her safe return to Washington. A telegram was received from Welles expressing his concern. It promised the Federal ironclad would arrive shortly, but did not specify what *shortly* meant. Richards hoped it would be in time.

Thursday and Friday came, a storm sweeping through the fleet to pound the decks and ruffle the water. The young captain paced the windswept deck, ignoring the rain falling heavily about him. Sewell's Point was a dark blur, often lost in the downpour. It would not have been surprising to see *MERRIMACK* appear, taking advantage of the inclement weather to hide its approach to the Union fleet. But the rebels were not of the same mind and the ship stayed in port.

The ironclad became an obsession. After all his prayers for action, the thought was now dreadful. He could not walk the deck without his eyes turning to the southwest. He prayed the fuss would be for nothing.

On Saturday, the sun shone brightly after the passage of the storm. It was warm, the coming spring bringing the men to the main deck. The rigging of *COHOCTON* and the other ships became strewn with clothing as the vigil continued. Every sailor in the fleet took advantage of the warm weather to dry the clothes wet by the storm.

"Ahoy the deck!" It was Weeks shouting from the foretop. "Smoke around Norfolk."

LaForge appeared, pulling on his coat as he rushed to the deck. "Probably just getting up steam," he noted, staring towards the point.

Richards checked the tide chart at the helm, and glanced at his watch. "They will wait for the flood," he stated. "Around noon, I should think."

LaForge stood, his gaze locked with Richards'. Few words needed to pass between them.

"Get yourself dressed, RenError!." He thought of LaForge and his comment before the attack at Hatteras. "We will need to put on a proper show for the men today."

LaForge smiled, the action showing humor, fear and

sadness all at once. "As you say, John."

"And pass the word to the men, RenError!. If the order comes to clear for action, I want all these clothes properly stored and not just tossed about. We cannot allow such a fire hazard."

"Aye aye, *captain.*" The single word spoke volumes from his officer and friend.

Richards bent to the speaking tube. "Engine room!"

Wilson knew. "How soon?"

"Another two or three hours, lieutenant," returned Richards. "Stand ready."

"As always, captain."

Richards stood quietly. Now that things were actually happening, he felt almost relaxed. Far different from the nerve wracking wait of the past week.

"Ships moving south of the point!" shouted Weeks.

Richards withdrew his watch and checked the time. Over an hour since the first alarm. His original estimate was probably correct. It was another indication of the deep draft of their adversary.

"Call the men to lunch, Mr. LaForge," said Richards, his voice calm and clear. He made sure the waiting seamen heard him; made sure of the rimber in his tone as he spoke. "When they are finished, have them remove their laundry."

The smoke from the far side of Sewell's Point was easily seen through the telescope, yet none of the other ships in the squadron showed any signs of alarm over the movement from Norfolk. He remembered Jarret's words. Judson Caldwell was here, too, but his uniform was gray, not blue.

Shortly past noon, the Rebel ships became visible

beyond the point and moving into Hampton Roads. Richards' heart raced. With a telescope, he climbed into the rigging.

There were five ships. Four were gunboats, no bigger or better than those they had already faced. But the fifth was different. Long and low, the vessel was a combination of rust brown and dirty gray. No masts were visible and black holes marked the gun ports along her side. The vessel looked much like Jarret's drawing. Richards stepped down to the deck.

"She is out," he said quietly to LaForge. "Call the men to quarters."

Hurried movement was finally seen on the three frigates. Signals flew on *MINNESOTA*, ordering all ships to prepare to sail. Both *ROANOKE* and *ST. LAWRENCE* called for tugs as smoke belched from the flagship's stack.

There was an impatient wait for the larger vessels. *ROANOKE*, whose engines were disabled, and *ST. LAWRENCE*, a sailing vessel, were dependent on the tugs in the narrow waters of the Roads. And while they waited, *MERRIMACK* steamed across the Roads directly towards Newport News, where *CUMBERLAND* and *CONGRESS* were anchored.

Richards watched the ironclad's slow, direct progress, fuming at the delay of the frigates. Finally *ROANOKE*, towed by a small, smoking tug, gathered way. *ST. LAWRENCE* followed. Then *MINNESOTA* slipped her cable and passed her two sisters. *COHOCTON* steered in behind the flag.

"Van Brunt is in a hurry," commented LaForge.

Richards grunted. "He had best watch what he is about! Too many shoals to move that ship around in such a rush!"

There was a roar of gunfire ahead. *CONGRESS*, a sailing frigate of fifty guns, fired a full broadside at

MERRIMACK. The ironclad returned the fire in a slow, measured fashion, uninjured by the weight of metal thrown against it. The rebel's course was for CUMBERLAND. Though only a sailing sloop of twenty-two guns, she carried the newest and biggest weapons in the squadron.

"My God!" The words came from Simpson, standing atop the rail for a better view. "The rebel is going to ram her!"

Sails appeared on CUMBERLAND, but they were too few and too late. Her broadside roared but the shells exploded without affect on the iron side of the Confederate ship. The ram struck the sloop dead amidships, CUMBERLAND heeling at the impact. MERRIMACK backed away, and it was obvious the sailing sloop was grievously injured. She settled, laundry still strung about her rigging. CONGRESS drifted, cable cut and heading for the protection of Army batteries mounted along the shore.

"She is everything you feared, RenError!," said Richards. "Everything and more!"

"Over there!" LaForge stabbed a finger at the flagship.

Men aboard MINNESOTA were picking themselves from the deck, for the frigate had slammed hard aground. Richards cursed under his breath and checked the other two ships astern. To his amazement, they were also stationary.

"Get to your guns!" he shouted, oblivious to the scant feet between them. "The fools have run the whole damned squadron aground!"

By now, CONGRESS lay deliberately aground near the batteries. All guns, both ashore and on the vessel, fired continually against the MERRIMACK. But Army and Navy alike, none affected the ironclad. Even CUMBERLAND, very low in the water, continued to work her guns with no visible damage to the rebel. The Confederates, confident in their armored vessel, sat bow on to CONGRESS slowly firing shells into the grounded frigate. Richards was pulled from the sight by Simpson.

"Flagship, sir! They want us to pass them a cable!"

"See to it, lieutenant!" returned Richards, raising his voice above the sound of cannon.

Deftly reversing course, the steam sloop slowed while passing the length of line to *MINNESOTA*. A guideline was tossed and successively larger diameters of cable were fed out as they halted astern of the frigate. It seemed hours before the main tow cable was passed across and made fast. Full steam was ordered and, though the water boiled madly about the sterns of both ships, *MINNESOTA* failed to budge.

Meanwhile, the scene of the battle worsened. Only *CUMBERLAND*'s topmasts stood above the water when Richard's looked back to her, the stars and stripes still flying at the main. *CONGRESS* was aflame and *MERRIMACK* continually fired into her, ignoring the white flag at the stern. Sailors climbed down the side of the stricken frigate, struggling for the safety of shore. Richards watched helplessly while his ship labored vainly to pull *MINNESOTA* free.

"We aren't getting anywhere!" Simpson's words were all but lost in the crash of guns. His eyes were fixed on the towering height of the frigate astern.

"Keep at it. We shall need her cannon if we must fight this beast!" returned Richards.

"Here she comes!"

Weeks made the comment, drawn from his position at the forward rifle by the fury of the battle off Newport News. The *MERRIMACK* turned from the burning frigate and headed east, making for *COHOCTON* and her grounded charge.

There was an explosion of splinters aft on the frigate when a shell struck. At first, Richards feared they were already within range of the ironclad. But the roar of the cannon to starboard drew attention to three of the rebel gunboats. Their captains had moved into a position where they could shoot at the frigate without receiving any fire in return.

"Enough of this!" Richards' frustration erupted into a flurry of activity. "Weeks, get to your gun! Cast off the tow and steer for those bastards!"

There was a flash of axes against the cable attached to the mainmast as other crewmen scurried to clear the heavy line. It parted with a crack and snapped out the aft scuttles like an angry rattlesnake.

Released of *MINNESOTA*'s deadweight, *COHOCTON* leapt forward. With the sloop rushing upon them, the gunboats fled, one passing down their starboard side.

"Fire as you bear!"

First one, then another of the cannon roared. A shell splashed close astern of the boat, followed by a clean hit forward. The small warship was sheathed in smoke for a moment before running clear. A second shell struck high amidships, where the pilot house might be. It was not until then Richards thought of Caldwell.

He lifted his glass and trained it on the damaged ship. Little could be seen other than blurred figures rushing to and fro. He shifted to another gunboat. There was a tall figure at the stern, looking over the battle with a telescope. It might be Judson, but he was too far away to tell. Richards lowered the instrument.

"*MERRIMACK* is closing, Captain." Sims said the words softly, but they carried through the noise of battle clearly.

Richards took a deep breath. The ironclad was headed for the grounded flagship. Aboard *MINNESOTA*, the crew worked their ten-inch Columbiad. A solid shot from the giant gun clearly struck the side armor and bounced off the enemy ship.

A terrier before a rhinoceros, Richards prepared to attack. He opened his mouth to speak, but stopped as the armored ship slowly swung around. *MERRIMACK* moved away from the grounded ships and towards Sewell's Point. Lengthening shadows across the deck showed the rebel could not risk grounding in the shallow waters in the ebb tide. The battle which seemed to last no more than minutes had taken over three hours. He rubbed his eyes, smarting from the haze of burned powder in the air.

"Secure the guns," he said. He felt relief: relief the battle was finished for the day. He did not think of the morrow. "Reverse course and slow to a third. Steer for the flag."

"Aye aye, C\captain." Sims showed relief at the turn of events. Richards could not blame him.

"RenError!?" LaForge was there, waiting for his orders. "Have the men stand down and prepare my boat. I am sure the commodore will need to talk."

The flagship's main deck was bedlam, crewmen scurrying about as stores and guns were transferred aft. Van Brunt met Richards quickly at the entry port, and Marston from the *ROANOKE* was also there.

"She is badly stuck." The commodore continued to speak while his eyes followed the laboring sailors. "You were going to attack that thing, were you not?"

"Yes, sir." No other explanation was necessary.

"Brave, lad, very brave. You would not have accomplished anything. I received a report our ironclad left New York two days ago." Van Brunt was no longer commenting to Richards. He spoke to himself, but the words were aloud. "She should have arrived by now! If she is not here in the morning, I fear the entire fleet shall be lost."

"There is little we can do against the *MERRIMACK*,

commodore," commented Marston.

Van Brunt eyed Richards. "And what do you plan when she reappears?"

"I plan to attack." The words were flat, devoid of emotion. "Is there any other choice?"

The commodore shook his head in disbelief. "She sinks a fifty gun frigate, and you plan to attack with an eight gun sloop!"

Richards moved closer, his voice intense. "We have talked about it, commodore. We will attempt to board and carry her by storm."

He did not know what to expect from his suggestion, but it was not laughter.

"See to your ship, Richards," said Van Brunt, chuckling. "I will have a captain's call later. You can present your ideas then."

"One more thing, sir," said Richards. "The man Jarret. His information was correct."

The commodore nodded in agreement, his face deathly serious. "You are right, commander. I will send a note to the fort to have him released."

Richards ate a quiet meal with his officers that evening. Few words were exchanged about the battle. The results of a fight the next day appeared obvious. They finished and the young captain went out on deck.

All the tugs were astern of *MINNESOTA*, assigned to the flagship after freeing their charges and returning them to Ft. Monroe. For all their efforts, the giant ship remained hard aground. The crewmen unloaded the ship's stores, laboring in the light of the flaming *CONGRESS*. While the drama unfolded in the deepening night, two ships approached from the east, but only the first showed a light at its masthead. The other's light was close to the water.

The first was a tug, a cable stretched taut astern. The second vessel was impossible to identify in the poor light. It was an oddly shape raft with some structure at the center. Smoke drifted from two short stacks aft, and the dim shape of men moved about the deck. The queer creation halted between the frigate and sloop though no anchor was visible. It took several minutes to decide this was the long promised ironclad from New York.

The flames from *CONGRESS* reached up the masts of the doomed ship. They lit the area as *COHOCTON*'s boat crossed to the meeting aboard *MINNESOTA*. The crew muttered about the Union ironclad as they rowed past her dark shape towards the grounded flagship. On reaching the deck of the frigate, Richards recognized a familiar face near the rail. Lt. John Worden captained the ironclad.

"John!" said Richards, slapping him on the back. "John Richards, remember? Last April in Pensacola?"

Worden examined him with weary eyes before awareness slowly bloomed. "*COHOCTON*! I thought I recognized the sloop." He rubbed his eyes and forced them to focus on Richards. "It has been almost a year since we met, but I owe you a debt of gratitude. Your friend, Judson Caldwell, interceded for me to gain my release from prison last year."

"I am glad I was able to help." The exhaustion etched on Worden's whole frame was evident. "Bad trip?"

"Bad?" The lieutenant let out a nervous laugh, the sound bordering on hysteria. "Damned near sank in a storm off New Jersey. I hope she fights better than she sails." He contemplated the strange shape, barely visible in the flames.

"*MONITOR* is like nothing you have ever seen." His words were soft, directed mostly to himself. The intent of the monologue seemed to be to bolster his own belief in his odd little ship. "The central casemate has two eleven-inch Dahlgrens and rotates to fire in any direction! Forward there, you can hardly see it in this light. The little casemate is the pilot house. No sails, of course. She is completely steam driven, everything from propulsion to ventilation. Anything to be damaged in a fight is inside the ship. She is an engineering marvel, Richards. A thing of the future."

"How much armor?"

"*Eight inches!* Eight full inches on the turret," repeated Worden, enthusiasm growing. "The rebels will not have a gun to go through that!"

"Can you stop MERRIMACK?"

Worden's face was tired, lit on one side by the lamps on the MINNESOTA and more fiercely on the other by the blazing ship. It showed no answer, just a calm resolve.

"We shall see," he replied.

Van Brunt appeared and asked the assembled officers below. His once lush cabin was stripped of all but the barest essentials. And while the other men stood, Van Brunt paced his features stern and strained.

"My engineer doubts the ship shall refloat on the morning tide." He stopped near the commander of the Federal ironclad. "Lt. Worden, it will be up to you and MONITOR to stop MERRIMACK when she attacks."

"That little nondescript toy?" asked Captain Marston of the ROANOKE. He snorted in the direction of the little ship. "After what we saw today, MERRIMACK will blow it out of the water!"

"We shall leave that for the morrow to discover," said Worden, an earnest intensity to his words. "Meanwhile, gentlemen, I have had no sleep for the past two days. Might we continue?"

Van Brunt unrolled a chart of Hampton Roads and the

Chesapeake. "We must stop it here, gentlemen. If that thing escapes into the bay, there is nothing to stop her from proceeding up the Potomac and firing on the capitol!" He hit the map with his fist. "The whole seaboard would lay open to it!"

He examined the captains of the wooden ships. "We have all seen what happens to unarmored ships. Tomorrow, you will stay anchored near Ft. Monroe and leave the battle to the MONITOR. If the ironclad is lost, we are all that stand between her and Washington."

The words were clear. Both *ST. LAWRENCE* and *ROANOKE* were dependent on wind or tugs for movement. Could Van Brunt expect the crews of an unarmed tugboat to face such a crisis? *COHOCTON* was the only ship in the squadron capable of maneuvering freely. She must face *MERRIMACK* if *MONITOR* was destroyed.

"We cannot allow *MERRIMACK* to escape the Roads. Here she is restricted, hemmed in by the shoals and tide. Destroy wooden ships she might, but better than allowing her to roam the open seas!" He ran a hand through his thinning hair. "It will be iron against iron in the morning, but the rest of the fleet is the bulwark protecting the Republic! Luck to you all."

They emerged on deck and even the senior captains allowed Worden to leave first, retiring to his small, untested warship to await the dawn. A massive explosion split the night, pieces of the *CONGRESS* hurled far and wide by the force as the flames found her magazine.

Richards watched the remains of the vessels falling into the water. *Wood against iron.* There were the results for all to see. And as he passed *MONITOR* on his return, he wondered at the outcome of the next day.

MONITOR and *MERRIMACK*

CHAPTER SIXTEEN

COHOCTON changed considerably during his absence. With time to work, the topmasts and topgallants were removed, along with all the yards. Gaffs were rigged to each of the masts, so they and the foresails were the only canvas now carried. In the morning, the sloop would rely completely on steam, reducing the chance of death and injury from falling rigging.

Richards stayed on deck, pacing in the chilly night air. The sky was strangely empty, with so much of the masts and rigging removed above him. Sims appeared, carrying a mug of coffee. Richards took it and sipped the hot liquid gratefully.

"Am I keeping you awake, Sims?"

"No, Sir. I guess I don't feel much like sleepin' tonight either."

Richards drank the coffee slowly, staring off towards

Sewell's Point. Sims remained silent for several minutes before speaking again.

"Pardon me, captain, but we're gonna' have to fight that thing in the morning, aren't we?"

The events of the day were obvious to the crew. To fight the *MERRIMACK* was to die, yet it might be necessary to ask them to do just that in the morning. Even knowing this, Richards remained noncommittal.

"It depends on how well the *MONITOR* does."

"Beggin' your pardon, cap'n, but that cheese box on a raft ain't gonna' hurt the *MERRIMACK*."

Richards grinned at the phrase. "Cheese box?"

Sims paused, embarrassed. "It's what some of the men forward called her."

"Perhaps that is all she is," returned Richards. The black iron ship was hardly discernable in the dark. "But my money is on her, Sims, and you can tell that to the men forward."

"I'd like that. More coffee, Sir?"

He handed Sims the mug. "If you please. Then get some sleep. I fear I shall be up the rest of the night."

Sims delivered the coffee and left. All was dark around the ship, but Richards was well familiar with the area. Much of his life was spent on the waters in and around the Chesapeake. The smoldering ashes of *CONGRESS* were a reminder of the night the year before when he had last seen Norfolk. *CUMBERLAND* had been there, towed out by Paulding and *PAWNEE*. *MERRIMACK* had been there too, burned to the waterline and sunk at the dock.

Now that same ship prepared to return from its grave and send them to theirs. Before, it had been the *UNITED STATES* in ashes; now it was the *CONGRESS*. And he was still here with *COHOCTON*. Richards continued to pace, his mind a restless flurry, tortured by his willingness to attack the rebel ship. Was it really necessary or pure bravado on his part? He was still not sure as the bright line of dawn marked the eastern horizon.

"You had best get below for some breakfast, captain," said LaForge from the dimness behind him. "They shall be down early because of the tide."

"Thanks for the reminder, RenError!. Let the men sleep 'til seven. Make sure they get a hot meal."

"Of course, John."

Richards ate and shaved. He felt none the worse for his sleepless night on deck. By seven-thirty, the lookouts reported smoke from Norfolk. At the same time, smoke rose from the *MONITOR*. The two short stacks noticed the night before were gone, and Worden stood near the small pilot house at the bow. Richards picked up the speaking trumpet.

"Godspeed, John!"

Worden acknowledged the comment with a wave, and then disappeared into the structure. The strange ship was ready. *COHOCTON* weighed anchor and joined the frigates.

The rebel ironclad appeared at eight, moving slowly beyond the point. Only four gunboats returned this day and they stayed close to the southern edge of the Roads, appearing content to let the ironclad do the fighting. The ironclad cruised east, skirting the shoal which grounded *MINNESOTA*. Once clear, it turned west for the flagship, the obvious first target. During its slow, purposeful approach, *MONITOR* cleared the frigate and placed herself across the path of the rebel warship.

There was no way to tell if the rebel crew was prepared for the apparition. After continuing on course for a while longer, MERRIMACK turned and fired its entire broadside at the Union ship. Most of the shells flew harmlessly past the turret, the only noticeable target on the queer ship. Those that struck exploded without any visible effect. There was a surge of hope when the little ship moved forward, its two guns roaring out their defiance.

The battle became thunder and smoke. The ships, each impervious to the others' guns, circled and fired, attempting to discover a weakness within their opponent. After an hour of combat, the area was covered by a growing cloud of gun and coal smoke. At times, the antagonists were just dark shapes marked by the flash of their guns or the darker explosion of a shell against iron plate.

The men's spirits rose as *MONITOR* stalemated *MERRIMACK* at every turn, frustrating the rebel ship's attempts to reach the wooden *MINNESOTA*. A second hour passed with no signs of injury to either vessel. For a short while, only one gun fired from *MONITOR,* but it was a temporary lapse and there was no visible reason for the interruption. Then it became clear the *MERRIMACK* was stationary.

"She's aground!" shouted Simpson. *COHOCTON*'s crew let out a loud cheer and jostled each other still further for a better view of the fight.

MONITOR lay close behind its adversary, firing shot at point blank range while *MERRIMACK*'s guns could not be angled to engage her. The situation lasted for several volleys before *MERRIMACK* managed to free herself and chase after *MONITOR.*

Shot and shell flew around the two ships. A dark orange flash near the bow of *MONITOR* indicated the explosion of another shell. No damage was obvious, but hopes fell when the strange little vessel set a course into shallow water out of reach of the rebel ship. The hit was near the pilot house, but Richards had no time for thoughts of Worden.

MERRIMACK headed east, away from *MONITOR* and *MINNESOTA*. Its course was for the ocean, and Richards felt a chill in his spine. With *MONITOR* nursing her wounds, only one ship lay in a position to engage her.

There was a moment, but only that, as Richards saw the Confederate ironclad turn in their direction. A lump formed in his throat, knowing what needed to be done. He swallowed and looked away, away for only the briefest instance to look at the open water, the clear sky. He knew it would be the last time he saw those simple pleasures: saw the wavelets crackling on the water; the sun glinting from across the sea. He swallowed again before turning back to his ship, to his men. His back straightened; his voice firmed.

"Call to quarters!" he ordered, looking to the helm. "Ahead one-third, Sims. Guns to starboard!"

There was a second while the men just looked at him as the sloop gathered way. Then naval discipline asserted itself and the sailors ran to stations. The ship filled with the rumble of the carriages and the guns were run out. Richards faced the *MERRIMACK*, afraid to look into the eyes of his men. The old thrill of going into action rose in his chest while *COHOCTON* strained towards the rebel ship.

"Steady!" The course was a straight line through the quiet waters of Hampton Roads. *MERRIMACK* approached from the starboard quarter. Richards bent to the speaking tube, marveling at the calm in his voice. "Engine room, I shall be requiring full steam shortly."

There was no delay to Wilson's tinny reply. "We are ready, captain."

A burst of smoke came from the forward end of *MERRIMACK*'s casement when the gun spoke. A shower of splinters ripped across the deck from where it struck forward, cutting down several men where they stood. Cries of the wounded followed. A moment of pandemonium swept the gun deck before LaForge's voice rose above it, cutting through the confusion. The voice was clear and strong and Richards was glad he was there.

"Prepare to fire!" A second shot from the ironclad whistled overhead to fall well beyond the ship. "Aim for the gun ports. Fire as your guns bear! Sims, port your helm!"

COHOCTON cut across the path of the oncoming ironclad, matching their broadside to the Rebel's single bow gun. The forward thirty-two banged out, followed by a deck rifle. Along the length of *COHOCTON*, the seven guns in the broadside fired in a staggered salvo. All the shells struck the front of the enemy ship, covering it with dark blossoms of exploding metal. When the smoke cleared, the forward gun jutted upwards at an impossible angle, knocked from its carriage.

"Good shooting!" shouted Richards, pulling down hard on the engine room repeater. "Hard port and full ahead!"

COHOCTON heeled into the turn. *MERRIMACK* turned slightly and loosed its broadside into the sloop. For an instant, Richards experienced hell as the ship erupted in explosions. The air filled with flying, screaming splinters of material. A gaff and some of the remaining rigging fell, adding to the confusion and destruction.

The three port guns fired a reply, the heavy roar of the thirty-two's lost in the surrounding chaos. The shells struck but did no damage to the sloping sides of the ironclad. The terror and confusion of the first hits had barely subsided when another broadside crashed in. Then there was silence as *COHOCTON* pulled ahead and crossed the Rebel ironclad's course in the opposite direction.

"All guns port side!"

The main deck was wreckage; mangled bodies intermingled with struggling wounded. The aft rifle lay on its side in the midst of its shattered crew. Those less badly injured pulled themselves towards the masts, clear of the sailors attempting to swing the remaining gun. Others were pushed and pulled out of the way as the rifle was reloaded and turned to port. Few men moved around the weapon, a testimony to the effectiveness of the rebel shells.

"Fire as you bear!"

The words were hardly out of his mouth when one of the thirty-two pounders fired forward, quickly followed by another and the deck gun. There was a deeper sound from the Dahlgrens aft. The men struggled to reload the deck piece when MERRIMACK fired again.

The ship reeled from the impact of the shells. Masts and rigging crashed to the deck. The air was alive, filled with shell and wood splinters. The ship shook to a muffled explosion and Richards was knocked from his feet by the force. A cloud of steam burst from below, followed by the screams of men scalded by the heat. These mingled with the cries of those already wounded.

Then COHOCTON drifted, losing way as the screw slowed. Richards regained his feet and searched for his antagonist. The MERRIMACK turned away, heading west to the refuge beyond Sewell's Point. He wondered at the change when two shots rang out from port. MONITOR closed on the rebel, sniping at the heels of the larger ship while she withdrew. Richards brought his attention back to his command.

COHOCTON settled. Her deck possessed a leaden feel, even in the placid waters of the Roads. She still carried some way, and the lighter color of the water ahead indicated a shoal close to the surface. If they grounded the vessel there, it might prove possible to salvage her.

"Sims!"

But the man was not there. The wheel and all around it were gone, wiped away by a shell hit. What remained of the steering gear would not control the crippled ship.

The men moved in a daze, helping their wounded comrades. There was a wisp of smoke forward. Flames spread from one of the hits.

"The pumps, damn it!" pointed Richards, his throat dry

from the rasp of gunpowder. "Man the pumps!"

The crewmen reacted slowly, stunned by the short, devastating fight. The steam powered pumps were destroyed and it took several minutes to rig the hand driven ones. A stream of water shot from a hose, trained on the growing blaze by the remaining crew, the wounded helping as best they could. Others pulled injured shipmates to safety. The ship scraped bottom and the deck assumed a strange, solid list.

Richards called for the surgeon but word came Ambrose was dead. He found Weeks lying to one side with a leg horribly mutilated. Wilson had died with the boilers, scalded to death in an instant.

The sailors gained on the fire, much needed help arriving from the two frigates. With the situation in hand, Richards went below to discover LaForge's situation. Between decks was a butcher's shop of blood and flesh. The deck was awash from water through the open gun ports. Wounded lay everywhere, their moans accompanying the clank of pumps. Potter and Jigs cried openly next to the broken body of another powder boy. Richards wished he could do the same.

LaForge's smashed body lay near the rear Dahlgren. By him lay the new midshipman. *Robins:* odd he should remember the name now. He considered it for a moment before returning to his duties. Simpson was wounded, appearing with an arm in a sling and his head bandaged. Leaving the young lieutenant in charge, Richards returned to the main deck wondering how he escaped the destruction of his ship unscathed.

The blaze was soon extinguished, leaving the forward deck smoldering. The blackened deck and hull added to the sense of loss and annihilation. Boats from *ROANOKE* and *ST. LAWRENCE* moved the wounded ashore while Richards compiled a list of the dead.

"How many, cap'n?" Hardy's words were soft, as if

they might be overheard.

The gunner had a bandage tied tightly about one arm, but the wound did not seem to affect him. Richards looked over the roster, the faces appearing in his mind to match the names.

"Too many. Forty dead and another fifty wounded." He became aware of the wrecked ship about him. "Add one more dead," he finished drily. "*COHOCTON*."

"Aye, cap'n," agreed Hardy, more than a touch of sadness in the old man's voice. "But we showed them rebs!"

Richards looked at the battered man, unable to comprehend the words. "Showed them what, Mr. Hardy?"

"That we'll fight, sir," returned the gunner without hesitation. "We'll stand up to 'em, whatever it takes!"

Richards did not answer. Instead, he walked to the stern, unable to bear the sight of the wreckage forward. If there was an answer, he did not know it.

Was it worth it?

He felt weak, his previous excitement blasted away by *MERRIMACK*'s guns. He had no answer, but one point was clear in his mind, standing above all else. It gnawed and preyed on him. He had loved every terrifying second of it. He felt the loss of his friends, but was driven by fear - fear that, when called upon, he would do it all again.

The small boat pulled away from shore and headed for the wreck of the *COHOCTON*. Richards stood at the stern, seeing the boat but paying no real attention to it. He was still shocked, stunned by the events of the previous day. It was only mid-morning on March tenth, but the ninth seemed a hundred years distant. Only the growing line of carefully wrapped corpses on the sloping deck proved it was less than twenty-four hours previous.

Richards tried to concentrate on the boat, watching the sailors dig the oars deep into the water to propel it forward. It was so close the muscles in their backs could be seen working as the oars bit into the clear sea. He shifted his gaze to the man at the stern holding the tiller. He was dressed in a civilian suit but maneuvered the boat with a professional ease worthy of notice and admiration. And while familiar, Richards could not set a name with the face.

The boat touched on the port side where the deck angled close to the water. The main deck was so low the civilian only had to use two rungs on the ladder to gain it. He surveyed the shambles on the ship momentarily before spotting Richards at the stern.

The newcomer was short and squat, his barrel shape indicating great strength. The prominent Burnside whiskers on the side of his face contrasted sharply with the bald expanse across the top of his head.

"Commander Richards?"

"Yes?"

"Gustavus Fox." He stuck out a massive hand. "If I may shake the hand of a very brave man, captain."

Richards shook it, feeling the hard calluses across the palm while recalling their brief meeting the previous summer.

"What can I do for you, sir?" The voice was subdued and barely audible.

"You are to return to Washington with me. *Today*." The blunt words were a surprise. He was unsure what to think of the orders, but Fox continued before he could ask for elaboration. "I saw the fight yesterday. A noble action, boy. Truly noble - but you stood little chance."

Richards agreed. "It was not much of a fight."

"No one could have expected better, but you're wanted

in Washington. We are to leave this afternoon and we must see Captain Van Brunt first. So if you could get ready..." Fox's words trailed off, obviously expecting instant obedience to his commands.

"My ship!" protested Richards. "The men..."

"Will be cared for," answered Fox. "You no longer have a ship to command, boy. We're to begin salvaging tomorrow. Now hurry; time is short!"

Richards went to collect what remained of his belongings from his smashed cabin. Fox called down to him when he reached the gun deck.

"By the way, Richards! Rebecca Welles accompanied me from Washington. She is waiting at the fort!"

He sorted through the wreckage and found a few serviceable items of clothing. He stuffed them into a damaged kit bag and returned to the main deck. He was met by Hardy and the remaining crewmen.

"Beggin' your pardon, sir, but the men and I have something to say."

"Yes?"

Hardy cleared his throat. "We're proud to have served with you, cap'n. When you get your next ship, we'd like to serve under you again."

There was a murmur of agreement among the sailors. Richards discovered it was difficult to speak. He waited, gazing at their faces and trying to commit them to memory. He did not want to forget any of them.

"Thank you. You are a good crew. I only wish things could have ended better."

"This is for you, cap'n," said Hardy. He held out the ship's ensign, battered, torn and burned, but still neatly folded.

Richards took the flag. How many more of these would there before the war was finished? He knelt to place it in his bag, holding the flag with reverence. He saw Potter, standing slightly behind Hardy, the youngster's face still blackened by powder.

"Still like the Navy, Potter?" The words were soft, a private communication from man to boy.

"Aye, dir!" The words were contagious, almost unbelievable considering their surroundings.

Richards caught some of the feeling and smiled. "Take care, Potter."

"Yes, captain!"

Richards stood to face Hardy. "Look after the boy for me, Elijah."

"You can count on it, captain."

Fox sat in the boat. Richards tossed his bag down and stepped from the COHOCTON. He settled next to Fox while they were pulled towards the grounded MINNESOTA.

Richards stared at the COHOCTON. She was low in the water, the deck tilted sharply towards them. Small waves washed into the gun deck. She was a sad sight and he could not help but feel he had killed her. He forced his eyes away and looked at their destination.

Fox kept a constant monologue on the short trip, speaking in quick staccato sentences of the battle and the need for more MONITOR-type warships. Richards feigned interest but cared for neither the sights nor the conversation. He was impatient to see Becky and to find what fate held for him.

A steady flow of boats moved around the MINNESOTA, removing supplies and equipment in the attempt to refloat the massive ship. The MONITOR lay near the frigate, men moving lazily about her flat deck. The ship appeared ready for battle, but dents and powder burns were evident on the turret. Some men worked at cleaning those away.

Van Brunt greeted the two men in his cabin, now even emptier than two nights previous. He wore the look of exhaustion but tried to be enthusiastic with Fox, while hiding the embarrassment of his ship's situation.

"And when will she be afloat?" asked Fox, ignoring formalities and getting straight to the point.

Van Brunt's answer was meek. "One, maybe two, days."

"Then north for repairs," said Fox. "I'd not like to see the damage you've done to her bottom!"

Van Brunt did not answer. Instead he sat, waving the two men into the chairs set up in the otherwise empty space.

"Captain," said Fox, "I need the orders issued to the squadron on the night of the eighth. We've lost three ships here and there will be a hearing in Washington. Commander Richards could face a court martial."

The words were a physical blow. It was the first indication his career was in jeopardy. The commodore considered carefully before replying.

"The orders were for the MONITOR to engage the MERRIMACK. The wooden ships were to stay under the guns of Ft. Monroe and keep clear of the battle."

"And you, commander?" demanded Fox. "What is your story?"

"The MONITOR withdrew from the action, apparently damaged. The MERRIMACK turned east, away from the MINNESOTA and towards the bay. I understood Captain Van Brunt's orders such that we were to keep the ironclad from escaping and threatening the capitol or the eastern seaboard. I attempted to stop her as best I could."

"Are you saying your orders were to stop the MERRIMACK?"

Richards looked to the captain, but Van Brunt refused to meet the younger man's gaze. "I understood we were to prevent the MERRIMACK's escape if the MONITOR lost the engagement.. The *MONITOR* withdrew from the action. Mine was the only mobile ship in the squadron."

Fox leveled his eyes on Van Brunt. The captain stiffened under the gaze. "Are you willing to place your orders in writing?"

"Yes."

"Do it! We will wait on deck."

Fox stood and was out of the cabin before Richards realized the interrogation was completed. He followed Fox, waiting in the bright sunlight for Van Brunt to deliver the papers which could ruin his career.

"It doesn't look good, boy." Fox examined the wreck of the *COHOCTON*.

"I followed the orders as I understood them. You can ask Marston and Purviance if you like."

"You can be sure I will," returned Fox.

Van Brunt appeared and handed Fox the envelope. Without comment, Fox placed the papers in his coat pocket and went to the side of the ship. Richards climbed down next to him, his mind in turmoil.

"John Worden was there, too," said Richards as they passed the *MONITOR*. "He will help clarify the situation."

"Lt. Worden was wounded in the battle, blinded I believe," returned Fox. "He is on his way to Washington."

Richards lapsed into silence. It was the first he had heard of Worden's injury. The picture of the shell hit at the bow of the *MONITOR* stood clear in his mind.

Two women were standing on the dock as they neared Ft. Monroe. From her dark hair flowing in the breeze, Richards recognized Becky at once. With horror, he realized Lorraine was next to her. He met her expectant gaze when he climbed to the dock.

"RenError!?"

The single word needed no answer. Richards' silence confirmed her fears. Her voice wailing something in French, she dropped to her knees in tears. Becky knelt next to her, speaking softly, trying to comfort her. Richards knelt also, placing a firm arm around her shoulder. Fox watched the scene in silence.

"My first officer's wife," explained Richards as they helped the woman to her feet.

Fox nodded his understanding and slipped a powerful arm around her waist to help her walk to the fort. He spoke softly in French, letting her cry freely on his shoulder while they crossed the intervening ground. It was a surprising turn for the gruff and brusque Assistant Secretary of the Navy.

Richards watched them leave, Rebecca standing silently at his side. They stared at each other for seconds, like strangers meeting for the first time. Suddenly, she was in his arms, weeping. He pressed her close, warm salty tears burning his eyes as he buried his face in her hair.

"I thought I would never see you again." He spoke in a harsh whisper.

"I saw it all," said Rebecca. "I was terrified."

He held her tighter. "It was terrifying... beautiful... horrible..." he choked, unable to continue. "*The devil himself*," he said at length. "Like fighting Satan himself. All those men and we barely hurt the damned thing..." Again tears burnt his eyes. "I had to do it. I would do it again..."

"I know, I know." She sounded soft, consoling. "You did what was needed."

"I liked it - loved it!" He pushed her to arm's length and stared straight into her eyes. "As if my whole life were for nothing but that!"

"John, you would not have done it if it were not necessary!" Her words caressed his ravaged thoughts, but

D. A. Joy

his eyes saw past her to the COHOCTON. "I could never love a man so cold he could not care," she continued. "You care for your men. I feel the pain. You do care!"

He pulled her close again, considering her words. "I am to face a court martial in Washington."

She was as shocked as he had been. "Whatever for?"

"Disobeying orders; losing my ship. Van Brunt says I was not following his orders when I attacked."

"Father will not allow it!"

"Gideon cannot prevent it. It is up to the Navy now."

She shook her head. "It does not matter; not to us."

"It is my life!" he protested.

"I will marry you if you were but a seaman." She was firm and her tone allowed no discussion. "We *will* set the date when we reach Washington."

Richards let out a sigh. How could he dissuade such an attitude?

"We will see," he answered.

The sun lay on the horizon as the yacht weighed anchor. The small ship moved towards the bay, a steady stream of smoke from the small stack.

Richards was at the bow, his arm around Becky's waist. They coasted past the remains of the COHOCTON. He wondered what miracle had kept him from injury and death on her deck. He was swept by a wave of doubt, a fear he misunderstood Van Brunt after all. He forced the thought from his mind; he was sure of the action he had taken.

Becky remained silent, not interrupting his thoughts of the wrecked ship. Then he looked down and gave her a small, determined grin and she pulled herself closer.

The yacht left the shelter of Hampton Roads and

entered the more lively waters of the Chesapeake. The ship pitched and Richards helped Becky to her small cabin. His future was uncertain: Washington was now the key to his life. But Richards' resolve hardened while walking across the deck. He face this like any fight of the past year. And like any of those, he would see it through.

THE END

ABOUT THE AUTHOR

D A Joy is a graduate of the University of Nebraska at Omaha Writer's Workshop with a Bachelor of Fine Arts in Creative Writing. Don has written stories since he was a child and started writing his first book in high school. He has worked as a business analyst and project manager across the country while still living in Nebraska. Outside of work, he maintains a range of interests including history, reading, films, and hobbies such as building models from ships to planes to starships, and participating in local and national competitions. Other interests include science, astronomy and the investigation of unexplained phenomenon.

"A Sudden Thunder" and "The Narrow Fury" are the first in *The Richards Line* of novels dealing with the naval history of the Civil War – or the War Between the States. They combine a deep knowledge of the naval aspects of the Civil War to paint the first years of the war through a combination of actual historical events combined with typical actions to present a personal view. Beyond the war, these are also the stories of men's service to their countries and the impact on their lives, friends, family and loved ones. Future novels will show the progression of the war, presenting the views of both northern and southern participants, and how life continues even under those harrowing circumstances.

"Murder in Whitechapel", his first published novel, combines a life-long love of Sherlock Holmes stories with an interest in the darker side of humanity displayed by Jack the Ripper. It provides Holmes' view of the pursuit of the serial killer in London using only his keen intellect and without the aid of modern forensics. And while Holmes is a fictional detective, the case surrounding Jack the Ripper and the murders is dealt with using the actual facts and suspects known to Scotland Yard in 1888.